Gretna Green by Sunset

A Rakes on the Run Novel

Sydney Jane Baily

cat whisker press
Massachusetts

Copyright © 2021 Sydney Jane Baily

First Paperback Edition
ISBN 978-1-938732-49-2

Published by **cat whisker press**
Imprint of JAMES-YORK PRESS

Cover: Erin Dameron-Hill
www.EDHProfessionals.com

Book Design: Cat Whisker Studio
Editor: Chloe Bearuski

DEDICATION

To Murray
My new furry friend

You're home!

ACKNOWLEDGMENTS

I'm so grateful to this book's beta readers for their help and suggestions: Toni Young, Judy Rosen, and Heather Brinkley. And I never tire of thanking my beloved mom, Beryl Baily, for all her love and support.

PROLOGUE

1816, London

An insistent banging awakened Philip from a sound sleep. Sitting upright, his heart pounded until he realized it was neither gunfire nor cannon blast. Merely a thoughtless arse on his doorstep on Cavendish Square.

Glancing at the mantel clock, he swore aloud. It must be some cork-brained tippler who had no idea of the hour and needed a swift kick and a reminder of what constituted civilized manners.

Sighing, he glanced down at his soft pillow and then out at the dawn's rays already cresting the sash of his window. As a major in the British Army, with three years engagement in the Peninsular War against France, fighting alongside the Spanish and Portuguese, Philip thoroughly enjoyed his comfortable bed. Anyone or anything that took him from it—save a beautiful woman—was most unwelcome.

His butler, Mr. Cherville, would be in his dressing gown by now and ascending from his basement dwelling to see who was knocking. Swinging his feet onto the floor, Philip wrapped his naked body in a silk banyan, donned slippers, and yanked open his bedroom door.

This had better be a matter of life or death!

CHAPTER ONE

Lord Philip Mercer could not stop pacing the parlor of the magistrate's private residence. For a matter as delicate as the one that plagued him, he had decided to seek out the powerful official at his home on Russell Square. The terraced house with all its comforts was exactly as he'd expected of the upper-middle-class Sir William Bright, a man who might end up presiding over a court session involving Philip's future.

Unfortunately, while the magistrate was not there, a prying servant was.

He'd discovered the pretty maid halfway up a ladder in the magistrate's study with a dusting cloth tucked under one of her arms, reading a book which she was obviously supposed to be cleaning. Although she sported a lacy cap, her hair was haphazardly braided with much of it loose and hanging down around her slender shoulders instead of in a tidy knot. She had a smudge on one cheek and wore a rumpled apron over a dress too fetching for a servant.

Philip's next impression was that he'd encountered a barely tamed creature without the social graces to leave him alone. It was as if the young woman had never seen a man before, so intent was she on speaking with him, staring at him, and even following him around when he paced into the front hall and back again.

It was when he had done this for the third time, turning abruptly on the polished floorboards and nearly knocking the maid off her feet, that he finally exploded.

"Will you leave me in peace?" Then softening his tone, he asked, "Did you say Sir William was expected to return soon?"

The brown-haired female with hazel eyes didn't seem the least put off by his abruptness.

"He will return when he is able. I am certain."

That told him nothing, and Philip fingered the calling card in his pocket. Five more minutes and he would give it to her with the request she have the magistrate send him word when he was available.

A quarter hour earlier this shapely housemaid had descended the ladder after another maid had shown him into the study. He'd noted at once the household had no proper butler and filed away the knowledge as indicative of Sir William's income and the magistrate's potential for bribery, should it come to that.

After returning the book to its shelf, the curious female had come down to greet him and offered him a chair and a cup of tea, both of which he'd refused. Instead of returning to her duties, she'd begun to pester him incessantly.

Ignoring his request for peace, she asked him yet another question.

"Are you on the run, sir?"

"I am not a *sir*," he pointed out, hoping to put her in her place. "I am Lord Mercer."

"My apologies, *my lord*. Are you on the run?"

"What on earth can you mean by such a strange question?" Philip demanded, wondering if she were daft in the head. "From whom or from what?"

She stared at him, and her large eyes, more green than brown, did not blink for a few seconds. Then she said, "I recognize your name from *The Morning Sun* and *The Times*.

3

You were linked with Miss Waltham at a house party in Twickenham, and none too favorably."

He grimaced. The Grub Street papers were ruthless. Even the servants had heard of his latest scandal.

"You read the papers, do you?"

"I do," she confessed with glee, and he supposed she had little else in her humdrum existence from which to derive pleasure. "I love the gossipmongering and the rumors. Who is doing what, and all that. It's not my world, and therefore, everyone is just like a character in a story."

Then she gave a snap of her fingers. "You're a baron, are you not?"

Good God! He was surprised they didn't have his height and weight listed, too. But the maid wasn't finished with him.

"I couldn't help but wonder if you were here to turn yourself in privately for some nefarious deed, something to do with Miss Waltham. Or mayhap you're here to ask Sir William to look after your affairs while you fled?"

What an impudent chit! On the other hand, she was just comely enough to get away with it. Besides her large, sparkling eyes, she had full breasts atop a pleasing figure from what he could tell where the apron was tied around her slender waist.

"The only thing I am running from is Miss Waltham's irate father," he told her. "He reputedly has a good aim."

"What did you do to his daughter?" she asked.

Philip nearly growled. *This wench could not hold her tongue!* What's more, she was asking him too many personal questions. He might have a word with the magistrate when he arrived regarding the quality of his help.

On second thought, he decided to plead his case and see how it sounded, for it was the bald truth.

"I vow what you read in the gossip column is a case of mistaken identity," he said.

"You were never with the lady in question?" she asked.

The maid sounded like a solicitor. Philip coughed.

"I might have enjoyed a kiss with her, but nothing else."

She raised her eyebrows. "Such as?"

All at once he wondered if she knew what else could be done or whether she was an utter innocent. Regardless, he wasn't about to discuss such things.

"I did not get Miss Waltham in the suds. That was another man," he vowed.

The maid nodded again, looking sage beyond her years.

"Do you know who it was, this *other* man?"

Philip shrugged slightly, noticing how she took in his movements before staring him in the eyes once more. She was an inquisitive, watchful, and strange chick-a-biddy, to be sure.

"I know *of* him. I have it on good authority who the scoundrel was from the servants' grapevine. I'm sure you know how reliable and swift that is."

She nodded in agreement. With all her questions, her luscious mouth was probably one of *the* most reliable and swift of all. As soon as he left, undoubtedly she would bolt below to the servants' quarters to tell the magistrate's other help what she'd learned.

In fact, it might be a good idea to tell her a little more. Mayhap, Philip would be believed once the gossip grapevine began whispering about *his* side of the tale.

"I believe Miss Waltham is protecting her lover," he added.

"And her parents blame you," she guessed. "But why?"

"From the kiss. Alas, we were seen by her mother from the drawing room window," Philip confessed.

"How terribly exciting!" the maid exclaimed.

"No, it is not. It is terribly irritating, not to mention dangerous from my perspective. Miss Waltham won't say it is *not* me, thereby throwing me to the wolves. There were a number of single gentlemen at the house party, but only I was seen kissing her."

"Worse and worse," the young woman said, but she was smiling as if it were a game, which irked him tremendously until she asked, "Do you love her?"

Shocked, Philip shook his head vigorously. "Of course not!"

"Why do you say it like that, my lord? Why 'of course not' as if you couldn't possibly love someone you were kissing?"

"It is not that." He lifted his hat from his head, ran a hand through his hair, and then replaced the brim. "I suppose it seems obvious to me and, thus, should be to you. If I loved her, then I would allow myself to be trapped into marrying her. However, I have no feelings for her at all. I merely kissed her because she was alone on the terrace and looked as though she wanted to be kissed."

Philip could see that interested his interrogator.

"That seems a rather weak reason. So you sloppily pressed your lips to a stranger's?"

How outrageous—as if she were a judge of how to kiss! He had done things she could never dream about, and he was beginning to wish he could show her one or two of them. He hadn't felt as tempted by a maid since he was in his teen years. Since then, he'd taken his pleasure either with available ladies of his class, both willing young vixens and frustrated widows, or more often with Cyprians.

Nothing was more enjoyable than paying for a night with an experienced whore who could—and would—do anything, leaving him free to walk away when finished without looking back.

With the maid's greenish-gold eyes fixed on him, he felt the urge to explain.

"Miss Waltham and I were not strangers. Her father and I have a business arrangement. Moreover, we'd eaten dinner within five feet of one another more than once, and we'd played charades. And there was nothing *sloppy* about the kiss. If I were to demonstrate, you impertinent rattle-pate, you would agree. In any case, we shouldn't be discussing this. It is crass. Vulgar even."

"Kissing isn't vulgar," she protested.

Ah-ha! She wasn't quite so innocent. Maybe that's why he found her enticing.

"You are correct. It is not, yet discussing it most certainly is, especially talking about a lady. I don't speak at my club about such things for I am a gentleman, and I don't wish to speak any more about such things with you."

He folded his arms.

"I see what you mean," she said. "Discretion and honor and such." When she paused, Philip hoped she would finally leave him alone.

"Do you think Miss Waltham wishes to marry you?" she asked, continuing her investigation.

He sighed. "I believe she is in trouble up to her earlobes and isn't thinking clearly. It has been my experience that most young ladies do not."

MIRANDA WOULD HAVE BEEN annoyed at such an unfavorable statement if she didn't partially concur. Her own sister was a ninny. Grace had never cared for anything more than playing cards and discussing fashion. Besides, having a verified rake at her disposal was too wonderful to ignore without getting as much out of him as she could. Stomping off in a huff over an impudent slight to the female of the species would get her nowhere.

She wanted to write a little starry-eyed story, maybe even one of those stimulating novels women were always warned about, only for her favorite romantic-minded cousin to read. And Lord Mercer was the perfect font of information.

"Do you think people would read a book if it didn't contain Miss Austen's perfect comedy of manners or Mr.

Defoe's and Mr. Swift's adventures?" she asked him. "I suppose you don't read novels anyway, my lord."

He stared a long while before he looked away.

"When did you say Sir William might return?"

"One never knows," Miranda told him, intending to be vague to keep the man from hurrying off.

"Sometimes he is gone for hours," she added. "Sometimes just a short while. He might come through the door to help you within a very few minutes. But let me understand you. If Miss Waltham holds her tongue, then she shall not be pressed to marry the scoundrel, as you call him. On the other hand, she might end up married to you if you're not unlucky enough to be killed in a duel by her father."

"Unlucky?" Lord Mercer echoed. "I would consider such an event a great deal worse than unlucky."

She waved her hand, dismissing his words. "I fail to understand the reasoning behind the lady's silence. It helps no one. You might die, and she will still be disgraced and alone. Or you may live, and she'll be forced to wed you, and she won't end up with the man she loves. That is, if she does love the scoundrel. And vice versa."

"Vice versa?" he repeated, frowning.

"It means something along the lines of a change in the order."

"I know what it means," he snapped.

"Then why did you ask?"

"I did not," he professed. "I wondered to what you are referring."

"I see." Miranda hoped to be clear for she was truly trying to understand this other woman's motives. "I mean if the scoundrel loves her, too, he won't end up with Miss Waltham unless she confesses to *his* involvement. Neither of them wins by her silence. And thus, I wonder why she does not simply tell the truth?"

"It is a world which you do not understand," he said superciliously.

Lord Mercer was probably right, and Miranda was ever so pleased he was going to explain it to her.

"If Miss Waltham were to let on about the existence of another man apart from myself, with whom she was seen in an embrace, then she would be considered irreparably immoral, loose, and sullied, and the scoundrel would be considered dastardly beyond reform."

"Are *you* considered dastardly?" she asked.

He smiled sheepishly. "Everyone knows me for a man of the Town. I cannot deny it, but I am also a gentleman through and through. Miss Waltham must have thought me too convenient an excuse to pass up, but I would never ruin a young lady and then leave her to face the consequences alone."

He crossed his arms. "If Miss Waltham drags me into the suds with her and, as you said, hopes I die or at the very least I refuse to marry her, then the man she loves can step in like a crusader from days of yore. He will look to be the epitome of heroic self-sacrifice when he weds a woman already ruined by another."

"By you?" she asked.

Lord Mercer sighed. "Precisely, except I did not." To her surprise he muttered softy, "But I should have."

Miranda could not help the little shiver that whisked through her at the notion this lusty satyr regretted *not* tupping some young lady, merely because he could have.

Taking his measure again, from his impressive height to his thick tawny hair, handsome face, and broad shoulders all the way down to his trim waist and firm, muscular thighs, she came over all hot.

Better not to think of such matters. Instead, she focused on the young lady's machinations.

"What a clever plan Miss Waltham has," she remarked.

"You sound as if you admire this conniving wench."

Miranda considered. "I presume the lady has few options."

Lord Mercer grunted. "I suppose you're correct. Regardless, I don't intend to be one of them."

"I wonder what the scoundrel thinks of all this."

"I have no way of knowing his opinion," Lord Mercer declared, "nor do I care."

Miranda stepped forward, unable to help her enthusiasm. "But you should, my lord. *He* may be your solution. Why don't you speak with him?"

He laughed at her. Finally, he stopped and said, "You believe I should speak with the rogue about how he may or may not have ruined Miss Waltham?"

"Yes, naturally." She couldn't see why he didn't think that a perfectly sound notion.

"I suppose now is a good time to tell you *he* is a marquess's son."

Miranda blinked. "And what does that signify?"

"You jest," Lord Mercer said. "He won't take kindly to being accused. If he wanted the young lady, he would have stepped forward and made his intentions known."

"Perhaps he is unaware of her trouble," she pointed out.

"How could he not know?" Lord Mercer was pacing again.

"Perhaps she has no way to tell him. Mayhap Miss Waltham is being watched like a mouse by a hungry owl," Miranda explained. "Most females are."

His lordship crossed his arms and came to stand before her.

"That is precisely how females are supposed to be watched, from the highest-born lady to the lowliest, slovenly housemaid. And that includes you, left to your own waywardness as you appear to be."

Miranda gaped. "Me?" *When had this become about her?*

"You are alone with a man considered to be something of a scapegrace," he reminded her, "and no one is the wiser."

Lord Mercer took a step closer. "Why are you allowed to flagrantly flout the customs of decorum?"

Miranda felt a shimmer of excitement. "Do you intend to kiss me, my lord? Is that why you moved toward me? It is most exciting."

She wasn't surprised. She'd been told she was pretty with something about her that caught a man's eye.

The baron grimaced. "When you dissect my every action and ask a hundred infernal questions, it is off-putting. And when you forget that you are meant to display a modicum of trepidation as any sane female, yet instead welcome the notion of my taking a liberty with your person, then the answer is no. That is not how this is done."

Miranda felt the hollow ache of disappointment. While she had received precisely two kisses in her life, being kissed by a dashing rake would be an excellent experience, and what could be safer than receiving said kiss in her own home?

"Please, then, tell me precisely how this is done," she begged, "but hold on a moment." Rummaging in the pocket hanging off her apron, she withdrew a square of paper and a pencil. She'd nearly forgotten she was wearing the unflattering garment while helping tidy her father's office. Still, even in disarray as she was, this raffish man might kiss her!

Currently, however, he was gaping at her writing implements.

"Whatever are they for?"

"For the story, of course." She cocked her head. *Had he been listening?* "I thought I explained that."

He shook his head. "You are well-educated, too much for your position in life. It's almost a shame."

Miranda couldn't help chuckling. "I am perfectly normal in all regards. I simply wish to entertain my country cousin and her brother with an amusing tale."

"At my expense," he grumbled.

"Only because you are here and seem to be full of interesting things to tell me. Why, there have been at least five already."

He took another step closer.

"What are you doing now?" she asked.

"You *do* look immensely kissable."

A tremor of warmth shot through her. "Like Miss Waltham at the house party?"

Lord Mercer shook his head. "Quite the contrary. She looked like she *wanted* to be kissed. Since I was on hand, I obliged, not realizing she might be waiting for another who would do far more than that."

Far more? Miranda swallowed, thinking she would like to hear about that as well, but another time. Both his unfamiliar closeness and the look in his dark-brown eyes quite mesmerized her.

"Are you saying I do *not* look like I want to be kissed?"

"I am saying that with your sweet lips and big eyes, even with that silly piece of paper awaiting your scribblings, you appear exceptionally kissable."

Then he paused. "*Do* you, in fact, wish to be kissed?"

She took in a quick breath. "I confess I hadn't thought too much about it, but now I must say I am pleased by the prospect."

"You are an odd fish for a housemaid."

A housemaid? She nearly laughed, belatedly realizing his misinterpretation of the situation. *And who could blame him?* After all, he hadn't found her seated in the parlor working on her needlepoint.

Before she could explain, his next step brought him within touching distance. His fine wool trousers got lost in the draping of her apron and her cotton dress. The inner warmth became delicious heat, making her feel flushed to the core. He *was* going to kiss her!

Slowly, Lord Mercer wrapped a hand around each of her upper arms and drew her against him until her breasts were crushed against his fitted jacket.

"How thrilling!" she proclaimed before closing her eyes. All the better for her other senses to take in these new sensations. She could smell a manly scent of sandalwood and lime, different from her father, who always had the aroma of tobacco clinging to him.

Where the baron's hands gripped her, she tingled beneath his fingers, and she would swear she could feel his heat like a brand upon her skin, despite his gloves.

After what seemed an eternity, long enough she nearly opened her eyes, finally his mouth touched hers.

What a zesty treat!

Miranda knew the instant it became more than an amusing experience to tell Helen, her cousin with whom she was closest in all the world. When Lord Mercer tilted his head, the kiss became her first "real" kiss. Her insides sizzled, and she would vow there was a direct path from his lips to her nipples and down to the juncture between her thighs where she now throbbed.

Feeling his teeth graze her lower lip, she moaned.

"What in blue blazes?"

Miranda snapped open her eyes at the sound of her father's voice. At the same time, all contact with Lord Mercer ceased as he dropped his hands from her and backed away.

Turning to her balding, spectacle-wearing sire, she greeted him fondly with a wave of her fingers. Luckily, he was both an indulgent parent and a reasonable man.

"Good day, Papa. Lord Mercer is here to see you on an important matter."

CHAPTER TWO

Papa! The devil take him for a fool if he hadn't just stupidly kissed the magistrate's daughter. *And been caught!*

Philip had brought it upon himself this time, except he'd been correct. Miss Bright *was* extremely kissable! She smelled good and had the softest lips he could recall. None of which excused him letting his baser nature take over.

"I offer my sincerest apology, sir," Philip began under the magistrate's stony gaze. "It was . . . that is . . . ," he trailed off. It had been an impetuous action, to kiss a pretty maid only to find out she was not a servant.

What could he say?

"Papa, I only wanted a kiss so I could write a story for Helen. Lord Mercer was kind enough to cooperate. Besides he didn't know I was your daughter. He thought he was kissing our maid."

The magistrate appeared confounded. "Kissing Eliza? But you look nothing like her!"

"No, Papa. I didn't mean he thought I was actually our Eliza." Then she laughed, and Philip wondered if she was dicked in the nob for neither he nor her father were the least bit amused.

"His lordship merely mistook my appearance."

"And no wonder! Why on earth are you dressed in that manner?" Sir William raised his voice. "Didn't that half-wit, Mrs. Emblin, teach you anything at her Ladies' Seminary?"

With that Miss Bright, appearing perfectly calm, untied her apron from behind and then unpinned it from the top of her dress before folding the garment over her arm. As she did, a gum elastic for erasing her wretched graphite scribblings and a small knife for sharpening her pencil fell to the floor.

As a gentleman, Philip leaned down to retrieve the items, catching her floral scent again as they nearly bumped heads when she stooped to do the same. Thrusting her writing tools into her hand, trying hard not to touch her bare skin, he backed away quickly.

"Thank you, my lord," she said, giving him a sweet smile that caused his insides to lurch through some feminine magic he couldn't fathom. Then she turned to her father again.

"No, Mrs. Emblin did not teach me, Papa, because *I* didn't attend. That was Grace. Please don't get in such a state. You know how easily you become out of sorts."

Worse and worse! Philip wished he had never come.

"Having two daughters will do that to a man," Sir William said to no one in particular. In fact, the magistrate seemed to have momentarily forgotten Philip until he suddenly sent him a scowling look.

"Are you here to ask for this one's hand? She's meek, mild, and knows her place. Can't you tell?"

"I . . . that is, . . . I . . . ," Philip didn't know what to say. He didn't want to insult the man by telling him his daughter seemed like a forward minx and was, if not the last person he would consider marrying, then fairly low on his list.

To his consternation, the hoyden laughed at Philip's discomfort, which seemed intolerably disrespectful not only to him but to her father, too. However, the older man merely sighed, took off his hat and gloves, even shrugging out of his jacket, all of which he handed to his daughter since there was still no butler and now no maid in sight either.

Then the magistrate stared at him, and Philip realized he still hadn't answered.

"No, sir. I came about another woman."

"Well, you're too late. My eldest was married last year."

"No, sir," Philip tried again. "I am here to speak with you about a lady who is not one of your daughters."

"Why?" Sir William demanded. "What's wrong with this one? You seemed to like her well enough when your mouth was upon hers."

Miss Bright gasped. "Papa! Please. You're embarrassing his lordship."

Philip stared, agog that this chit would speak to her own father in such a fashion, while the magistrate didn't bat an eye. He wasn't sure what to make of this madhouse. If Sir William wasn't a well-respected man of law, one who presided over a petty sessions court among others, then Philip would have made himself scarce when the winsome female first started asking him questions. Even then, if he could bow out without causing offence, he would do it.

"It was a mistake, sir. I did, indeed, believe Miss Bright to be your maid."

The magistrate grimaced. Immediately, Philip wished he had not said anything so stupid. It made him sound like a dastardly predator who went after those who were powerless, which he was not.

"I was dusting when he arrived," Miss Bright chimed in. "And then he told me how he is being blamed for ruining Miss Waltham. But he swears he didn't." She looked at Philip and nodded in his direction.

Clearly, she thought she was helping, but he could almost feel the magistrate's hostility emanating like waves of heat from a well-stoked stove.

"You see, Lord Mercer merely obliged the lady with a kiss," Miss Bright continued, "and nothing more. Someone else ruined her."

Philip wished he could stop her talking, but that was like wishing he could hold back the ocean. The magistrate's visage had grown ever more grim at her words. Yet instead of throwing Philip out of his home, he took his daughter to task.

"You cannot behave like this," he said to her in a scolding tone before adding, "with such carelessness." Then the older man shook his head. "You will never get a husband if you go on in this way. You shall only attract *his* type."

Philip didn't enjoy being considered the dregs of marriageable material, but the magistrate had the right of it. *His* type, as the papers liked to point out, was not the marrying kind. At least not yet. There were too many lovely ladies to taste and titillate.

Regardless, he should not have tried to enjoy a sensual encounter with this particular one. Nor could he imagine how he would now ask for the assistance he needed to clear his name, but he would do it anyhow.

Without any further preamble, the magistrate said, "Leave us, and I will talk to his lordship."

Philip waited, but Miss Bright didn't even pretend to obey.

Ignoring his daughter's insubordination, Sir William turned to him.

"What do you want?"

Philip couldn't quite believe he was going to ask him for anything after being caught kissing the man's daughter—a kiss so simple and sweet he'd lost himself briefly.

"As Miss Bright mentioned, I am Lord Mercer of the Mercer barony in Guildford. I am here on a delicate matter." He shot the magistrate's daughter a look, hoping she would go away. Her presence would only make it worse because of their indiscretion.

"I have heard of you," the magistrate said.

Philip feared he would be hoisted on the petard of his own scandalous reputation. But the next question was of an entirely different nature.

"You were in Europe in the war, yes?" enquired Sir William.

"Were you?" Miss Bright asked. "Why didn't the newspapers mention that when they go on about your more questionable deeds?"

Philip wondered how she had become a sharp and needling thorn in such a short time.

The magistrate narrowed his eyes, then he gestured toward the parlor instead of his study.

Unfortunately, behind Sir William went his very troublesome daughter who seemed to be made of tar, so fixed was she upon sticking with him.

"Perhaps we could speak in private, sir."

The magistrate shrugged but said to his daughter, "Fetch me a cup of tea and one for the baron while he tells me his woes without your interference."

"But, Papa, I already know all about his woes. I shall ring for Eliza." And she wrapped her slender fingers around the bell pull with an insistent tug that somehow caused a spark of desire to shoot to Philip's loins.

Coughing, he looked away.

He was correct. Miss Bright was troublesome. She had disobeyed her father. *Again!* The magistrate didn't seem to notice or to care. Nor did he wait for his daughter to take a seat. The balding man sat heavily upon a winged chair and put his feet on a velvet ottoman.

"I've already had a busy morning, my lord," Sir William said. "In order for me not to look unbearably rude, please take a seat."

"Thank you," Philip said, but he remained standing, watching Miss Bright.

He might be a riotous rake who'd just displayed dreadfully poor judgment, but he would not dismiss all civilized behavior. He waited while she poked her head out the doorway and spoke with someone who'd come along the passageway, presumably regarding the refreshments.

"Take a seat, dear," her father ordered, seeing Philip's conundrum.

"Oh, I see," she remarked and finally did as she was told, sitting upon the couch.

At last, Philip could follow suit, and he did—taking the other winged chair, which was as far from Miss Bright as possible.

"Go ahead, my lord." This prompt came from *her* and not the magistrate.

Before he could say anything more, however, she asked, "Are you truly an officer? Where did you fight?"

Frowning, Philip could hardly ignore her without insult although he didn't particularly care to speak about the war, especially in front of a female.

"I am an officer, yes. A major—"

"Major Mercer," she said, and to his astonishment, she chuckled softly. "It has a lovely alliteration."

Was her father going to allow her to keep gabbing like a magpie?

The man had put his head back and closed his eyes. Perhaps he was sleeping.

In the next instant, he knew the magistrate was awake for he said, "My daughter wondered where you served, my lord. If you don't tell her, she'll only ask again."

Philip found himself locked in a battle of the gazes with Miss Bright, who merely smiled and waited.

"Mostly, I was on the Iberian Peninsula with Wellington. I served with him at Vitoria and then right through the last battle at Waterloo." For a moment, Philip's sight was clouded by smoke and flames and men screaming.

"Waterloo!" Miss Bright exclaimed, drawing him from his reverie.

"Tell me," the magistrate prompted, his eyes now open and narrowed, "what do you need from me?"

Philip cleared his throat. "To put it plainly, I have been wrongfully accused of ruining a young lady."

Silence met his declaration. The irony was not lost on any of the three of them. After an excruciatingly long and awkward pause during which Miss Bright continuously flicked the edge of her paper with her finger, the magistrate sighed.

"Is that right?"

"Yes," Philip muttered.

"*Wrongfully* accused, you say?"

"Yes, I do say. The accusation goes far beyond a mere kiss," Philip added, wishing he hadn't let his glance flit over to the last lips he'd kissed. Swiftly, he yanked his gaze back to Sir William. "The charge is far more damming, and I swear it was not I."

The magistrate steepled his fingers. "I do not know you at all, and thus, I cannot take your word for it. Nevertheless, your service to our country goes a long way toward putting you in good standing."

"I believe him, Papa," Miss Bright chimed in. "He told me all about it. The young lady in question *wanted* to be kissed, you see. His lordship merely did as she wanted. He has no reason to lie to me."

"And did you also wish to be kissed?" the magistrate asked his daughter, holding her in his gaze.

Philip watched the young woman close her mouth firmly while her cheeks turned a perfect shade of dark rose. Just when he hoped she had finally gone silent for good, she sighed and spoke.

"I suppose I did," she admitted.

Philip almost fell off his chair at her admission.

"But his lordship said he was going to kiss me because I looked kissable, *not* because I wanted to be kissed. It's a brilliant distinction that I didn't understand until he explained it."

Philip wished he could clamp his hand over her mouth as firmly as he'd kissed it. She had no common sense, no awareness of when to hold her tongue. That was plain.

The magistrate's glance flew to his.

Philip flinched. *What could he do?*

At last, shrugging, he felt like the mischievous youth he'd once been at Harrow public school.

"Again, I offer my profound apologies. Your daughter was speaking of romance and asking many questions, and I can only say I was carried away by fleeting madness, being severely worried about the situation with Miss Waltham."

He stopped talking as it didn't sound any better no matter how many times he or Miss Bright discussed it. He had behaved badly, and there was no defense.

"Hm," Sir William said, and then the maid came in with the tea tray.

When they all had a cup in hand, Philip hoped the magistrate would offer his professional assistance, but again, it was the daughter who spoke.

"Please, Papa, won't you help Lord Major Mercer?"

Philip couldn't help smiling at her convoluted use of his title, even when she continued prattling.

"I suggested someone speak to the other man in question. Perhaps she hasn't told the scoundrel who ruined her, and so he along with her parents are entirely in the dark."

"And the scoundrel is?" asked her father, looking directly at Philip.

"Lord Rowantry, sir."

"The marquess's son?" The magistrate frowned slightly.

"Yes, the very one," Philip said.

"Oh my, then you are in a mud puddle, aren't you?" And Sir William sipped his tea, seemingly unconcerned.

"Yes, I believe I am. Moreover, there are reasons I cannot simply gainsay Miss Waltham and declare her to be pulling the long bow."

"I beg your pardon?" asked Miss Bright.

"Lying," her father explained. "And why is that, my lord?"

"For one thing, I am not in the habit of insulting young ladies, and I would find it to be beyond distasteful."

"Oh, very good," Miss Bright said. "You see, Papa, even a notorious rake can be a gentleman."

Was it possible she might choke on her tea and be rendered speechless? Philip could only hope.

The magistrate merely grunted, and Philip continued.

"Also, I have recently gone into partnership with her father and his brother. They have a fleet of cargo ships, and I'm counting upon them to bring lucrative freight from France. I have no wish to lose my investment nor my deposit, and so far, our deal has not been compromised."

"Even though Miss Waltham has been," Miss Bright said quietly.

Philip glanced sharply at her, but she wasn't making fun of him. She was simply enjoying a play on words.

The magistrate sipped his tea silently and appeared to be contemplating the situation. He looked from Philip to Miss Bright a few times.

Philip could only hope the ill-advised kiss hadn't ruined his chances of receiving the aid of this powerful man. With the court magistrate on his side, Miss Waltham and her father, Lord Perrin, would be obliged either to offer up some evidence or remove any shadow of doubt from Philip's reputation, at least regarding this transgression.

"The family's solicitor came pounding upon my door declaring all sorts of utter lies," he added, recalling being dumbfounded by the false accusations.

He honestly didn't want to confront the young lady, nor embarrass her. But with the magistrate's help, Philip would demand she come forward to state her claim. She would have to declare before her parents, God, and Sir William that Philip was the blackguard who'd ruined her. He doubted Miss Waltham would have the fortitude to publicly vow they'd made the two-backed beast.

22

At least, he hoped not. He might be a rakish Corinthian, but dishonesty was another matter altogether. And he liked to believe most people weren't duplicitous, especially not ladies of good breeding.

"I intend to have a successful import business," Philip added, for stating it made it seem as if it were still possible. At the same time, he was loath to elucidate the true importance of his new brandy endeavor to the magistrate.

"You seem to be a determined young man," Sir William said, still eyeing him with the same hazel-colored eyes as his daughter.

"And yet the papers talk as if you spend all your time enjoying yourself," Miss Bright said, sounding mystified.

Philip glared at her, but he had to defend himself. "During the day, I believe I work as hard as anyone."

"And during the nighttime?" the magistrate asked, reclaiming Philip's attention.

Blast! Regardless, he would continue to speak the truth. "I suppose I know well how to entertain myself. London is a marvelous city, and I missed it greatly while I was away." He would leave it at that.

At last, Sir William set down his cup. "I will help you on one condition."

"Yes?" Philip basked in relief until he noticed an unsettling glint in the man's eyes.

"You will escort my daughter exclusively for the rest of the Season."

CHAPTER THREE

"Papa!" Miss Bright exclaimed before Philip could respond.

The magistrate lifted a hand to halt her protest, if that was what she'd been about to do. Then the man stared expectantly at Philip.

"Why would you want me to do that?" The question left his lips before he thought better of asking it, but why would any father trust him with his female offspring?

"To launch her, of course. It must be properly done with you as escort and a chaperone for every assembly. Not a whiff of scandal, mind you, merely your respectful admiration while taking her to every choice event and bringing her home safely. You may even dance twice of an evening if you wish."

"Papa," Miss Bright said again, shaking her head, unable to look Philip in the eyes. "Why would you ask Lord Major Mercer to do such a thing?"

The magistrate raised an eyebrow, and Philip understood at once.

"In order to bring suitors flocking to see what all the fuss is about," Philip guessed, eyeing her again.

"Precisely," her father said.

Miss Bright was a pretty enough chit, honey-brown hair, those curious verdant hazel eyes, and a full lower lip that would make most men think of one thing.

Besides all those attributes, she had a figure that was rounded in the right places.

The magistrate coughed, and Philip realized he had spent too long assessing Miss Bright, sizing her up as he would prime horseflesh at a Tattersall's auction.

"It's a good plan," he announced.

"Is it?" Miss Bright asked doubtfully.

"The bucks will come running if they are anything like the young men of my day," the magistrate said. "As soon as I started to pay attention to your mother, God rest her soul, so did the other single coves, every Tommy Tit and Jack O'Dandy." Then he looked at Philip. "Naturally she chose me anyway."

"Naturally," Philip echoed, starting to like the man. "For the entire remainder of the Season, you say?"

The magistrate nodded.

"And in return, you'll get me out of my plight?" Philip pressed.

"As long as you don't disgrace my daughter in any way. No dishonor, shame, or even the smallest smudge to her reputation."

"She will be with me, and my reputation is not that of a saint." Philip hated to remind him, but it was the truth.

"Fair enough, as long as you don't practice your raffish ways on her, she won't be tainted. It will seem as if she has tamed a wolf. All the better. Everyone will wonder how she did it. Moreover, they'll see her in the light of being someone quite extraordinary."

As she already is, Philip thought. Then he rose to his feet and leaned over to offer the magistrate his hand.

MIRANDA WATCHED HER FATHER shake Lord Mercer's hand with her mouth hanging partly open. Normally she would have protested their belittling discussion. At least, she might have demanded they treat her as though she existed rather than talking about her and settling her future as if she were not present.

However, she thought about what she would gain from the arrangement and snapped her mouth closed. She hadn't gone along with any of her father's previous plans to marry her off, mostly because they hadn't involved an interesting baron.

The year before, despite how obtaining a ticket for Almack's had been next to impossible, her father had called in a favor. Thus, holding "stranger's tickets," as they were named, Miranda and her older sister, Grace, had attended on two successive Wednesday evenings the year prior. There were easily five hundred in attendance at each ball. Men pranced and posed. Ladies giggled and batted their eyelashes.

Miranda ended both evenings wishing she hadn't wasted her time, although her sister had found a suitor who offered for her almost at once. Consequently, Grace was now married—happily or not, Miranda couldn't say as her sister had been whisked away to the north country of the Yorkshire Dales and hadn't been seen since. Her letters indicated she was content, and her husband doted upon her.

Whereas two unmarried daughters had been a tremendous worry, with one taken care of, her father had been less insistent. When he'd tried to get her to attend a ball with his sister, her widowed Aunt Lucinda, she'd refused. Her father had allowed Miranda to decline his offers to get her out into society. And lately, he'd stopped trying.

Not that she didn't want a husband and a family of her own—it was simply how awkward and forced the whole ballroom experience had felt.

Yet with a nobleman as her escort, everything would be different. Instead of Almack's curated but public balls, she would attend the private Mayfair ballrooms. *How exciting!*

Miranda could hardly imagine what stories she could tell her cousins once she began rubbing elbows with the quality folk. All those people she read about in the society column would be directly in front of her in the flesh.

And already, there was Lord Mercer's surprising kiss to be described.

Of the men who had tried to kiss her, this stranger was one of only three who had succeeded, and he was the first who hadn't made her want to wipe her mouth and rinse it with her father's best wine.

This was what happened, she supposed, when one loitered mid-afternoon in an apron and kept company with a rake. And now she would do so for weeks, except without an apron. And amazingly, it was at her father's behest.

When the men finally turned to her, she managed to present to them a neutral expression before taking a sip of tea and even shrugging a little. Inside, she was bubbling with the thrill of this endeavor. Whether she found a husband or not was of little consequence. She would experience a great deal in the meantime.

Her father narrowed his eyes, clearly having anticipated her protest and staunch resistance. Lately, she had told him she would rather read in her room than waltz. Instead, she nodded.

"Very well," she said and left it at that.

Lord Mercer nodded, too, as if he'd expected nothing less of a dutiful daughter. Finally, her father relaxed.

Let them both think her docile.

"She'll need ball gowns," her father said, once more addressing Lord Mercer.

"Surely you don't expect me to dress your daughter," the baron protested.

Her father crossed his arms. "A small price to pay in comparison to the large cost of supporting a wife and babe," he shot back. "Anyway, don't you want the female on your arm to look like a diamond of the first water? Or would you prefer she accompany you dressed in rags?"

Miranda smiled. She usually wore better than rags. On the other hand, she had only two acceptable evening dresses made for Almack's, and neither of them new.

"We can't have my Miranda being embarrassed," her father continued.

"Miranda," Lord Mercer echoed thoughtfully, and she shivered upon hearing her name on his lips.

He had kissed her, and therefore, a measure of intimacy had already occurred. Nevertheless, hearing him say her given name aloud, especially in front of her father, made her cheeks grow decidedly warm.

"Hm," her father said, apparently also noting the infraction. "Remember, you will treat her with respect and utmost decorum."

Lord Mercer put his right hand over his heart and gave a shallow bow in confirmation.

"When shall we begin?"

MIRANDA BARELY HAD TIME to send a missive to her cousin Helen, which would be shared with her other cousin Peter, announcing her unexpected turn in fortune. They would most excitedly be awaiting each and every letter describing her attendance of the remaining six weeks of the Season. For while she shared a special bond with her female cousin, Peter had also been known to appreciate good London gossip.

The following day, in the company of her father's sister, Aunt Lucinda, Miranda infiltrated the exclusive establishment of Madame Devy's at the juncture of Grafton and New Bond Street. The experience of choosing fabric for so many gowns was practically overwhelming. While being measured, Miranda mentioned the first event was within the week, and she would need an evening dress.

"Unheard of!" exclaimed the modiste, shaking her head.

"Impossible!" cried the head seamstress, throwing her arms up.

However, when Aunt Lucinda pointed out how this was for the Baron of Mercer, a war hero, suddenly everything became possible. Miranda accepted this development was not due to the service he'd performed for his country but rather that he was known to have a sizable estate and upward of thirty-thousand pounds a year.

"His lordship may need a wedding dress for a bride someday soon," Madame Devy mused.

"An entire *trousseau*," the head seamstress added in a tone of excitement, "and plenty of gowns for his new baroness."

Miranda thought them mistaken. The baron most definitely did not wish to have a wife, and if she captured the interest of some single gentleman over the next six weeks, then her father would pay for anything she needed up until the wedding day.

Like any young lady, Miranda also acquired a dozen new pairs of soft doeskin slippers for dancing and just as many pairs of gloves.

"Stockings!" her aunt announced, scanning the list she kept pulling out of her reticule as they traveled between Wood, which manufactured ladies' fashionable shoes, and Harding Howell & Co. for a new parasol. "Shawls, two new spencers. Oh, and we must see about a riding gown, something with a very full skirt."

Miranda hoped Lord Mercer knew the extent of a woman's wardrobe for a Season, far beyond a few ball gowns. *Would he be annoyed?*

Two days later when he stomped into their front hall and was shown into the parlor where she was answering a letter from Helen, she had her answer.

"These bills were dropped off at my house." He waggled a few account slips in front of her. "You must cease outfitting all of your friends, for that can be the only explanation as to how you could have spent a fortune in such a brief period."

"Gowns are not cheap," Miranda told him, thinking he looked very fine even when in a great tweague. "But I believe you'll find those bills are less expensive than a wife and baby."

"Don't you go using that same tired argument upon me. Besides, it doesn't give you license to fleece me. Let me have a word with your father. Is he here?"

Miranda wasn't sure if she should tell Lord Mercer they were alone. Her father's words about the utmost propriety between them rather knocked her preference for a casual friendship upon its head. From then on, they would probably never have a private moment, and all her questions would have to be done in the presence of her aunt.

"I assure you, my lord, I purchased *only* what was necessary."

"Gloves in *every* color," he stated, slapping the papers against his palm.

"To match each of my dresses," she explained.

He paused. "Do they have to?"

"I was advised they ought to whenever possible."

"And if not possible?" he asked.

"Then I will wear white, of course."

"Of course." Then he glanced at one of the bills again. "Do you ride, Miss Bright?"

"Not as yet, no." She was looking forward to doing so, especially with the major by her side. She was certain he would sit a fine horse.

"You're not much of a horsewoman, then?" he asked, his voice mild.

She shook her head.

He pounced in a louder tone, "Then why am I paying dearly for not one but two riding gowns? With matching hats!"

"And a crop," she confessed. "But only one, as well as a single pair of riding boots. I had no idea how attractive they were until I tried them on."

He stared at her, then looked down at the bills, then back at her.

"Do you not intend to take me riding in Hyde Park?" Miranda asked.

He frowned. "I suppose I shall. And if I understand this arrangement, you will wish to borrow a gentle mare from my stable. Unless you have already purchased one and I have yet to receive the bill from Tattersall's."

Seeing his expression and hearing his exasperated words, Miranda laughed.

"I promise you, my lord, I did not buy a horse. And we do own a carriage and a pair."

The baron's nostrils flared. She thought he might even have shuddered.

"You will not ride with me on a carriage nag. I will provide you with a suitable mount."

"Very well. Do you still need to speak with my father?"

"No," he said.

"That's good because he is not here," she confessed, "and if he came home now and found us, I believe this is precisely the type of behavior of which he would disapprove. Our being alone, I mean."

Lord Mercer suddenly had a hunted look on his handsome face and took a quick step away from her.

"You should have told me at the outset. And then the appropriate thing to do would have been to call a maid to stand with us."

"It is too late now," she reminded him, eager to write down every nuance of their encounter as well as how fine he looked in his cream-colored, buckskin breeches that molded to his impressive thighs.

"In any case, my lord, I have a letter to write, and it is urgent."

"Are you dismissing me?" he demanded.

"Not if you have something more to say." She stared up at him. "Do you?"

He pursed his lips. "I shall pick you up for Breadalbane's ball at eight o' clock on Friday. Please be ready. I hate to be kept waiting, and make sure you have a suitable chaperone. I cannot afford to risk your father's ire and, thus, his help."

"Yes, my lord. That is the plan." Aunt Lucinda would undoubtedly be ready by the stroke of six and seated in the parlor awaiting her chance to take the baron's measure.

"*We* shall see you then."

PHILIP CLIMBED INTO HIS carriage feeling out of sorts. He knew Miss Bright meant her and her chaperone when she said "we," but he'd heard tell the Virgin Queen, Elizabeth, referred to herself in the plural. It rubbed Philip roughly, especially when Miss Bright had all but sent him away over some blasted letter-writing nonsense.

That young woman needed to be taken down a peg. Bringing her into his world of well-bred ladies would suffice. Let her see the females with whom he usually mingled, not to mention with whom he shared his bed. Each and every one was glad of his company!

The next forty-eight hours crept by with Philip dodging anyone who seemed to be a representative from Lord Perrin or his brother Waltham. Sir William said he would send a strongly worded letter *after* the first assembly providing all went well.

Finally, Philip was at Miss Bright's door again, hoping his money had been well spent and she would be presentable to the *bon ton.*

What if she'd chosen a garish pattern or a color unbecoming an innocent young lady or even an unsuitable style with a neckline that left her cat's heads on display?

Not that he wouldn't like to see such an exhibition, but he didn't want to be responsible for keeping her respectable for six weeks if she was an outlandish flirt.

Ushered into the parlor, Philip was rendered not only speechless but thoughtless, too, with his head emptying of anything except the incomparable sight that greeted him.

CHAPTER FOUR

"Mercer," Miss Bright's father greeted him, and Philip had to tear his gaze from the young lady who was literally shimmering.

Still, he was at a loss for words. He could barely recall his own name. Luckily, he didn't need to provide it. All he had to do was mumble something.

"Good evening." And then he went back to staring at Miss Bright, whose lips were moving. He had to make himself listen and not merely gawk at her radiance.

"Good evening, my lord," she said, curtseying perfectly.

He must have seen a gown like it before—a pale rose iridescent silk with silver flowers embroidered across the bodice and around the hem, but if he had, he'd never seen a more beautiful woman wearing it. Her light-brown hair was dressed up in that mysterious way only women knew how to do and which men could only destroy by pulling out the pins.

Her loose curls, with a silver ribbon artfully arranged throughout, made him itch to feel their silky softness.

"Yes," he murmured, entirely bewitched. "Isn't it?"

"I beg your pardon." These words were from a stranger, so he ignored the biddy in dark gray satin until Sir William coughed and Miss Bright lowered her gaze.

"Good evening, Miss Bright," Philip managed, sounding more like himself, and then he turned to the woman who must be her chaperone.

"I don't believe we've been introduced," he said, offering an inclination of his head.

"This is my sister, Mrs. Cumbersome," said the magistrate.

Mrs. Cumbersome? Philip had to use all his born-and-bred gentlemanly manners not to snicker. Most chaperones were a pain in the arse, but this one was actually branded as such. He feared she would live up to her name.

"A pleasure to meet you," he said.

More a female version of her brother than an older Miss Bright, Mrs. Cumbersome gave a shallow curtsey while looking him up and down.

"There's a smudge of mud on your right boot, my lord," she said, and that was all before looking to her kin and announcing it was time to leave.

"Your slippers and shawl are in the foyer," the older woman added to her niece. "Well, brother, I hope this was a good idea." Then Mrs. Cumbersome nodded to the magistrate, took Miss Bright by the hand, and marched from the room.

Philip looked down at his boot. *By God, she was right!* His valet was faultlessly dependable, which meant he must have soiled his boot between home and the Brights' modest drawing room. Moreover, he now knew exactly how keen the chaperone's eyes were, and he would be careful not to forget.

Drawing a handkerchief from his pocket, he spat on it, bent down, and rubbed away the offending smudge. When he straightened, he made eye contact with the magistrate, who looked entirely amused.

"Better you than I," Sir William said, then took his seat by the hearth. Philip noticed the man had a book and a glass of brandy at the ready.

"We are waiting, my lord," came the bluff and nettled voice of Mrs. Cumbersome.

Philip swallowed before nodding to the magistrate and catching up with the women at the door. Not a butler but the same maid hauled it open, and Philip followed the ladies outside, hoping his horses' manes were brushed and glossy enough for the aunt and his carriage waxed to perfection.

After he assisted first Miss Bright and then Mrs. Cumbersome into the carriage, he climbed in behind them. Making sure the lamp was lit, he sat back and surveyed his new companions. First, he turned to the chaperone.

"There is mud upon my carriage wheels, too, but it is London, madame. Thus, I hope you'll forgive me."

The lady narrowed her eyes as if trying to decide whether he was making sport of her.

Miss Bright seemed to have a permanent expression of excitement. It made her eyes sparkle, and somehow, her lips seemed to glisten. *Her kissable lips!*

"The days have crawled by until this instant," she said. "Yet I feared the modiste had not enough time to make my dress."

Philip was glad for the new dress. His money had been well spent after all.

"Miss Bright, if I did not say so before, let me tell you I am most impressed with how you have turned out. I am certain you shall draw single gentlemen by the wagonful."

Mrs. Cumbersome cleared her throat.

"That is," Philip amended, "I'm sure you will have precisely a decent amount of attention as befitting a young lady of your good breeding."

"I am certain my aunt will make sure I am not overwhelmed by the number of my admirers," Miss Bright said before sharing a smile with him.

"Do you know what to expect?" he asked.

In response, she said, "I have been to two balls at Almack's."

"This will be nothing like them," he promised. "First, it will be a smaller affair. There will be only nobility and their guests. You mustn't speak to anyone with whom you haven't been properly introduced. And once you have been, then you may dance with that gentleman, although I recommend not more than two dances lest you wish tongues to wag. And you must never leave the ballroom with any man."

"Of course she won't," said Mrs. Cumbersome.

Philip continued, feeling like he was once more on the battlefield advising his troops.

"Music will most probably start around eleven. If there is any waltzing, it will be the last set before we dine. There will be supper at two—"

"At two? In the morning?" The magistrate's daughter looked amazed.

Philip cocked his head. "Naturally. When would you have it, Miss Bright? At two in the afternoon?"

"No, but at Almack's," she began.

"At Almack's, you had thinly sliced bread with a whisper of butter or some crumbly cake to revive you when famished. This will be a proper dinner for two-hundred and fifty."

"Gracious!" said Miss Bright.

"I told you it would be smaller than Almack's. Are you disappointed by the number of guests?"

"Quite the contrary," she said. "I am amazed that anyone has that many chairs."

MIRANDA TRIED NOT TO let her mouth drop open, nor to stare at any one thing for too long. Breadalbane House, the largest of the three houses fronting Park Lane, was everything Almack's was not. When Miranda had approached the latter with her sister, she'd seen an unassuming building, and the interior truthfully had not been much better.

The Earl of Breadalbane's home at Number Twenty-One, however, was impressive from the outside through to its elegant interior. A large brick façade with stone accents welcomed her on Lord Mercer's arm with Aunt Lucinda walking behind. The entrance hall was filled with flowers, and Miranda felt as if she were transported to another realm.

Just beyond the foyer, a large circular staircase, itself decorated with garlands of white roses and laurel leaves, brought them up to a chain of three assembly rooms in which other guests were already sauntering from one to the next. The third of these, a drawing room, was the largest with an elaborately plastered ceiling.

Miranda was fairly fizzing inside, staring up at the meticulously painted central panel with blue sky, clouds, and cherubs, committing it to memory. When she finally lowered her eyes, everywhere that there was fabric, whether upon a chair or a window dressing, it was white damask.

"How on earth can it be kept clean?" Miranda wondered, thinking of the dust and ever-present soot.

Lord Mercer laughed. "I cannot imagine."

"I think it is one of the finest houses I have ever been in," Miranda confessed, ogling the gilded mirrors which made the room brighter and larger, as well as the fine paintings, the sculptures, the bronzes, and other *objets d'art* on pedestals either prominently displayed or tucked into alcoves.

Servers came by with trays of glasses.

"Not lemonade," Miranda guessed as Lord Mercer handed her one as well as to her aunt. They each sipped. "Definitely not Almack's. I am thrilled to be here."

"You fit in perfectly," the baron told her. "Let me introduce you to people I know so you will be able to socialize with them and to accept dance partners."

Miranda let him take her around the room for the next hour and a half to meet the quality folk of his world. The reaction was nearly always the same as both lords and ladies tried to figure out if she was anyone important.

By their expressions, they were puzzled at her being with Lord Mercer, even when she was identified as a magistrate's daughter. Doubtless, they didn't consider that enough to warrant her entrance into high society on the arm of a well-liked wealthy baron who was also a revered army officer.

After they'd gone halfway around the room, she would swear she could hear murmurings in their wake.

"Are we causing a stir, my lord?"

"Not to worry," he said. "The women wonder what type of threat you may be, and the men hope you don't have your heart set on me because they want to have a chance with you."

Miranda laughed. "And the truth is neither. I am obviously no threat to these ladies, and despite a room full of gentlemen, my heart is firmly my own."

In fact, no one else in the room came close to measuring up to the dashing major. She could hardly believe he was her escort.

"You may give your heart away before the Season ends," came her aunt's voice from behind. Miranda had nearly forgotten her.

Both she and Lord Mercer startled at her aunt's words before stopping at the next small group. By the time the musicians began playing, her head was spinning with faces and with names, mostly titled, many she'd read in the gossip columns of the newspapers delivered daily to her home.

Oddly, now that she could put faces to the familiar monikers, they seemed like regular people, or as regular as those who held most of the country's wealth could be. True, they wore the finest silks and satins and dripped in jewels, and that was just the men. The women were equally togged in fashionable twig, while also sporting feather aigrettes and waving fans around as if directing an orchestra.

Yet up close, Miranda could see how utterly ordinary they were. She had expected them to be glowing with some noble light. Instead, despite how each heaped a helping of flummery upon one another, Miranda had seen more good-looking people working at the Covent Garden stalls, and that was no lie.

As the baron had predicted, it was past eleven when the first notes of "The White Cockade" caused them all to take their places under the brilliantly lit chandeliers. Lord Mercer made sure she was in the right spot. Miranda would swear he was the most striking gentleman there, and the most thoughtful.

The Earl of Breadalbane and Lady Ann Cantrell led the rest of the dancers at the front of the procession. Miranda was pleased for the dancing lessons her father had pushed upon her and Grace in preparation for Almack's. While she was not perfect, nor did she make a fool of herself. She was in fact concentrating on not making a misstep when a hurrah went up from the crowd.

Glancing around, she immediately bumped into the back of the woman in front of her as they crisscrossed the floor.

"What's happening?" Miranda asked Lord Mercer after she recovered her place.

Leaning close, he told her, "The Prince Regent has arrived."

At her first private ball, and the man who would be king was attending! She almost wished she could hurry home and write it all down before she forgot a single detail.

"You look pensive," Lord Mercer told her.

Trying to appear calm, she asked, "Will I meet him?"

"If you wish. Prinny adores meeting beautiful ladies."

Lord Mercer considered her beautiful! *What a treat!*

When the long dance ended, they found Mrs. Cumbersome, and the three of them went in search of the Prince Regent. Lord Mercer headed into the thick of loud talk and raucous laughter in the next room, parting the throng with his determined stride. At last, he stopped in front of a tall portly man with pudgy cheeks and dressed to the nines.

"Your Royal Highness, good evening."

"And to you, Mercer. Still enjoying civilian life, wot-wot?" The Prince Regent's gaze had already passed off of the baron and was dancing across Miranda to her chaperone and quickly back again, fixed firmly upon her . . . décolletage.

"I wish to introduce you to Miss Bright," Lord Mercer continued. "Her father is the magistrate Sir William Bright of the Queen's Square Court."

"I say, is he now?" The Prince Regent held out his hand palm up, and Miranda had no choice but to place her fingers upon it. A thrill trickled through her at touching royalty, even though they both wore gloves.

"I am very pleased to meet you, Your Royal Highness." She sank into a low curtsey, and beside her, Aunt Lucinda did the same. Miranda only hoped her aunt could rise without assistance.

When they were both standing upright again, she said, "This is my father's only sister, Mrs. Cumbersome."

"Is she?" But the Prince Regent's gaze remained upon Miranda. "You *are* a spruce filly."

She opened her mouth, then closed it, wondering if she was supposed to compliment him in return. That, however, seemed presumptuous.

"I thank you, Your Royal Highness." There was already so much to write about she cursed herself for not bringing paper and pencil instead of a fan and dancing slippers.

"This one's a good one to have in your pocket, Mercer," the Prince Regent added, winking at her.

Miranda wasn't sure what he meant, but she was beginning to feel like a shop display. He might be of royal blood, but he also seemed rapacious with his bold stare and knowing smile. The respectful regard of one of the law clerks who sometimes came home with her father to an evening meal seemed preferable.

How did one politely escape the presence of a prince?

The Regent solved the problem.

Turning to the baron, Prince George announced, "I tell you what, come to the card room with me for a few minutes, and then I'll leave you alone the rest of the evening to be with this charming chicken."

Miranda could see by the glance Lord Mercer sent her that he wasn't entirely at ease with the prince's arrangement.

"If you and Mrs. Cumbersome—" he began.

The Prince Regent laughed, interrupting him. "I am certain your new lady-friend and her chaperone know how to comport themselves without your instructions, *Major*. This isn't a battlefield. Come along. I am tired of standing."

With that, the Regent nodded to Miranda and to her aunt, and they both sank into another curtsey before he turned away, moving with a slight limp.

"Gout," Aunt Lucinda whispered into her ear.

"I shall return as soon as I can," Lord Mercer promised before strolling after Prince George.

"The Regent behaves as if he were already a king," Miranda said after they'd returned to their place by the tall windows in the ballroom. "And not a modern king, either."

Her aunt made tutting sounds, but then she began to survey the room.

"Don't fret over Prince George's childish manners," Aunt Lucinda said. "Let's get you partnered for the next dance."

PHILIP PLAYED A HAND of cards with Prinny and a few old chums before being allowed to excuse himself. He doubted Miss Bright would intentionally get up to trouble. Then again, she was like a rough gem and many of the single men there would wish to polish her. Upon entering the ballroom, alas, he saw only her chaperone.

"Mrs. Cumbersome, where is your niece?"

"She danced with a young man you introduced her to, Lord Lowry."

Philip nodded. "Good." The man was harmless and considered upstanding by all. However, Lowry was across the room talking to another young lady. "But where is she now?"

"She went with Lady Harriet Beaumont to promenade the three rooms. I gave my permission since the young lady is an earl's daughter and she wished to introduce Miranda to her sister."

That would be fine, Philip thought, *except Lady Harriet had only a brother, and a randy one at that!*

CHAPTER FIVE

P hilip knew the game the Beaumont siblings played. They traced their lineage back to the dawn of Britain, or so they claimed, and they enjoyed nothing as much as putting down those whom they considered upstarts—or *mushrooms*, as the newly monied were called.

In the case of a young woman such as Miss Bright who was innocent to the ways of a Mayfair evening, the still-unmarried Lady Harriet would enjoy lessening the competition by helping to ruin her on her first foray.

Except Lady Harriet was playing with the wrong debutante. Miss Bright's father could toss a Beaumont into Newgate as easily as any light-fingered bubber. Philip glanced around the ballroom and determined the magistrate's daughter was not there.

"How long has she been out of your sight?" he asked.

"Merely five minutes," she said, but catching his worry, Mrs. Cumbersome frowned. "I believe you should go in search of my niece."

Hurrying through the other two rooms, also vacant of Miss Bright's shimmering figure, Philip went down the stairs. The dining room was already set up with tables and full service. Empty save for servants, he searched the other two rooms prepared to accommodate those who didn't get seated at the main table. They, too, were empty.

Rushing outside, he prayed he wasn't too late. If Miranda Bright was ruined at the first event, the magistrate would have his hide. Their deal would be finished before it had barely begun, and his brandy would be the least of his worries.

At first, Philip saw only gatherings of men, and then he heard female laughter.

Sure enough, behind a yew hedge, he found his quarry in a small cluster of young ladies, including Lady Harriet, with whom Philip had once enjoyed the briefest of sensual encounters in a garden very like this one.

No, wait—that was Lady Astrid. He'd dallied with Lady Harriet in an alcove on the third floor of a house in Piccadilly. He vividly recalled the painting next to her head. While they were kissing, his mind had wandered to the fine representation of a man atop a chestnut horse. Philip had realized at that instant he wasn't actually interested in her and had never again attempted to get her alone.

To his relief, the group of females seemed to be doing nothing more than chatting and drinking champagne. *How extraordinary!* And Miss Bright, who was the one presently speaking, looked perfectly at ease.

Every head turned toward him as he approached. All their faces lit up with varying degrees of interest, except Lady Harriet's which transformed into a scowl. Regardless, Miss Bright was the one who boldly stepped forward.

"Lord Mercer, there you are," she said as if he was the one who had gone missing. "Do you know all these ladies or shall I make introductions?"

He had to hand it to her. She was behaving as if she'd been born to the *bon ton* like a duke's daughter. Taking another look at the other three, he said, "I believe I have met everyone here. Good evening, ladies. A fine evening, in fact. But the ballroom is sorely lacking your feminine presence."

Lady Harriet Beaumont glanced slyly between him and Miss Bright, then she nodded.

"We must do our duty to our host and hostess, or the swells will end up forced to dance with each other."

Her friends laughed, and the three moved off toward the terrace doors. Miss Bright went to follow, but Philip stopped her.

"You should have stayed with your aunt," he chided.

Her hazel eyes widened. "I was perfectly safe."

But he thought about what could have happened if he had been right about Lady Beaumont's intentions.

"You cannot leave your chaperone, or you may end up alone with a man."

Miss Bright put her delicate hands upon her hips, causing her gown to pinch and show him her slender figure. Then she cocked her head.

"Do you mean exactly as we are now, my lord?"

Philip looked around and swore under his breath. They appeared decidedly suspicious behind the shrubbery, and he could easily reach out, draw her to him and kiss her. He'd done it at least a dozen times that year with that many women. Moreover, even knowing he had to protect her from scandal, he very much wanted to hold this sparkling minx in his arms, feel the curves contained by her pink-of-the-mode, fashionably low bodice, and taste her soft lips again.

Except her lips were flapping like a hummingbird's wings.

"If you had not hunted me down, Lord Mercer, I would be safely enjoying a delightful conversation with those ladies. Did you know they use their fans to communicate, not with each other but with men, especially with the men they fancy?" Then she snapped her gloved fingers.

"Unquestionably, you knew! No one ever told me this before, but you must have been on the receiving end of a lady's fan message many times, telling you she wanted to meet or wanted to be kissed."

Philip was growing increasingly uncomfortable with this discussion.

"Can you be silent?" he ground out.

"*Pish!* Silence," she scoffed. "There's no point to it, is there?"

Point to it!

"What on earth do you mean? Of course silence has a point, woman! The absence of your incessant chattering."

Instead of looking miffed she smiled.

"I know what silence is, but when two people are together, why be silent? Alone, you can contemplate. But surely the reason for two or more to gather is to communicate, discuss, chat, share. How on earth can one do any of that silently?"

All at once, impulsively, *stupidly*, he drew her close.

"I can assure you, Miss Bright, two people can communicate quite well, better even, *without* talking."

Her green-gold eyes widened, and her pretty lips formed a small *O*.

"Yes, I understand," she said, leaning back so she could look into his eyes rather than at his cravat. "I know all about that type of thing," Miss Bright assured him rather shockingly.

Did she? Besides their kiss at her house, how many had she shared? And with whom?

Philip didn't know why he cared. In any case, he believed her knowledge stopped at a kiss while, at that instant, he longed to do more—a flyer against the garden's stonewall came to mind. And yet he knew he must behave.

"Do you see what you've done by disobeying me?" he groused. "I would ask you to remember that this arrangement is *not* merely about your entrance into society. It is about *my* future. The stakes are high, and I would appreciate if you would not go out of your way to be in bad bread!"

He had uncharacteristically raised his voice, but he feared she wasn't taking him seriously.

"Listen to me, Miss Bright. I do not intend to be pushed into marriage by some female who sees me as a convenient way out of her own trouble. Even if that female is you. Do you understand?"

"I do," Miss Bright said, looking very agreeable. "You are still annoyed with Miss Waltham and hence snapping at me like a crabby turtle. I was merely in a group of ladies whom I can only suppose are respectable. It wasn't as if I went off with someone such as yourself, my lord."

She let that sink in while he dropped his arms from her. Then Miss Bright gave him a saucy smile, which unexpectedly inflamed him, before she turned on her heel and retreated to the security of the interior.

With the force of habit, Philip nearly called her back. After all, they were alone and hadn't been discovered. It seemed a waste of a good opportunity.

"Recall the brandy," he reminded himself, thinking of the sturdy ships which Philip hoped would carry his newly produced brandy from France to British shores on a regular basis. Above all, he needed the magistrate to prevent any bad blood between him and Lord Perrin and the rest of the Waltham family.

Following Miss Bright and her pleasing rump, he vowed not to let himself be forced to marry Miss Waltham, who didn't tickle his fancy the way a certain other female did, even if he would get a very good deal on shipping costs for the rest of his life.

PHILIP DIDN'T LET THE chit out of his sight for the rest of the evening. And he enjoyed having her in his arms during her first waltz. Miss Bright giggled when they began, what with him placing a hand on her back, before she became serious while trying not to trip him or step on his toes.

Soon, she was moving smoothly around the ballroom while he muttered an occasional "right," "left," or "head up."

For his part, with her as his partner, he preferred it to the contra-dances they'd been doing earlier. She was a good height, nice to look at, and smelled like a meadow in spring. The only thing more enjoyable might be a ballum rancum, during which the Cyprians wore not a single stitch of clothing while dancing with the men who were fully clothed. It was exciting and arousing for about two dances, and then even that became tedious.

The last time he'd gone to such a dance, he'd felt a little embarrassed by the other men pawing at their partners or exclaiming rude compliments, and had ended up taking his chosen female upstairs to a private room for a proper swiving.

For a few brief moments, he imagined Miranda Bright naked as a needle in his arms. Dancing would be acceptable, but tupping would be inevitable.

"My lord," she said.

He brought his attention back to the present. The music had just ended. He bowed and she curtsied, and Philip led her from the floor. Another man was ready to be her partner, yet he had the strangest sensation of not wishing to release her.

Shaking his head at his own ridiculous flight of fancy, he watched Lord Stadden, a man he knew from his club, take her in his arms for the next dance. There would be waltzes for the following forty minutes before they dined. Philip snagged another partner and whisked her into the thick of things, both in order to perform his duty as a single guest and also to keep an eye on Miss Bright.

In truth, it was hard to look away. Yet he couldn't fathom why he found her the most alluring female in the entire room, nor could he deny it was so.

〜

MIRANDA SET HER QUILL in the ink stand upon her writing desk and wiggled her cramping fingers. After she'd finally arisen from her bed at half past eleven and had a cup of tea and a buttered bun with jam, she'd gotten directly to work. Having filled both sides of a piece of stationery in her tiny, meticulous scrawl, she was considering writing in the other direction on the same page.

"We're not paupers," she reminded herself, reaching for a fresh sheet of paper. It would be a kindness not to make her cousins have to turn the paper this way and that to read her spicy tale.

After the very late supper, the gathering ended. By then, it was four in the morning. I am not exaggerating, dearest Helen and Peter, too, if you're listening to your sister's reading of this letter.

The Prince Regent departed with Lady Ingram-Seymour-Conway, Marchioness of Hertford. I cannot but confess a public affair seems odd to me. Everyone knows she is the wife of the Marquess of Hertford who was, until very recently, the king's Lord Chamberlain of the Household, and yet no one raises an eyebrow when the Prince Regent and his lady behave as a married couple all evening.

How can a man let another, even a future king, go about Town with his wife? Moreover, how do the Hertfords stay married when the marquess knows he is being cuckolded weekly? I vow I would not be able to bear such humiliation.

Miranda had already written about the lovely house on the edge of Hyde Park. And she'd been unable to contain her excitement regarding her first-ever waltz. Wrestling with herself over how deeply to describe the sensations of having the baron's hands upon her, she settled for saying that dancing with a man in such close fashion was a stimulating experience.

No need to mention how her other partners after him for the rest of the waltzes hadn't made her body pulse with longing as he had.

Lord Mercer also claimed her for the final waltz before they went downstairs to eat, escorting her to the table and drawing out her chair.

At that point, her aunt was in a different room entirely, but no one could think anyone might be up to mischief while eating. The baron had been correct about the food. Although it wasn't as many courses as at a dinner party—in fact, only white soup, fresh bread and butter, and roasted pork in cream sauce with peas—still, it was a world away from the thinly sliced dry bread she'd eaten at Almack's.

All this she told Helen, eventually even disclosing how she felt warmer than normal in Lord Mercer's presence, and as if her skin had suddenly become too tight. It was hard to explain how it was a pleasant sensation, but it was. She would rely upon her cousin's discretion not to read those words to Peter.

After making a small but detailed sketch of her ballgown for Helen's amusement, she set the sheets of paper aside. That evening, after dinner, she would tell her what the music had been, at least what she could name, and then tomorrow, Miranda would send off her long letter.

Her cousins were stuck in the countryside of Northampton, with little amusement. Peter, who was the elder of the two by just a year, had survived a terrible riding accident and spent most of his time restricted to the family's parlor or his first-floor bedroom, or occasionally he went out in a pushchair. And Helen was devoted to her brother, keeping him company as much as either could bear.

Whatever Miranda could do to amuse them both, she would happily do.

However, it occurred to her as she rose and stretched that her cousins might become envious if she only went on concerning her own exciting experiences. She vowed to write more about the nobility she met and especially of Lord

Mercer's interesting behavior should he ever exhibit the raffish conduct for which he was infamous.

In the garden the night before, she'd hoped for a kiss such as her father had interrupted, but the baron had been on frustratingly good behavior.

After changing into something suitable, a soft cotton dress with a solid green bodice and a subtle green-and-cream stripe skirt that gathered directly under her bosom, Miranda went downstairs to their modest parlor and waited. Lord Mercer had explained how a number of the gentlemen with whom she'd danced the night before would pay her a visit that day. Since the assembly had continued as late as could possibly be, their social calls would also be later than usual, sometime around three o'clock instead of between eleven and one.

To make things as respectable as possible, she had their maid-of-all-work, Eliza, on notice to come and sit with her when the first caller arrived.

After an hour, feeling famished, Miranda hoped she wouldn't be caught by her callers in the middle of eating a serving of their cook's chicken pie, and hastily tucked into a plateful alone at the dining room table.

Before she was halfway finished, she heard an arrival in the front hall. Jumping to her feet, she dashed through the adjoining door to the parlor, clasped her hands in front of her, and waited. Eliza appeared first and then . . . Lord Major Mercer!

CHAPTER SIX

H er emotions went from confusion to happiness to disappointment and back to excitement.

"Lord Mercer, miss," said their maid handing her his calling card.

"Yes, I can see him." She didn't mean to sound snappy, but she was aware how in the upper-class homes, a butler would have collected the calling card and brought it to her to decide whether she was "at home."

Softening her tone, she said, "Thank you, Eliza," before turning to the impossibly handsome man in the parlor. If anything, he looked even more dashing by daylight than he had the night before.

In fact, he seemed to be growing ever more of a rum cove each time she saw him.

He bowed shallowly. "Good day, Miss Bright. I hope you are well."

"I am, my lord. Good day to you. Would you care for some tea?"

"No, thank you. I won't stay long."

When her maid forgot her earlier instructions and went for the door, Miranda called her back.

"Eliza, take a seat." She looked around. It was out of the question for her to sit with them. "Over there, if you please." She gestured toward an ottoman at the other end of the room, pulled into place when her father wanted to put his feet up, but which currently held a stack of newspapers.

With big eyes fixed upon Miranda, their maid did as she was told, not even moving the papers but sitting firmly upon them.

Amidst the sound of crinkling, Lord Mercer stared at her, and Miranda quickly took her seat so he could do the same.

"I had a wonderful time," she volunteered. "Did you enjoy the evening?"

"I did," he said.

She could see he had something on his mind. "Is there aught amiss?"

He hesitated. "It is not usually my position to play the nanny, but when you meet with your gentleman callers, you ought to have a true chaperone. I'm afraid the help, no matter how dedicated, does not qualify."

They both heard another round of scrunching paper as Eliza settled herself.

"My aunt was too exhausted from the early morning conclusion to the assembly. Hopefully she hasn't worn herself out for the entire Season," Miranda added. "Yet it is neither here nor there. I have had no gentlemen callers, except for you."

She was rewarded with a genuine look of astonishment.

"But how can that be?" Lord Mercer demanded.

She shrugged. "I suppose that is for you to say, my lord. My father thought your attention would draw a flock of suitors, as he said. I can only assume the fault in the plan rests with me."

She tried to speak lightly as if it were unimportant. After all, she hadn't wanted or expected a Season anyway, nor was she desperate for a husband. But her disappointment must have shown.

Leaning forward with earnest, Lord Mercer declared, "You were the most desirable woman there, I promise you."

She sat up straighter, a tremor of happiness running through her. Quickly, it dissipated. She must recall he was using her to get her father's assistance.

"If that is the case, which is highly unlikely, then why did no one come? I believe you are only humoring me."

"No, Miss Bright, I swear it." He rubbed a large hand over his chin, considering. "It must be because you favored me with a contra-dance early in the evening and then two waltzes. One more than your father allowed, by the way, but apparently Mrs. Cumbersome cannot count."

Miranda laughed. He'd succeeded in lifting her mood.

"Then our three dances," she began.

"Scared off the swells and blades," he finished. "They are in awe of me."

"Naturally," she agreed, biting back a smile at his vanity. After all, it was true. He had been the most attractive man at the ball. Not noticing her hint of amusement, he continued.

"The problem is you showed me too much preference. Consequently, the others believe they have no chance to gain your affections."

Miranda considered this. "Do you think so? Truly?"

STALLING FOR TIME, PHILIP nodded sagely and crossed his legs, folded his arms, and even cleared his throat. He should have accepted the blasted tea. It would have given him something to do with his hands.

In truth, he hadn't a bloody clue why she didn't have a line of callers on her doorstep. The way she'd filled out that dress, her graceful dancing, her lilting laughter. If he'd been interested in gaining a wife, he would have fought tooth and nail to be the first one into the foyer that morning.

He certainly hoped the lack of suitors wasn't due to some shallow reason such as her being a magistrate's daughter and not having the best Mayfair address.

"In two nights, at Vauxhall, you must allow me to plead my case loudly and then you must brush me off."

"I should cut you? In public?" She looked shocked.

"Well, not too badly since I will still bring you home and escort you to the upcoming picnic on the grounds of Syon House. Just rump me," he advised, and immediately he conjured a notion of her sweet bottom tucked against him as they lay together in tangled sheets. *'Zounds!*

He was rewarded with her laughter, and strangely, he was happy in turn to have caused it.

"You do put me in a good humor, my lord. And I believe I can return the favor. My father drafted a note which his clerk will have written up today. It insists on your behalf that Miss Waltham has inadvertently involved you in a case of mistaken identity, for such it surely is, and that it must come to a swift resolution. It was well written," she added.

"Did you write it?" he asked, for something in her tone bespoke of pride.

Her hazel eyes twinkled. "I may have had a suggestion or two," she allowed.

The rustling of paper caught his attention. He'd all but forgotten the maid, which was one reason servants weren't good chaperones. That and the fact their employer could simply force them to lie. They weren't credible vanguards of a ladies' reputation in the least.

With that in mind, Philip rose to his feet.

Miss Bright also stood and followed him to the door. "I must say, I am thrilled to be going to the Vauxhall Pleasure Gardens."

He nearly brushed it off, but then a thought struck him.

"Don't say you've never been before?"

She hesitated long enough to know her next words were going to be something of a fib.

"Of course I have," she said, tilting her chin before adding, "but never at night."

He nearly laughed in her face, but that would have been rude. He couldn't get himself to take her to task for lying, nor tell her the owners no longer opened it to visitors during the day.

Instead, he let her save face. "Then we are a perfect pair, Miss Bright, for I don't think I have ever been there in the light of day."

Her expression was priceless, and he stared at her wide eyes and rosy cheeks a moment. Then he explained.

"While some might go there for a breath of fresh air as you did, when I need such, then I go to Hyde Park upon my horse. And if I need more, then I go to Richmond Park or leave the area for my estate in Guildford. Do you know of that area? In Surrey?"

She shook her head. "Not really."

Philip knew a sudden impulse to invite her to visit his family's country home, but a young lady at a house party was what got him into trouble in the first place. He needed to keep his attention on the task at hand, and that meant giving her a successful and uneventful Season.

"Knowing Vauxhall as I do, I cannot help but think of its evening activities as the sole purpose for existing," he said. "Accordingly, I would hate to go when the sun is up and be disabused of its magical qualities."

She smiled. "I'm sure I shall not recognize a blade of grass at night, and you must show me everything."

"I will," he promised and took his leave.

Actually, he would not. Certainly not the Lovers Walk or the Dark Walk or any of the covered walks, either. They all spelled trouble, especially if she were seen to be strolling along any one of them with him. In fact, he had no intention of letting her go beyond the Supper Boxes in the Grove or see anything more exciting than the Turkish Tent and the fireworks. She would encounter nothing to which her father could object.

Obviously, he couldn't do anything about the caliber of other visitors. Anyone who could pay the three shillings admission price—or jump over one of the walls—could get in. Some of his friends, both lords and ladies, enjoyed Vauxhall for the very titillating experience of rubbing elbows with those whom they normally wouldn't come into contact. It seemed a benign environment to interact with all walks of life, including merchants and the *demi-reps*, and the price of such titillation was coming across the occasional pickpocket and hearing bear-garden jaw from the seediest sorts.

MIRANDA DIDN'T HAVE TO knock at the Beaumonts' door, for it opened effortlessly as she approached the four-story, five-bay brick house on Grosvenor Square. A stern butler took her card, which was in fact her father's with her name scrawled across the top.

"You may wait here, miss," he said and mounted the stairs.

Miranda hardly had time to admire the expensive furnishings and the pretty wallpaper before he returned and asked her to follow him. Up the staircase, he led her into a formal drawing room, the pale-yellow walls of which stretched high above to a white plaster ceiling with crown molding.

"Miss Bright to see you, my lady," and then he bowed and left her.

Miranda was surprised to find she was the only guest. The invitation had been vague as to what sort of a get-together this would be.

Lady Harriet Beaumont stood to welcome her and even held out her hands as if they were firm friends instead of new acquaintances.

"So glad you could come," her hostess said.

"It was kind of you to invite me and most unexpected." When Lady Harriet's note came not long after Lord Mercer left two days earlier, it went a long way to soothing the sting of not having any other male callers.

"Sit, please. I have tea ready, but we can have coffee if you prefer."

"Tea is fine, thank you. I am partial to it above coffee." *Best manners,* Miranda reminded herself, taking the offered place upon one of the two sofas. She was representing the Bright name before nobility and must carry herself as well as her father when he was seated in judgment upon the bench.

"But why unexpected, Miss Bright? We had an introduction at the ball and even an amusing discussion after I introduced you to my other friends. We all thought you most charming."

"Thank you. I enjoyed everything about that night, not least of all meeting you and Lady Emily and Miss Pratt."

Lady Harriet poured their tea. "I had not realized you'd arrived *with* Lord Mercer until he came to fetch you from the garden."

She didn't ask a question but merely left her statement hanging as she leaned across the low table and handed the saucer and cup to Miranda.

Luckily, Lord Mercer and her father had decided upon a story. "His lordship is an acquaintance of my father's. He offered to escort me to a few events since my father despises such things."

"I see. How nice. I must admit I never thought of Mercer as the type to do something out of the goodness of his heart. Therefore, I must caution you to beware. Only because I know a thing or two about his type."

"His type?" Miranda asked politely while knowing already what she meant.

"I hope I'm not making you uncomfortable, but he is one of the well-known rakes of our social circle. He's known to prey upon innocent females for his own prurient desires."

Prurient? Miranda thought it a very good word and would use it the next time she wrote to Helen.

"I am aware of the baron's reputation," she assured Lady Harriet, "but I appreciate your words of warning. I confess to being a devotee of the sillier sections of the newspapers, and his name has come up several times."

Lady Harriet's face broke out into a smile. "Do you enjoy a good pot of gossip-water?"

She seemed to be a kindred spirit, so Miranda nodded and added, "I do, in fact. *The Times* is my favorite but also *The Morning Post* and *The Gazette*. I seek out the most interesting ones and clip them to send to my cousins in the country."

Lady Harriet looked puzzled.

"They don't get the London papers at my uncle's home in Northampton," Miranda explained.

Lady Harriet's frown deepened. "Whyever not?"

Miranda hid her smile. Her uncle had balked at the expense of the news coming from Town, and since it was always "stale" as he declared, he didn't bother with any but the financial news. But she didn't wish to explain all that.

"I know only that my cousins greatly appreciate the tidbits I send. I hope you don't think me foolish, but I am also writing about where I go and what I see this Season and sending them such tales as I can make most amusing in my letters."

"Are you really?" Lady Harriet leaned forward. "And are you naming names?"

For her cousins, Miranda certainly did, but she didn't want Lady Harriet to think her terribly imprudent.

"I suppose I could disguise them the way the newspapers do."

Lady Harriet nodded approvingly. "A good practice but futile, don't you think? We all know who is who, but it offers the veneer of privacy and discretion, I suppose. Is Mercer in your letters?"

Miranda was taken back. "Why, yes. I can hardly leave him out as he is my escort."

Lady Harriet sipped her tea. "I applaud you in your endeavor to entertain your cousins. I recall the other night that you were a good storyteller. Are you as good a writer?"

Miranda felt her cheeks warm but answered truthfully. "I have been told I am."

The young woman opposite her considered for a few moments.

"I have an idea I think you will find agreeable. After a few weeks of balls and outings, picnics and whatnot, you might turn your letters into a novel."

Stunned, Miranda nearly choked on her tea. After all, Lady Harriet's suggestion was in keeping with her own wish to write a short story, based on real life. When she could speak, she asked, "Not for the public, you don't mean?"

"If you're a good writer, why not share it so we can all be amused? Do you know why the newspapers put the nobility and the mushrooms in its columns?"

Before Miranda could ask why there would be mushrooms mentioned in the society pages, Lady Harriet answered her own question.

"Because the nobs like to be talked about, as do the half-swells and chicken nabobs. They love the notoriety. Why, they even send word of their own antics to the editors in order not to be left out." She shook her head disapprovingly.

"Really?" Miranda asked. She'd always assumed the opposite.

"Not *my* family, you understand," Lady Harriet continued. "We don't need any more fame or accolades. That is why you've never seen our names in the papers, I would warrant. At least not connected to any scandal." She paused. "Have you?"

"No," Miranda agreed. "I never have."

"Then as long as you don't discuss my family, I would highly support your endeavors. I shall explain how best to change the names while making clear by other means about whom you're writing, with a physical description and some obvious clues."

Lady Harriet sat up straighter. "In fact, let *me* be your patron." She tapped her chin. "It will be great fun. You can write your stories about the Season, and then I will pay for it to be printed and distributed."

This was all happening too fast. Miranda had a feeling there was a reason this had not been done before. She needed to rein in Lady Harriet.

"I am not sure my father would wish me to become a published writer."

Lady Harriet shrugged away the protest. "Then write under a clever disguise. Let's think of one. I think you ought to remain female as you shall be a more sympathetic figure should anyone become annoyed."

"Annoyed?" Miranda echoed.

"Never mind. I don't know what I was thinking. As your patron, I will make sure everything goes smoothly. As your friend, I will steer you away from trouble." She smiled, and Miranda relaxed.

After all, Lady Harriet knew her way around the *haut ton* in a way Miranda never could. Now, the earl's daughter was thinking aloud.

"Bright makes me think of *luminous, beaming, vivid, blazing.* Yes, Miss Blaze! What do you think?"

Miranda didn't know what to think about this turn of events. She had a patron and was writing a novel that was really a gossip column in disguise. Yet she hated to disappoint Lady Harriet, who had shown her such kindness. Moreover, she couldn't see any harm in going along with her.

"Miss Blaze seems suitable," she began.

"Of course it does! Miss Marian Blaze. No one will ever suspect it's you. And people will be passing it around as a gift at Christmastime."

"Oh," was all Miranda could say. It hardly seemed the correct gift for a time of peace and good will.

She added, "I promise I shall think about your offer. But for now, I would prefer to write only for my cousins."

Lady Harriet sighed. "Whatever you say." Then she grinned. "I know I will change your mind. Oh, Miss Bright, let's make it grand!"

CHAPTER SEVEN

As Philip made his way into the Custom House on Lower Thames Street, he reminded himself of two things. Firstly, he was innocent of any wrong-doing where Miss Waltham was concerned. Secondly, he was a man in possession of some damn fine brandy, and he needed to bring every drop to Britain.

Few knew how poorly his estate had been handled while he was on the Continent fighting Napoleon's army, and he wanted to keep it that way. If he didn't quickly become a man of business with the same acumen as he had been a successful soldier, he would lose his family's estate by year's end. And he didn't intend to let that happen.

Instead, he planned to exploit the brandy business to its lucrative fullness and refill the drained Mercer coffers. To that end he had spent a sizable sum buying an existing wine distillery in southern France that had produced brandy for a decade. The pale amber *brantwijn*, or "burnt wine" already aged in barrels was the finest Philip had ever tasted. When he'd returned home, he had given a shipping deposit to Waltham.

If they had a falling out, Philip would not be able to start again unless the man gave him back every penny without delay. And even if he did, no one had offered him as favorable terms.

At that point, his only option was to return to France and drink every last drop himself.

With that cheerful thought, he navigated the warren of one-hundred and seventy offices on three levels, getting lost once before he opened the heavy oak door to the rooms that housed Waltham Shipping. In the first office, two clerks sat at two desks, their heads down, scribbling away. The very act of writing reminded him of Miss Bright's ridiculous paper and pencil that she always had with her.

Both young men looked up, and then, upon seeing the caliber of the person who'd entered, probably noticing Philip's fine silk topper and rich blue coat with gold buttons, one rose quickly to his feet.

"May I help you?"

"Lord Mercer to see your employer. He was to meet me here at two o'clock." Pointedly, Philip pulled out his pocket watch by its gold chain from the small, hidden fob pocket in the waistband of his trousers. It was exactly fifty-nine minutes before two.

"Yes, my lord. He is here." The clerk adjusted his cap and went to the door on the far side of the room, tapping twice.

"Come," came the response.

The clerk opened the door.

"Lord Mercer, Mr. Waltham."

Mister? Philip heard a chair push out, and then the figure of Lord Perrin's brother appeared in the doorway.

"I'm surprised to see you here," were the man's opening remarks.

At such a greeting, both the clerks' heads swiveled from their employer to Philip.

Although taken aback by the brusque reception, he merely raised an eyebrow. He was innocent, Philip reminded himself, yet he was so used to having taken outlandish liberties with females, it was difficult not to feel guilty.

"Your meaning?" Philip demanded. *He might as well get the worst over with.*

The clerks looked at Mr. Waltham.

He scowled. "For one thing, the last time we met was at my brother's club. Gentlemen don't often come here for meetings."

The man was correct. Philip didn't make a habit of going somewhere like the Custom House to do business. One of his friends had introduced Philip to Perrin and his brother, Waltham, after having imported some wine on a much smaller scale using one of their ships. They had all met over drinks at Boodle's.

"You would rather I had met you at the club?" Philip asked, using his best bored voice as if the success or failure of his brandy endeavor was of little importance. If anyone knew it meant everything to his future, he would lose all his power.

The clerks' attention shifted again, but Waltham didn't answer.

"In any case," Philip continued, "I expected to meet with the viscount himself."

Mr. Waltham drew himself up taller. Then he sniffed.

"I understand you're in some trouble with my niece."

Two heads whipped round to face him.

Philip sighed as if the tedium might make him slide to the floor that very instant and fall into a deep slumber.

"You understand incorrectly." *Should he say more?* He might explain himself further, but not with the clerks taking it all in as if at a cricket match.

Mr. Waltham blew out his cheeks, then pursed his lips, all the while making a great show of taking Philip's measure.

Two could play at that game. Philip crossed his arms and waited. Either he would be invited into the blighter's blasted little hole of an office in the next ten seconds, or he would be off in a noble huff.

In eight seconds, the man stepped back and invited him in.

With a nod, Philip strode past the clerks, took a seat in the most comfortable chair, and he and Waltham got down to it.

"My brother decided not to meet with you," Waltham began. "At least not here, not about business. Better you should make an appointment, go to his home, and ask for permission to marry his daughter."

Better for whom? Philip wondered.

"I have no intention of asking for your niece's hand," he said firmly. "There is not any reason for it, nor do I believe it is truly what she wants."

Philip thought about what Miss Bright had said. Perhaps Miss Waltham was actually in love with Rowantry, the Marquess of Delham's son.

"My niece doesn't know her own mind, nor can she be allowed to make such a decision."

Philip was shocked. He knew families who arranged marriages when the children were still in leading strings, but to hear an uncle coldly dismiss the feelings of his adult niece seemed cruel.

"My brother," Waltham continued, "is determined our ships shall not bring your brandy until this matter is settled."

"You have taken my money," Philip reminded him.

Waltham sighed, removed his spectacles and rubbed his eyes. After carefully replacing them, he said, "It shall be returned if necessary. Money is nothing compared to honor."

"You do not have to explain to me about honor, sir. I was an officer in the king's army."

"Your actions here in London as I've heard them described are not those of a decent soldier."

"Careful, Waltham. Your brother may be a viscount, but you are walking over thin ice. If you wish to make an accusation, then I suggest you, your brother, and your niece do so publicly before the magistrate and bring proof. But if you personally are calling my honor into question, then I suggest you get your affairs in order and secure your second, for we shall meet with pistols."

Waltham paled. "Now, now, my lord. I am doing no such thing. Even the great Admiral Nelson and the Duke of Wellington had mistresses. But you must have pity on the girl."

"Pity her, yes. Marry her, no. I shall not be blackmailed nor coerced," Philip insisted. "Did you not receive a letter from the magistrate of Queen's Square Court?"

"I was with my brother when he received it. The magistrate wants my niece to step forward before the Season is out and before everyone, including you, leaves Town. He said he would help adjudicate the matter. But my niece is not inclined to press it any further."

"Then the matter is settled, and our business association can continue," Philip said, glad to know Sir William's letter had helped.

Waltham shrugged. "I for one believe in keeping one's personal affairs out of one's business dealings. But you must understand my brother cannot ship your brandy while there is a rumor you have ruined his daughter. His sense of honor is as great as yours."

"Currently, there is no accusation to which I can respond and clear my name," Philip reminded him. "It seems we are at an impasse, at least until the Season has concluded. At that time, if Miss Waltham has not accused me formally, then as the magistrate suggested, she must drop the matter. The threat of it cannot hang over my head indefinitely like the sword of Damocles. Nor can I wait longer than that for my shipment of brandy."

Philip not only had to keep himself out of trouble and make sure Miss Bright remained above any hint of immorality in order to keep the magistrate on his side, but he also had to hope Miss Waltham kept everyone guessing until it was too late to ensnare him.

"If you agree to marry my niece now," Waltham proposed, "then I promise you your barrels of brandy will arrive swiftly. Otherwise, they may fall off my ships in the Channel or they may end up in the cellars of this very building, where King George's officers store the seized wine and spirits of dubious quality or those lacking the proper import permission."

Philip rose to his feet. "I assume you speak in jest for those do not sound like the words of an honorable man."

"Unlike you and my brother, I am a simple man of business," Waltham said, his eyes alert and cunning. "I, for one, hope everything works out to your satisfaction, as I know we can make a good profit together. But my hands are tied, and I can do nothing for you until you marry my niece by the Season's end or she chooses another."

Philip left feeling as if the enemies were outflanking him despite Bright's letter to Perrin.

The only sliver of light in the darkness of his situation was that he was forced to enjoy Miss Bright's company for the remainder of the Season. And that was no hardship at all.

THEIR NEXT EVENT WAS a much smaller dinner party, only fifteen couples, all strangers to Miranda except for Lady Harriet and her friend Lady Emily, and of course Lord Mercer. As there was to be no dancing, her aunt had been given the night off and her father escorted her to the home of Lord and Lady Hartwell, leaving her in the care of the married hosts.

Officially the baron's partner for the evening, Miranda felt not the slightest trepidation and looked forward to the experience with great anticipation.

Upon entering the upstairs drawing room, her gaze swept over the brightly colored silk and satin gowns before she spied Lord Mercer. He was speaking with a dark-haired young lady, and Miranda had the most uncomfortable jolt of jealousy.

Ridiculous! He was only her partner due to an arrangement with her father, and she would do well to remember that. But the young lady beside him was lovely and seemed to have commanded his full attention.

Miranda accepted a glass of wine and chatted with other guests to whom their hosts introduced her while keeping her gaze upon Lord Mercer. When he saw her, he smiled broadly, making her stomach flutter. Rapidly, he took his leave of the lady and left his place by the mantel, coming directly to her.

"You are unencumbered," he quipped after a bow over her hand, noting the absence of Aunt Lucinda.

She curtsied. "Indeed, my lord. After all, how much trouble can one get into in a drawing room or a dining room?"

His grin made her toes curl inside her dove-gray slippers.

"I would love to show you," he whispered, and her tingling toes were nothing compared to the sizzling shiver that went down her spine, tickling the juncture between her thighs.

The man was made of sin! What's more, whenever she was around him, she felt more than a little sinful herself. Her mind raced, trying to imagine what he could mean.

When everyone had a glass of claret in hand, their hosts made a short speech welcoming them all to dinner and to a night of entertainment, which consisted of a recital by the hosts' two daughters, both of whom had suitors present.

"The price of a good meal," Lord Mercer muttered into Miranda's ear. "Such a high cost will more than likely lead to indigestion."

He was incorrigible!

"Then you are fortunate the entertainment is coming *before* the meal," she said. "For I heard one of the gentlemen remark that the young ladies 'must sing for their supper.'

The man seemed to think he was making a hilarious jest. Regardless, I'm sure they shall be good."

While she had no experience with the talents of either young lady who would honor them with a song that evening, she didn't doubt they must have talent. *Why else would they sing in front of gentlemen upon whom they hoped to make a favorable impression?*

An hour later, Miranda was proven half wrong. One sister, who was the prettier of the two, could not carry a tune in a pail, as her father would say. And Miranda had to elbow Lord Mercer to keep him from muttering too loudly about his pained ears. She heard the word *cacophony* more than once from his lips.

At least he had the civility not to laugh out loud, which sadly was not the case in all quarters of the audience.

The other sister, surprisingly, had a bell for a voice, a pure tone that hushed the restless listeners when she began to sing. When her turn came to an end, they went downstairs to dinner.

"Thank goodness," Lord Mercer said as they found their assigned seats and he drew out her chair. "The entertainment in a private home is always a bit of a gamble and more often than not rather dodgy."

"Ssh," she said.

Suddenly, passing on his other side was the first young miss who clearly knew her failure in comparison to her talented sister. Her cheeks were still stained red. Miranda held her breath as the baron turned to her. He barely hesitated before gently taking the woman's hand and offering a polite bow.

"Lady Anna, I want you to know you set an example tonight with your courage and your persistence. Well done."

For a few seconds, the young lady appeared unsure. Then she considered his words. Miranda watched her digest the note of praise and his sincere admiration for how she'd put herself upon the "stage" for all to criticize. Finally, she smiled and nodded as he released her hand.

"I thank you, my lord. That is very generous of you."

"Not at all."

There was a moment's awkward silence. Luckily, the lady's suitor, who seemed more interested in her décolletage and pretty curls than in her voice, escorted her farther along the table toward its head.

When Lord Mercer took his seat, Miranda leaned close. "That was well done of you."

In an instant, his hand slipped onto her lap and squeezed her thigh. Yelping in surprise, she felt her own cheeks warm as many sets of eyes turned her way. Calmly, she offered a placid expression in return before raising her hands above the table cloth so all gazes would follow.

Peeling off her gloves slowly until the others guests became bored and looked way, she placed them in her lap and covered them with her napkin. By that time, the scoundrel had removed his hand.

"I cannot believe you!" she all but hissed.

"A quick demonstration of mischief in the dining room," Lord Mercer said quietly. "A lesson that will cause you to tread carefully and be wary of your dining companions."

She glanced slowly to her left. The gentleman beside her was . . . Beau Brummell! No, she knew he couldn't be the man himself as that intriguing gentleman had fled to France earlier in the year to escape his gambling debts and to keep himself out of debtor's prison. Yet for all she'd read in the papers and even seen in a sketch, this man was his close likeness.

Dressed to the nines in a dark-blue jacket and the whitest white, immaculately tied cravat, he had not a hair out of place and smelled almost as good as Lord Mercer.

"My lord," she asked, suddenly recalling he'd been introduced to her as Lord Pastille, "are you a dandy?"

She heard the baron cough behind her and hoped the word was not an insult.

"Why, if you take me to be one, miss, then I am pleased to say I am."

He was quite jolly and entertaining for the duration of the long meal. And he certainly didn't seem the type to try to touch her leg. Lord Mercer probably thought all men were as scandalous as himself.

After dinner, *three* hours later, Miranda learned the evening was not yet over. The men remained where they were as a servant brought in a tray of cigars and another carried a decanter of brandy.

The ladies, led by their hostess, retired to an informal parlor next door, for whipped syllabub, which was more dessert than beverage. With its frothy curd of lemon peel and juice, cream and sugar, all floating in a glass atop sweet wine, Miranda had never tasted it before. It was a fussy drink that took time to make beyond pouring from a decanter, and thus, it was nothing her father would ever instruct their cook to create.

Swallowing it with absolute delight, she thought it quite superior to most every other beverage she'd ever imbibed.

Seated next to Lady Harriet, Miranda kept her ears open and her mouth shut, soaking in the conversations, which were surprisingly *not* about other people but about dress styles, furnishings, and travel.

After what Lady Harriet had told her, Miranda expected within the intimate setting of a dinner party they would all start to gossip about those who were not lucky enough to be present.

After a while, she yawned, belatedly hiding it behind her hand. When their hostess skewered her with a disapproving look, Miranda realized she needed to shake the cobwebs from her head and excused herself. The nobility's hours were different than her own, and there was no denying this lifestyle took some getting used to.

Out in the hallway, she strolled to the back of the house overlooking the garden. It was partially lit but entirely unwelcoming as a chilly fog had swept in. When she turned, one of the doors opened in her path, and she startled. Realizing she was out of place, Miranda tucked herself behind the curtains and waited.

To her astonishment, a woman's head appeared, looking hither and yon. Miranda hadn't even noticed Lady Sarah missing from their gathering. The lady looked back into the room and nodded, then dashed out into the hall and scurried quickly along toward the parlor.

Miranda almost called out to her for the back of her hair was in a state of disarray. Too late, Lady Sarah opened and closed the door, rejoining their hostess's discussion of bonnets and spencers.

After the span of about ten heartbeats, Lord Pastille followed, his cravat no longer as perfect as it had been during dinner. He disappeared into the dining room across the hall.

Hm! Apparently, there was more than one rake at this dinner party. She didn't need to fetch her paper and pencil from her reticule. Miranda would easily remember to record this later, too.

Before she could leave her concealment, the dark-haired Lady Penelope, the very same with whom Lord Mercer had first been in conversation, exited the parlor, looked in both directions, and went into a different room.

What the devil! Salacious behavior was going on right and left, proving the baron correct. There was much mischief one could get up to at a dinner party. Pressing her cheek to the cool pane of glass, Miranda waited, not wishing to run into a man who might be about to come for a *rendez-vous*.

After a minute, she wondered if the lady's paramour was already inside the room. If such was the case, Miranda wanted to return to the safety of the parlor before the pair came out all flustered and disheveled.

Strolling back toward the assembly of women, the dining room door opened once more and Lord Mercer appeared.

CHAPTER EIGHT

Miranda's heart sank at the sight of him.

"The lady is in there," she told him, pointing to the correct door across the hall.

"I beg your pardon," he said, bemused.

She cocked her head. "It is not anything to me. I just didn't want you going into the wrong room and being disappointed. That one," she paused and pointed to where Lord Pastille had come from, "is empty."

"Is it?" Lord Mercer asked, taking her arm, walking her back toward it. "Are you sure?"

"Quite sure." Her fingers on the handle, she swung it open for him to see, and then found herself softly urged inside. When the door closed behind her, she was in utter darkness.

"My lord?"

"That was ridiculously easy," he said, sounding annoyed. "Why were you wandering the halls where any wolf might pounce upon you instead of being safely with the other sheep where you belong? Our hostess is utterly remiss! Do you understand what just happened and how easily you let me maneuver you into a place of ruin?"

Speechless, Miranda realized the danger she was in. Not with him, of course, but if he were someone unknown to her.

"I only wanted to stroll the hall for a minute. It was tedious and stuffy in the parlor."

"That is also the cost of attending tonight. You must bear all the awful parts that go with a dinner party."

"Why?" she asked, not liking the pitch blackness and taking a step forward. Unfortunately, she bumped into him, and his hands reached out to take hold of her.

"Why?" he repeated, his tone softening. "I suppose in order to enjoy the not-so awful parts."

How he located her mouth, she had no idea, but Lord Mercer's lips brushed hers. A second later, he cradled the back of her head with his big hand while his mouth firmly claimed her own.

She reached out and clasped ahold of him, hoping she wasn't disturbing the perfection of his cravat, like Lord Pastille's. Then, as his other hand swept down her back and grabbed the softness of her bottom, she stopped thinking of anything except the flames flickering through her body as he lifted her hips against him.

When his tongue demanded entrance to her mouth, she gave it. When his hand cupped her breast, she leaned into his palm, aware of a dampness between her legs. With her heart racing and her body trembling, she was ready for whatever he would do next.

Except step away from her, which he did, leaving her panting and longing for his touch.

Without any light, Miranda couldn't see him, but she could hear his breathing as ragged as her own. She affected this experienced man.

It should not please her, but it did.

"*You* are one of the wolves," she guessed.

"I am." His tone was husky. "But it's not I you need fear. At least, I did not think it was."

"I've been out of the parlor a long time," she said. "Someone may come looking for me."

He swore softly, and a sliver of anxiousness pierced her. This was no game. If she left this room and was confronted by her hostess . . .

"Go," he said. "And don't forget this lesson."

Saying nothing, she found the handle and cracked open the door. Seeing no one, she slipped out into the hall and hurried to the parlor.

Upon entering, she noticed Lady Penelope had not returned, and Miranda wondered if Lord Mercer would now go to that other room. Perhaps he'd had a pressing engagement for another assignation and such was the reason he had dismissed her so quickly.

Realizing many gazes had turned her way, Miranda made the mistake of putting her hand to her hair to discern its state. At once, she knew it was a telltale sign of guilt.

Their hostess's eyes widened as her face paled.

"Miss Bright," Lady Hartwell said like the sternest governess, "won't you take a seat?"

The blond-haired Lady Sarah had taken Miranda's place on the sofa next to Lady Harriet, who was looking at her with pursed lips and more than a hint of disapproval.

When she found another place on the edge of the gathering, Miranda hoped the evening was nearly finished as she now felt she'd overstayed her welcome. A few minutes later, when Lady Penelope strolled in, head high, looking at ease with every hair in place, their group was once more complete.

Not long after, Lord Hartwell and the other gentlemen came in. Miranda was fascinated to see Lord Mercer's expression. *Would he appear different? Perhaps ashamed?*

Not in the least. He glanced toward Lady Penelope, and Miranda thought a look passed between them. But he came directly over to her with a warm smile.

"Are you enjoying yourself, Miss Bright?" The banal question served to dissuade any gossip, she assumed.

"Yes, my lord. Thank you for asking. Although perhaps not as much as you."

He frowned slightly. "What have you ladies been talking about? Probably going over the foibles of menfolk."

"Gladly, the discussion hasn't once sunk to the level of discussing any of you. Do you think my father has arrived to retrieve me?"

"I am surprised at your lack of fortitude," he said a little stiffly. "I thought you would wish to remain to the bitter end so you can put it all in your letters to those country cousins of yours."

She glanced over at Lady Harriet, who was in turn watching them.

"I have witnessed plenty for my letters," Miranda promised.

His gaze flickered slightly. "Have you?"

"Indeed, my lord."

Lord Mercer grimaced, and from a plate of sundries on a side table, he popped a sultana into his mouth.

When she said nothing more, he asked, "Very well, tell me. What are these cousins of yours like?"

She nearly told him how she'd halted her extensive epistles in favor of a tale of a single young woman entering the elite world of a small group of Londoners—fictional yet using all the real people and situations she herself had encountered. However, that seemed a larger conversation for another time.

Instead, she answered his question.

"My cousins and my aunt and uncle have a darling house in Northampton. I am sure you would think it inferior to your own country manor, but I have always loved its comfort and charm. My sweet Helen, born a month after me, is closer to me than my own sister. She's a year and a half younger than her brother, Peter. He has a superior mind to most anyone else I have ever known."

This was met with a raised eyebrow.

"Do you fancy this cousin?" Lord Mercer asked bluntly.

She laughed. "Peter is as a sibling to me, and Helen and I used to tease him mercilessly like pesky young sisters."

"Why aren't they in London? And if he's as brilliant as you say, where did he go to school? What is his surname? Mayhap I know him."

"Garrard," she told him, wondering at his surly tone.

"Never heard of this genius."

"Peter hasn't left their country house in years. And Helen, being a devoted sister, has remained with him." She wasn't sure how much she wanted to disclose, as it was a source of some embarrassment for her eldest cousin. She thought of Peter's sharp brain and his extremely facile way of working out puzzles and everyday problems, even fixing things that broke, like a mantel clock. And then there was his aptitude for numbers and investing in the safe government funds, the "four percents," as he called them, along with his riskier, more profitable subscription to the London Stock Exchange.

"I never said he was a genius," she protested.

"Why are they hiding out?" Lord Mercer asked. "Is she hideously ugly and is he considered less desirable than a goat?"

Frowning, Miranda did not like this line of questioning. It was petty and unlike him.

"Helen is lovely," she said truthfully. "And Peter is quite good-looking."

When the baron's brows drew together and his nostril's flared, she realized her rake had a flaw running through him like a streak of sulphur in a coal mine. He was vain and thereby jealous of another male who might be smarter or better looking. It was an unexpected chink in his armor. *How curious!*

Not to soothe Lord Mercer's vanity but to defend her cousins' decision to remain in the country, she decided to tell him the truth.

"Peter was thrown from his horse when he was seventeen." She paused, thinking back. "That was . . . seven years ago. My sister and I were visiting. I can see it as if it were yesterday. Poor man."

Although, he had been barely a man then, more a tall, gangly youth. Peter had deserved better than the broken bones which left him mostly homebound and confined to an awkward Bath-chair when he did leave their manor house.

After the initial shock and a year of brooding, Peter had bounced back to being more like his previously good-humored self except with an edge and a different goal in life than he'd had previously, which was to go to Cambridge. Miranda wasn't sure what he'd intended to study. The only benefit to the accident, as her Auntie Lilah said, was that her only son couldn't go to war on the Continent.

Before Miranda could explain further, the butler announced carriages were waiting for three among their party, including her. Rising, she let Lord Mercer take her hand.

"It was my pleasure to be your escort this evening," he said.

"Truly?" And then before she could stop herself, she asked, "Wouldn't you rather have had a different partner for the evening?" She couldn't help thinking of Lady Penelope awaiting him in that room.

With that, she snatched her hand back and went to bid her hosts good evening.

As her father helped her into their carriage, Miranda wished she'd held her tongue and not sounded like a shrew.

"You're sighing, dearest. Didn't you have a good time?"

She thought of the two recitals, the delicious but long dinner, and then what came after in the darkened room. Her emotions had been up and down all night.

"Honestly, I cannot think why you consider events of the Season to be tedious, Papa." Settling back on the squabs, she tried to quell her swirling sentiments that Lord Major Mercer had stirred.

In a perfectly ordinary tone, she added, "The conversation occasionally was dull, but the creamy pottage and the roast chicken were excellent, as was the fruit and cake trifle for dessert."

No need to tell him of the eye-opening misbehavior she'd witnessed, not to mention her own impossibly improper actions. Either would put an end to any further outings with her handsome rake.

PHILIP HAD THE HELP of his skillful valet whenever he was leaving his home, but he had long hated to be fussed over upon his return. Thus, alone in his room, he began to shed his attire, tossing his cravat onto the dresser next to the *billet-doux* from the raven-haired Lady Penelope.

Shaking his head at how that certain tryst had been thwarted by Miss Bright, he found he didn't mind too much. Kissing the magistrate's daughter had been as intensely satisfying as many couplings he'd had with a willing woman in a salon or dressing room.

She took his breath away and made his heart pound when all he was trying to do was show her how terribly dangerous was her careless behavior.

His lesson had become all too real the instant their lips touched.

By the time he went into the salon for the arranged meeting with the awaiting Penelope who reclined upon a divan, he no longer had an interest in tupping her. Instead, he did nothing more than tell her she ought not to meet alone with a man of his character.

Undeterred, she'd pouted her lips and argued with him while drawing her skirts up her legs, inch by glorious inch. For all he knew, some other man had ruined her and she thought he was her way out, just like Miss Waltham.

"If you hope to tame or trap me, my lady, by offering your body, you are to be sadly disappointed. I bid you go back to the party before you are missed."

Ignoring the surprised and hurt look on her face, he'd returned to the dining room to finish his brandy. A few of the other men gave him knowing looks. He nodded, but wanted to roll his eyes.

What foul creatures his fellow sex were!

Long after he'd seen Miss Bright depart with her father, she'd flitted through his thoughts. Actually, she'd lingered there!

He knew he ought not desire her as he did. He should try to think of her as his ward for the next few weeks or even like a sister, and not as a luscious woman. Yet she was precisely that—warm and soft, full-breasted and, as his hand had discerned, she had a perfectly round arse meant for squeezing.

"Fool," he muttered aloud, having undressed down to his stockings, which he now removed before falling back onto his splendidly comfortable bed. She was his ticket to a lucrative brandy endeavor and was the only thing that stood between him and Miss Waltham's machinations.

Therefore, although Miranda was charming, sweet, and clever—not to mention alluring as any Cyprian—she was also innocent and naïve. And he must stop obsessing about her.

Groaning, Philip closed his eyes and tried to forget the taste of her and her fragrance. Mostly, he tried to banish her face from his mind. He ought to have tupped Lady Penelope.

Better yet, he ought to have stopped at one of his favorite houses and let a professional see to his urges, one who would neither point a finger at him, nor worm her way into his affections.

Too late! As usual, the bliss of clean sheets and a soft pillow stole him away to the land of nod, where he dreamed of a hazel-eyed beauty.

CHAPTER NINE

Miranda had hardly been able to sleep the night before or to think of anything all day except for Vauxhall Pleasure Gardens. Even the name seemed mysterious and thrilling.

Before Lord Mercer arrived at seven, she had already kissed her father's cheek, promised to be careful, and made sure her aunt was entirely ready. Accordingly, the baron had barely taken a step into the foyer when Miranda entreated, "Let us get going!"

Once settled in his carriage, she decided to pretend the indiscretion at the Hartwells' dinner party never happened. She'd written down every moment, and it was time to move on from his "lesson."

"Lord Mercer," she said to catch his attention since his gaze was fixated on the window and the view beyond. It couldn't be that he didn't want to look her in the eyes. *Could it?* "Will we go by boat?"

Aunt Lucinda gave a deep sigh, nearly a groan. A river crossing was obviously not her preference, but Miranda was keen for the short voyage across the Thames to Lambeth.

Lord Mercer dashed her hopes. "It will be quicker and more comfortable to go by carriage over the Regent Bridge."

Miranda supposed getting there more quickly was a fair trade. Perhaps they would go again another evening and she could insist upon the full experience of going by boat from the Thames northern shore.

"Although despite Prinny's pleasure at the bridge's name," Lord Mercer continued, "I believe it shall swiftly be renamed Vauxhall Bridge since that's all anyone is calling it."

When they crossed the newly built bridge, the view did make it an adventure, and soon, they were on the south side with Vauxhall Pleasure Gardens directly at hand.

Miranda was trembling with excitement. Off to the side, she could see some people arriving in wherries from the dock at Westminster or from London proper. She shook off her envy and entered through the proprietor's house. They didn't dally long inside, although she was shown a retiring room should she need it.

Then they stepped out the back of the house into the gardens. People ambled everywhere creating a gentle hum of noise, and wherever her gaze landed, there were prettily painted buildings and sculptures, arches and columns. Music floated from a round building that seemed to be in the center of the treeless area to her right.

"Gracious! It's the most wonderful thing I have ever seen," she said, only realizing she'd stopped in her tracks to gawk when Lord Mercer took her arm and urged her forward.

He gave a short laugh. "You haven't really seen much yet, Miss Bright. I will give you the grand tour, but first we must claim our supper box and order our meal."

Glancing behind to make sure her aunt was following, she let him lead her on.

"I believe I can smell the supper already. Eating outdoors at a proper table," she said. "How divine!"

"You're currently on the Grand Walk," Lord Mercer told her. "It continues all the way to the end of the establishment to the stone wall in the distance."

However, Miranda wasn't looking to the far end, she was glancing right and left at all the hundreds of people milling around.

"What is over there?" she asked, looking left.

"The Rotunda. It's quite a magnificent building," Lord Mercer told her, "and next to it is the Pillared Saloon. Just past them are the Chinese Temples and the Arcade. Later, we shall—"

"And on the other side?" she asked, scanning to the right of the promenade.

"There are many delights over there," Lord Mercer said.

Her aunt coughed behind them.

"That is to say, in the area called the Grove, the building that looks like a bejeweled crown is the Gothic Orchestra. Can you see the musicians on the upper level? Behind it is the Turkish Tent. Dancing occurs under the covered area between that and the supper boxes beyond. There are more supper boxes by the—"

"Where is the Cascade? I have heard much about its false waterfall." Miranda wanted to start running hither and yon to see everything.

"It's up this walkway, on the left in a copse of trees. You'll hear a bell strike at ten o'clock after the first concert, and then a surge of humanity will direct you toward the entertainment of the Cascade."

She turned to him at the sound of sarcasm in his voice.

"I take it you have seen it and are unamused."

Lord Mercer shrugged. "Don't let me spoil it for you. Yes, I have seen it, and it is splendid the first half a dozen times to be sure. It's not worth getting crushed in a veritable stampede, but we'll make sure you get to see it safely by being in that area before the bell strikes."

She couldn't contain her enthusiasm and clapped her hands together.

"What shall we do next? I want to see the Triumphal Arches and the fireworks tower—"

"And the fireworks, too," he said teasingly.

"Yes, of course the fireworks! What's the point of the tower elsewise?" She laughed. "And the Octagon Rooms and Handel's Piazza and what's the other one?"

"The Gothic Piazza."

But she had to quell her excitement until after they'd dined. Lord Mercer told her it was simply how things were done at Vauxhall. After crossing the Grove, they found their assigned supper box within the gardens' colonnades.

"And we have our own private painting." Miranda marveled at the work of art painted on the back wall of their box.

"There's one in each," Lord Mercer told her. "Take note of it, and you'll know which table to return to during the evening. Each one is by Francis Hayman. He was the artistic director for Vauxhall for a time in the last century. He also painted the Shakespearean scenes in the Prince's Pavilion." He pointed to the building next to the proprietor's house through which they'd entered.

"And the four huge victory paintings in the Pillared Saloon." He gestured toward the area on the other side of the Grand Walk next to the Rotunda.

"How ingenious to have a different painting in each box. Don't you think?" Miranda asked her aunt.

"I have seen them before." Aunt Lucinda leaned forward and took a closer look. "The milkmaids," she added.

Miranda nodded. "Very pretty milkmaids. It seems to be a May Day celebration."

Waiters moved quickly between the tables and the kitchens. Their meal consisted of carved cold meats and various salads of vegetables and fruit. Lord Mercer lifted his glass of wine to salute the start of a fine evening. Miranda joined in, but her aunt examined the food on her plate and shook her head.

"The ham slices are even thinner if possible than when I came here at Miranda's age."

They all laughed, but soon an expectant hush fell over the diners. Most knew what was to come. Even Miranda knew what would happen while they were dining at dusk.

"I can hardly wait," she said.

"Any minute," the baron promised.

As if his words had caused it to happen, a shrill whistle cut through the other sounds in the gardens. Lamp-lighters hurried to their stations throughout the Grove.

Miranda held her breath. The second whistle signaled the lighting of the cotton-wool fuses. In the gathering darkness, the flames could be seen traveling all around the gardens from one oil-lamp to another. In the span of two heartbeats, thousands of lamps flared to life in an array of colors including the one hanging from the ceiling in their own supper box.

The crowd erupted in cheers and clapping.

"That was the most marvelous thing I have ever witnessed," Miranda confessed, a quiver of awe still resonating within her.

"I must admit," her aunt said, "it was inspiring."

Miranda looked at the baron. "Even you, my lord, cannot ever grow tired of such a wondrous feat."

The lights were reflecting in his rich-brown eyes, and he smiled.

"I admit the lighting of Vauxhall is spectacular." Then he pushed away his empty plate. "Unlike the thinly sliced ham."

They laughed again and awaited their tray of cakes and pastries, which a waiter brought over. Miranda gave little attention to the sweet treats as she wanted nothing more than to partake in the dancing and then go exploring.

After the dessert course, they left their supper box, secure in the knowledge it would remain a sanctuary for the rest of the evening when they needed it, whether to rest between dances or as a place to order a beverage. And being by the dance floor, it was most convenient.

Under her aunt's watchful eye, Miranda allowed Lord Mercer to take her into his arms for a waltz. She should have known the manager of the Vauxhall Pleasure Gardens would feature the most sensual dance.

When she felt Lord Mercer's hands upon her, her heart skipped a beat. Her body was ready for him to hold her close. Her lips tingled as if he would kiss her in front of everyone.

Looking straight ahead in good form, still, she couldn't help but see his chiseled chin and wicked mouth out of the corner of her eye.

"This almost seems tame compared to Lord and Lady Hartwell's dinner party," she said.

He tensed under her fingers.

"You should not speak of anything that happened there."

"Why not? Will it happen again?" she asked hopefully, preferring the naughty kissing baron to this polite and proper one.

"It will not," he said before glancing down at her. "It cannot. Do you understand?"

Before she could answer, he whisked her around the floor toward the Turkish Tent. Miranda sighed. He could think what he wished, but her female intuition told her he very much wanted to kiss her again. And if he tried, she would let him.

After all, she had research to do.

WHILE MOST WERE STILL listening to the concert, Lord Mercer told her it was nearly time for the unique spectacle of the famous Cascade. Miranda urged him to hurry for she didn't want to miss a minute of it.

They walked toward the thicket, Lord Mercer on one side of her and her aunt on the other. There was nothing much else to see in the vicinity until they came upon a structure shrouded in a dark curtain. Workmen were already raising this, allowing Miranda to take a closer look.

There was a scene of natural beauty consisting of a bridge, a mill with its large wheel, and a bare cliff. But all was still and silent.

"Not impressed yet," she stated.

The baron laughed, but it was Aunt Lucinda who remarked. "Just you wait, my dear. I've seen it before and even I want to see it again."

They heard the bell over in the Grove, heralding the Cascade's entertainment and as if it were the flute of the Pied Piper, people came from every direction in the gardens.

Some pushed and shoved, but Lord Mercer held his ground, and Miranda and her aunt were shielded by him, standing at their back.

"I believe Vauxhall has become more and more unruly," Aunt Lucinda remarked.

Miranda didn't mind. The excitement of the crowd added to her own. In the next instant, concealed lamps were lit, and the scene before her came to life.

She gasped, and the sound was echoed by dozens of others around her as the fake waterfall for which the entertainment was named started up like magic, appearing to realistically cascade down the cliff's face. When it reached the bottom, it caused the mill wheel to turn. Accompanying this movement was the deafening roar of such a tumbling body of water.

Miranda couldn't take her gaze from the astonishing scene, especially when coaches and lifelike pedestrians, including smartly uniformed soldiers, appeared to cross the bridge at regularly timed intervals, all of them utterly artificial.

"Are you still unimpressed?" Lord Mercer asked.

"Absolutely not!" She glanced back to look at him and saw an older couple to his right. The lady had stooped shoulders and the gentleman leaned upon a cane. Neither could see past those in front of them.

Miranda was about to mention this to the baron when he noticed the pair at his elbow. Quick as a whip, he murmured something to the man before tapping the shoulders of two who'd come afterward and taken positions up front.

"Show your elders a little respect," Lord Mercer said. Not waiting, he assisted the elderly couple forward, driving the others aside.

With the lamps reflecting in the older lady's blue eyes, her face lit with pleasure to see the Cascade. The gentleman put his free arm around his wife's waist.

Glancing at Lord Mercer again, Miranda smiled.

The baron was a considerate man. She'd noted this before. Why she'd expected a rake to be selfish, she didn't know. Perhaps it was how he'd been depicted in the papers as caring only for himself and his own pleasure.

About ten minutes after the spectacle started, it was over.

"I wish they would begin again," she said.

The older lady to her right overheard her. "That's the wonder of the Cascade," she began in a thick Scottish brogue. "It's never on long enough that you grow bored of it."

Then she addressed Lord Mercer. "Thank you for allowing us to see it, young man. It's been many years since we came down from Edinburgh to witness it. When I saw the crowd, I feared our long trek had been for naught."

"My pleasure, madam," he said.

The older gentleman nodded his head in agreement before glancing in Miranda's direction and back at the baron.

"Good evening to you and to your wife, my lord. Mayhap you shall come again forty years from now to this very spot. There's nothing like a long marriage and a good woman to keep you young."

They departed into the darkness, the man leaning heavily on his cane and his wife grasping his free arm.

They left behind them an air of awkwardness.

Aunt Lucinda spoke first. "If only my Mr. Cumbersome had not had weak lungs," she said, then sighed before following the crowd out of the treed area.

Miranda and Lord Mercer exchanged a glance. He shrugged.

"Two of the few souls at Vauxhall who do not know me nor my reputation."

"You were very kind," she insisted. That was the reputation he ought to cultivate.

The baron's gaze lingered on her before he said, "Shall we move on? We have much more to see. And there's an extra treat this evening, maybe even better than this last entertainment."

Miranda couldn't imagine what might top the Cascade. After another hour of dancing, Lord Mercer ushered her and her aunt under the arches along the Grand South Walk until they stopped where a throng had gathered near its far end.

"Madame Saqui, late of the theatre at Covent Garden, is going to put on a show," Lord Mercer explained.

"Does she sing?" Miranda asked, gazing curiously at the fireworks tower still many yards away at the end of the walkway and the rope coming from its high point to a stake in the ground near their feet. Someone performing while fireworks were exploding seemed unusual indeed.

He smiled. "You'll see."

In a few minutes, the top of the tower was lit with lamps and a woman appeared, waving to the crowd. Many gasped while some women put their hands over their mouths in excited fear, but most everyone clapped.

"Madame Saqui?" Miranda guessed.

The baron nodded, and she kept her attention upon the figure perched atop the platform. She was dressed in an exotically patterned tunic of blue and gold that reached her knees, with pantalettes showing to her ankles. Upon her head was a headdress consisting of a tiara and a bloom of white feathers that rose in the air a good two feet.

Miranda grasped her hands together with anticipation, memorizing every detail for Helen and Peter.

While the strains of music rose again from the Gothic Orchestra in the Grove, Madame Saqui stepped off the platform. It looked for a moment as though she stood on air.

Miranda gasped, hearing it echoed all around her, until she recalled the rope that stretched at an incline all the way up to the performer.

"A rope-walker," she exclaimed. "What do you think, Aunt Lucinda? Isn't she marvelous?"

"I am terrified," her aunt said, grabbing Miranda's arm. "I don't know if I can watch."

"She hasn't fallen yet," Lord Mercer said. "I saw her at the theatre twice."

Miranda wondered when and with whom, although it was none of her business.

"But this is special," he began just before a firework exploded behind Madame Saqui, illuminating her figure so they could all see her clearly.

With her feathers waving gracefully overhead, she took a step forward and another back and then forward again.

"Why, she is dancing!" Miranda exclaimed, then held her breath, wishing the woman was already farther along the taut rope and closer to the ground.

"It appears to be a minuet," her aunt said. She was correct, for that's what the musicians were playing. A few minutes later, the music quickened, and Madame Saqui began to skip along the rope.

Her aunt added, "And now the gavotte!"

Madame Saqui had only the toes of one slippered foot on the rope while lifting her other leg in a jaunty kick. With her arms swaying, she seemed to be as light as air.

"Gracious!" Miranda said. "It appears she could fly if she wished."

Meanwhile, the fireworks continued overhead, showering the performer in a rainbow of colors—yellow, orange, red, then suddenly green and white.

The crowd cheered.

"I'm sorry to abandon my charge," her aunt said, "but this is leaving me a bundle of nerves. I cannot watch. It is madness! I trust you'll be safe among all these onlookers," she said to Miranda before giving Lord Mercer a particularly hard stare.

"She'll be perfectly safe here," he agreed.

Her aunt sniffed. "Then I will see you back at our supper box." With that, she turned from the fantastical performance.

"I, too, am worried for Madame Saqui," Miranda confessed, "yet I cannot possibly look away."

CHAPTER TEN

If it hadn't been for Madame Saqui, Philip would never have lost sight of Miss Bright. The thirty-year-old, famed rope-dancer was truly mesmerizing, having been practicing her craft in France with her parents since she was a girl. But that was no excuse for taking his eyes off Miranda. Not even for a second.

Nor would he have, regardless of how dainty and magical the French woman appeared. Yet somehow, Madame Saqui made eye contact with him, and he could sense she was going to use him in her act even before it happened. The fireworks continued behind her, the music swelled, and she ran on tip-toe the final yards down the inclined rope.

Sure enough, as Madame Saqui approached the end, she bent slightly at her knees and sprang into the air, directly at him. This was probably the most dangerous part of her act because she was relying upon a stranger. Luckily, he caught her midair.

"Twirl me, monsieur," she demanded, and suddenly, as if it had been planned, he found himself cradling her in his arms and turning in a circle while she threw her hands overhead, accepting the acclaim and applause of all those around them.

"Again!" she ordered, and he did as requested, enjoying her warm body against his and even appreciating the envy of the men in the crowd.

Finally, she said, "Enough. You may set me down."

Disentangling himself from the lovely limbs of Madame Saqui, who let her hands run down his arms and chest, Philip finally looked around for Miranda.

She was no longer in the vicinity.

Blast!

Philip recalled the last time he'd panicked when he had lost sight of her, and took a steadying breath. There had been nothing to worry about then and probably all was well now. Thinking she'd decided to rejoin her aunt, he returned to their supper box. Alas, it held only Mrs. Cumbersome.

"Where is Miss Bright?" he asked the older woman who had ordered herself a pitcher of the popular Arrack punch and already downed a portion.

"I came here twenty years ago and had the very same," she said, slurring slightly and looking at her nearly empty glass that had held the unique, distilled liquor of fermented palm sap, mixed with citrus fruit, sugar, and spice.

To Philip, the taste reminded him of a blend of spiced rum and inferior brandy.

Mrs. Cumbersome picked up the pitcher and refilled her glass.

"We called it *rack punch*. 'Waiter, more rack punch,'" she called out to the memory of a server from her youth.

Philip nodded. He imagined he might be equally in trouble with the magistrate for his sister becoming inebriated as well as for losing his daughter. A cold sweat broke out between his shoulder blades.

"This setting is more pleasurable than a ballroom," Mrs. Cumbersome blurted looking around at those who were dancing nearby. "Don't you agree?"

He couldn't help wondering how a woman with a brain could tolerate the tedious job of watching over another adult female. It was probably more exciting if one were the chaperone to a troublesome minx, although such a stressful task didn't sound appealing either.

Luckily, Miss Bright had been cooperative and obedient so far. He should stop worrying, except for the first time in his life, thinking of his deal with Sir William, Philip could appreciate what it would be like to have a daughter. Worse still to have a beautiful one with wicked rakes like himself around.

"Have you seen Miss Bright?" Philip asked again. After all, this was her aunt's main task.

At last, Mrs. Cumbersome set down her glass with a thump, focused her watery gaze upon his, and frowned as she caught on to his concern. Her face paled to a distraught pallor of bloodless white.

"Oh dear," she said. "I thought my niece was with you."

He clenched his fists at his sides. Miranda hadn't returned to the table even to tell her aunt where she was going.

"She slipped away in the darkness," he replied, unable to temper his annoyance while he scanned the dance floor as the first most likely place to find her. Suddenly, he was on high alert as if on the battlefield trying to spy the enemy over the next ridge.

"I think you ought to return to the proprietor's house and look in the ladies' retiring room. Perhaps our meal disagreed with her," he suggested.

"Yes, I shall at once. My brother will be most displeased with both of us," she announced, hurrying off across the grove with a wobble to her gait.

Philip growled in frustration. He hoped Mrs. Cumbersome didn't pass directly through the owner's house and fall into the Thames. Moreover, she would have to recall the painting of the milkmaids to return to the correct supper box.

Then he discharged her from his thoughts entirely for the more important matter of finding Miranda. Perhaps she'd gone to the Prince's Pavilion since she had expressed an interest in the Shakespearean-themed paintings.

Endearingly, she'd seemed as excited by the view from the recently built, iron-crafted Regent Bridge as she had by the famous Cascade, and by everything she encountered. He liked that about her. She hadn't a jaded bone in her attractive body. But curiosity was a dangerous thing for a young woman alone at Vauxhall. If she was at the Pavilion, then she was safe. Better he should search the worst possibilities first.

With that in mind, he headed down the Grand South Walk since that was where he'd last seen her. Hurrying farther from the well-lit Grove toward the now-deserted fireworks tower, he came to the darker sections of the Pleasure Gardens where no young lady should be.

Passing couples who were looking for secluded spots, they turned their faces when he went by. A few times, he had done the same thing with willing and savvy minxes, never considering a chaperone might be anxiously searching—or if he had thought about it, he hadn't particularly cared.

"Selfish bastard!" Philip muttered, knowing more than he should about the best places for privacy in public areas.

Half hoping he didn't find her anywhere in the vicinity but also hoping he did, because the suspense of not discovering her whereabouts was fraying his nerves, he inspected the large walnut tree with its cover 'of hanging branches. He peered behind a statue and even under a small decorative bridge. If one were tucked beneath it, those strolling over couldn't even tell. In his hunt, he found lovers in two places but not Miss Bright.

Ten heart-pounding minutes later, he spied her. While she was not with Lady Harriet and her friends this time, nor was she being debauched and ruined.

To his disbelieving eyes, she was entirely alone in the last place she ought to be, the Dark Walk.

Fury clouding his judgment, he snuck up on her, grabbed her by the arm, and spun her about to face him. She shrieked, stumbled, and fell against him. Feeling relief mixed with his anger at how she'd put herself in harm's way, he wrapped his arms around her and drew her close.

"Dammit all, Miss Bright!"

"You frightened me," she said against his chest, and her body trembled.

"Good! You deserved it. You frightened me first and for a much longer time."

Resting his chin atop her head, he simply held her, hardly able to believe his luck in finding her safe. Unless . . .

"Why are you in this place? Did you come with someone? Has anyone approached you or touched you?"

She leaned back in the circle of his arms. In the dim moonlight where there were no oil lamps, she gazed up at him, looking like any number of desirable women he'd had in this or another dark garden. Except she was Miss Bright, and for some reason infinitely more alluring

"Lady Harriet was beside us during the fireworks and the rope-dancing, didn't you see her?"

He hadn't, so he shook his head, still enjoying the feel of having her soft warmth securely against him. What's more, she was making no move to pull away.

"Just as the last fireworks were going off, she invited me to do some exploring. She mentioned other music, the Turkish band and the Pandean band, and even a Scotch one."

"I promised to show you everything," he reminded her, caressing her back.

"You were otherwise occupied," she said tartly, and he realized she was jealous of Madame Saqui.

"I could hardly let the lady fall."

"If you hadn't been staring at her with your tongue hanging out, she might have chosen someone else at whom to launch herself."

He chuckled. At the same time, a couple passed by, heads averted, and disappeared at a trot into an alcove of shrubbery.

"But how did you end up here?" he asked, feeling riled again.

"I know not. Lady Harriet said we would find the Pandean band down this path, but she must have become befuddled, as lost as I am. Then she stumbled upon a root in the dark and said her ankle was sore. She told me if I went along here, I would find assistance."

Philip was growing angrier on Miranda's behalf. Lady Harriet had purposefully sent her into danger. *That cunning hoyden!*

"And did you find assistance?"

"Well, no," Miss Bright admitted.

"That's because the only people on the Dark Walk are couples," he explained.

"The Dark Walk?" she repeated.

Just then, as if to prove him a liar, a sole figure came strolling along the path between the high hedgerows.

Instinctively, Philip hunched, molding her into his body and turning her away from prying eyes. But when the stranger passed, Philip glanced over his shoulder, and the man turned.

Lord Geoffrey Beaumont!

If he wasn't mistaken, brother and sister were playing games, and Miss Bright was their toy.

"I thought you said only couples," she began, her voice muffled as she spoke into his jacket.

"Unless there is a prearranged meeting. Imagine if you had been alone."

He felt her shiver and let her draw back.

"Thank you," she said meekly, looking up at him and raising her fingers to touch his cheek.

It was his undoing. Keeping one hand on her back, he slid his other to the base of her head, his large palm anchoring her in place.

When she parted her lips, he leaned down and kissed her. Heat shot to his loins, and his heart sped up the way it had when he'd been madly searching for her. But this time with pleasure. He didn't even have to coax her mouth open as she'd given him sweet access.

Slipping his tongue between her lips, he explored her warmth, feeling her tentative response. When the tip of her tongue slid along the length of his, Philip moved his hand from her back to her waist before stroking up to palm her breast through the thin silk of her gown.

"Mm," she moaned, the sensual sound inflaming him further. He rubbed his thumb over her nipple, feeling it stiffen. That wasn't all that stiffened, and he groaned in return.

Miss Bright giggled into his mouth.

Giggled?!

Philip raised his head. "Is something funny?"

"Only the noise you made, my lord, like I imagine a bear might sound."

She did little for a man's ego. But it was just as well. He'd gotten carried away. *Again!* And she hadn't had the wherewithal to stop him.

Where was her blasted chaperone? Mrs. Cumbersome was probably slumped over their table with her belly full of punch.

Was he supposed to be saint, escort, and nanny all at once? After all, he was a passionate man and she was a tempting female.

"Your chaperone must be worried witless. Let us go find her."

"What of Lady Harriet and her ankle?"

He swore under his breath, then aloud said, "I'm sure someone has found her by now and taken her back to the civility of the Grove." They walked swiftly to the other end of the Dark Walk where it intercepted the Grand Walk.

Turning onto it, they continued toward the lighted area, but soon, he would have to part from her to protect her.

"You must not be seen coming from this direction with a man. Do you understand?"

She nodded.

"Answer me," he demanded, feeling a tumult of emotions that would have him gladly call out Lady Harriet as a troublemaker and her brother as a libertine of the worst caliber. Undoubtedly, the slippery jackanape had intended to find Miranda alone and defenseless.

"Yes, my lord." At last, she sounded almost contrite.

"I'll watch you from here. You must go directly to our supper box, and when Mrs. Cumbersome asks you, you were with Lady Harriet and no one else."

"And if she asks me about you?"

"Tell her you never saw me. I'll return shortly having given up hunting for you."

"Yes, my lord," she repeated, softly. He watched her make her way to the Grove. He'd defeated the enemy this time, but had almost suffered the dearest casualty of all. Philip would be more careful the rest of the Season.

And he certainly needed to show some restraint around her. She had only to look at him a certain way, and he wanted to devour her.

And then he wouldn't have to worry about Miss Waltham's accusations or the Beaumonts' evil antics. With the magistrate against him, Philip would find himself laid by the heels in Newgate, paying good chummage for a moth-eaten blanket and a bowl of watery gruel, never to see daylight again.

CHAPTER ELEVEN

"I cannot believe I was out again last night. At this rate, I shall have worn out all my new slippers like those princesses from the fairy tale."

Miranda's father grunted and looked up from his papers.

"Have you found a husband yet? It's been a month."

She smiled at him. "It's barely been three weeks and no, Papa, but I've experienced many wonderful things. I am exceedingly grateful."

Balls and dinners, the theatre, and even twice a ride in Hyde Park—she had met many new people, seen the most wondrous sights, and done all of it in the company of her favorite male. *Lord Major Mercer had been a dash-fire escort!*

Moreover, she'd chronicled all of it and was turning it into a tidy little tale as Lady Harriet had suggested. Although, she couldn't help wishing she had a few more adventures like the one from the Dark Walk. Being in Lord Mercer's arms had been heavenly. He was like a Vauxhall lamp-lighter and his kiss was the flame set to the swift wick of her body's core.

When his lips touched hers, the sparks of desire seemed to have raced through her blood, igniting it to a fiery pulse.

It was a delicious, tempting, frustrating inferno that made her squirm merely thinking of him.

Yet after that night, he'd been nothing but polite, even standoffish, touching her only when absolutely necessary, offering his hand to assist her into his carriage or allowing her to rest her hand on his arm. And never once had he let himself be alone with her again.

Frankly, it had been a little disappointing, even though she knew he was on his best behavior for the sake of his brandy business. Were they to continue to keep company after the Season's end, Miranda wondered what might happen if she could, in fact, get the baron alone.

"You're meant to find yourself a husband," her father's voice broke into her wicked thoughts. "This might be your last chance to catch a wealthy one, my girl. You might as well snag a rich man as a poor man. Otherwise, you'll have to make do with some law clerk who comes sniffing around here, hoping to ingratiate himself in my court by courting you."

Her father paused then laughed at his own words.

"Court and courting, did you hear?"

"Yes, Papa," she said.

However, gaining a husband, while a pleasant dream, was not currently her goal. She had a book to finish, perhaps during her only Season of interesting events. Tomorrow, for instance, she would be among a party taking rowboats up the Thames toward Brentford, followed by a picnic on the riverfront of the Duke of Northumberland's Syon House.

Lord Mercer, of course, would be her escort. And just as assuredly, the other young men would start to pester her for the favor of her company. She was becoming used to it, and also to being disappointed in them. They were always lacking in some way—not as tall as the baron or not as broad-shouldered or not as humorous or intelligent. Their eyes weren't as glitteringly dark, or their mouths weren't as sensual. In all manner, they were inferior.

Besides, Miranda doubted her father realized how her close association with the raffish baron might be giving other gentlemen the wrong idea. At the previous ball, she'd received a knowing wink from one man while another had patted her backside by the potted palms, and most of them stared down her décolletage as if she'd given them leave to scrutinize her person.

And all the while, her Lord Major Mercer remained coolly aloof despite any encouragement from her. And sadly, there would be no cover of darkness to allow for a kiss while rowing or enjoying the picnic in the sunlight.

Just as well. She wasn't foolish enough to think if he did ruin her the way those other young women had allowed themselves to be debauched in the far reaches of Vauxhall's Pleasure Gardens or out behind the darkened hedges at the last ball, that Lord Mercer would follow up with an honorable proposal.

She had only to look at Miss Waltham as an example.

"You're scowling. I do not like it," her father said. "Fetch me a cup of tea, there's a good girl."

As soon as she did, she slipped away to visit with Lady Harriet. As before, Miranda was admitted at once, even without an invitation.

"I wanted only to make certain your ankle was not severely injured, my lady. I haven't seen you out since Vauxhall."

"You are a dear for worrying over me and my clumsiness, especially as I got us lost and then sent you off alone into the darkness. I was useless, stranded like a sailing ship on a windless day. My brother took me directly home."

"I believe I saw him going in your direction that night."

"Did you?" Lady Harriet looked interested. "He did not mention it."

"Lord Mercer kept me protected from prying eyes."

Lady Harriet cocked her head. "Did he? How chivalrous of him. Rather unlike his usual behavior. You have quite captured his interest, I dare say."

Miranda felt her cheeks warm.

"Not at all," she protested. "He is only with me because—"

"Why stop?" Lady Harriet said, leaning forward in her chair. "Do tell."

Miranda chided herself. She had promised her father not to disclose the arrangement. It certainly didn't put her in a good light, keeping company with a rake only because he had been coerced into doing so. And to make the situation perfectly clear, she would have to tell tales out of school about Miss Waltham.

Miranda loved gossip, but had never before had anything remotely of interest to tell to someone like Lady Harriet. Telling her new friend something personal about someone she didn't even know felt distinctly wrong.

"As I told you before, it is merely because of an old friendship between our parents." She would swear her cheeks had grown even hotter. Lying was not something she did readily or often. *Had she done it well enough?*

"*Hm,*" Lady Harriet said. "Again, it seems out of character for Mercer. Regardless, how is our writing endeavor coming along?"

THE NEXT DAY, MIRANDA wore not slippers but a pair of soft-leather half boots in a very becoming shade of blue to match her gown. The entire ensemble seemed most prudent for a day spent outdoors.

At the public landing on the north bank of the Kew Bridge, the small party of guests were greeted by their hosts, Lord and Lady Coxley. The couple had a close association with the Duke of Northumberland, at whose home they were staying for a month and on whose land the party-goers would enjoy their rustic meal.

Miranda found herself to be one of four single ladies, along with four single men including the baron who had gone to university with Lord Coxley and thereby had received an invitation.

Hers was a coveted spot in this exclusive gathering, which she appreciated even more when it turned out to be only two to a rowboat. The gentlemen would show off their manliness by rowing the ladies up river to the duke's property. Miranda would have nothing to do but sit in her new cotton dress, hold up her silk parasol, and pepper Lord Mercer with questions about what he did inside the hallowed halls of White's, since her latest fascination was with gentlemen's clubs.

Naturally she would include the information in the chapters of her novel, as she now thought of each letter she wrote to Helen and painstakingly copied before sending.

Lord Mercer spent a few minutes in a tête-à-tête with his friends. His head nodded once in her direction, before Lady Coxley peered past him to take Miranda's measure.

To her surprise and consternation, Miranda was paired with an earl's son. Lord Wesley had been eyeing her since her father had dropped her off by the bridge, and now they would be together in a small boat.

Worse, Lord Mercer had done it on purpose.

Trying not to let her disappointment show, she allowed Lord Wesley to assist her onto the comfortable cushioned seat of the rowboat. It even had a padded back, allowing her to relax.

"Are you ready, Miss Bright?" he asked cheerfully.

"I am. Thank you."

While he picked up the oars and waited for a footman to untie their boat, she purposefully didn't look again at Lord Mercer.

As it turned out, Lord Wesley was amusing. With the stone arches of Kew Bridge receding behind his head, he told her about his misadventures of the Season. Apparently, he was a tad clumsy yet so good natured, he didn't mind talking about it, whether tripping over a lady's foot on the dance floor or falling down a flight of stairs at Devonshire House.

Her happy smile was genuine when they eventually approached the grassy bank of Syon Park to rejoin their party. It had taken the better part of an hour, what with time spent letting Lord Wesley rest his arms while they floated along. The other guests had done the same, including Lord Mercer who kept his boat not too far off, while he rowed for Lady Emily, Lady Harriet's friend.

After that, they took a brief tour of the ground floor of the duke's magnificent home before spending time in the gardens. Northumberland himself was not there, but he'd given leave for Lord and Lady Coxley to play hosts.

Miranda walked with Lady Emily at her side down the path between the cultivated beds. The spectacular flowers gave off a dizzying fragrance.

"These roses!" Miranda exclaimed to Lady Emily. "I've never seen such magnificent blooms."

The other woman nodded, then leaned closer. "Did you enjoy your time with Lord Wesley? He's handsome, I dare say."

Miranda looked over to where the men were standing in a group, chatting.

"He is," she agreed, but her glance went to Lord Mercer and stayed there. He was without doubt the most mouth-watering man in this or any assembly. The rest paled by comparison as far as she was concerned.

"Lord Wesley was good company. And how was your boat trip with Lord Mercer?"

Lady Emily shrugged. "He was as he usually is."

Before Miranda could ask what she meant, the young lady added, "You know what I mean. If a man is not available for marriage, then it is practically pointless to converse for any length of time. One such as Mercer only wants women for a singular purpose. Thus, he hardly bothers to make himself agreeable."

Miranda hadn't found that to be the case. On the other hand, he was simply fulfilling a hand-shake pact with her father, not keeping company with her by choice. Consequently, she had no idea how he comported himself with someone like Lady Emily if he had no particular interest in her.

When it was nearly three o'clock, they were ushered to a picnic set out under two walnut trees. Clearly, it was meant to look artless and easy, but everything had been transported to the spot by harried servants. Not only the food and beverages, but the furnishings, large umbrellas, the table linens, and the dinnerware—all had been packed in baskets and trunks and brought to their patch of grass in wagons to be set out.

Once Miranda reached the shaded area, she closed her beloved parasol, leaned it against the tree, and took a seat where directed.

"Isn't this fun?" Lord Wesley said, coming over with the other men. "I can't possibly knock over a pedestal or a wall sconce in this dining room." With that, he tripped over a tree root that had made a slight bump in the grass and went sprawling, landing practically in Lady Emily's lap.

She shrieked. "Will you be careful, my lord?"

With his face beet red, he offered his sincere apologies and took the seat beside her.

Miranda hoped Lady Emily softened to him for it would be a wonderful tale to tell their children of how he "fell" for her.

Lord Mercer sat on her other side, and she caught the zesty fragrance of his sandalwood and lime cologne. She nearly leaned over to breathe it in more deeply.

"How are you faring this beautiful day, Miss Bright?"

"Very well." Recalling how he'd pawned her off on another man, she wondered if he was tired of her already. "How was your trip up river?"

Lord Mercer shrugged, glancing at Lady Emily deep in conversation with the affable Lord Wesley.

"As well as it could be. Mostly silence unlike when you are nearby."

Miranda gasped. *Had he just accused her of being a jabber-box?*

Then he added, "The tedium was broken only by the inanity of vapid remarks about her own clothing and her comfort, or lack thereof." He pretended to look behind them while whispering in her ear, "I was about ready to abandon ship and swim here."

She nearly spat out her lemonade as laughter caught her by surprise.

When the picnic came to an end and every last morsel of roast duck and ham pie, each crusty roll, and every spoonful of stewed fruit and forkful of plum cake had been devoured, it was time to row back. For propriety's sake, everyone switched partners, and now she was with Lord Mercer.

"I thought you would arrange for me to be with one of the other two single men," she said as he helped her into the boat.

"Not likely. I don't trust either of them. Only Wesley was good enough for you, despite being ungainly as a newborn colt."

"*Good* enough for me?" She settled onto the seat and started to open her parasol.

"Yes, recall your father hopes you find a husband. I thought Wesley might be a suitable match. Nice enough fellow and looking for a wife."

"I see." That made her feel better in a way. He hadn't dismissed her company out of hand but had her best interest in mind. Yet she would have preferred if Lord Mercer had her heart as his own target rather than hoping she gave it elsewhere.

A black blob appeared before her eyes, and she realized a spider had crawled into her parasol when it was resting against the walnut tree and was now dangling over her. Miranda knew it was foolish, but her aversion to spiders was intense.

Shrieking, she watched it descend toward her lap and tried to scrabble out of the way.

"Stop moving," Lord Mercer ordered.

She didn't answer but scooted right, then left, before finally dropping her parasol and standing.

"Miss Bright!" he admonished as the rowboat tilted. "Sit down."

The spider crawled out from under the silken folds of her parasol, moving directly toward her.

Feeling as if her skin were crawling, too, she yelled again and tried to move away.

"Miss Bright!" he exclaimed again as the boat tilted in the other direction.

Too late!

The boat that was already rocking with her erratic movements tipped over as she leaned away from the creepy-crawly, spilling her and Lord Mercer directly into the Thames.

CHAPTER TWELVE

"The deuce!" Philip exclaimed, foregoing the boat to save Miranda.

In two strokes he was by her side. The bank fell away steeply, and he couldn't touch the bottom. However, by treading water while holding her around the waist, he was able to keep them both from sinking.

"What on earth?" he demanded, while the female fish he'd caught spluttered out river water.

"A spider," she said, sounding sheepish and splashing her hands on the surface, apparently unable to swim.

"A spider!" He hadn't meant to yell, but really! *What a ninny!*

"I've lost my new parasol," she complained.

"And I've lost my patience," he said, kicking out toward the narrow dock from where they'd embarked. "Grab on," he said.

Luckily, although the other guests and their hosts were well away already, a footman remained who was able to help her out of the water. Then Philip hoisted himself up onto the dock. They sat side-by-side watching the bubbles come out from the boat as it drifted away.

"Are you well?" yelled Lord Coxley from many yards down the river.

"We are fine," Philip called out.

"Take our carriage back to Kew," Coxley yelled.

Philip rose to his feet, offering her his hand and drawing her up beside him.

"That was not well done of you," he scolded, then closed his mouth, speechless as he viewed her full figure outlined by her sodden gown.

Every inch of Miss Bright was on display as the pale blue fabric clung to her breasts, molded over her stomach, and—sweet Mary—tucked into the apex between her thighs.

He swallowed and glanced at the footman who was ogling her. Philip could hardly blame the young man.

"Let's get you inside Northumberland's house and see if a maid can help dry you off."

Apparently unaware of the display of her assets, she nodded and strolled ahead of him, giving a view of her backside that had him aroused before they reached the rose gardens.

"I really liked that parasol," she called over her shoulder.

He was starting to like that spider who'd caused the mishap and struggled to wipe the silly grin off his face.

Once inside the back entrance, they stood in silence, and Philip tried to keep his glance off of her.

"Where is everybody?" he wondered.

"When the cat's away," she began.

"I take it you think the servants are the mice playing somewhere in the house."

She shrugged and unwittingly showed him her dusky nipples through the fabric.

"Are you growing chilled?" he asked.

"I am," she confessed. "How did you know?"

He looked away. "Just guessing."

Making a decision, he took her hand, mounting the backstairs two at a time. They wandered along the corridor, and still, no servant came into view. This was a rake's dream and, thus, Philip's nightmare. Every ounce of blood in his body was singing with desire.

With trepidation, he opened a door and peered inside. Luckily, it was a bedroom and it had a wardrobe. He dropped her hand and headed for it.

"Thank my lucky stars," he said upon seeing women's dresses. She stood beside him and peered in.

"I cannot simply steal someone's clothing."

"You can't parade around outdoors like that," he insisted. "And I can't take you in the Coxleys' carriage soaking wet. You'll stain the squabs. More importantly, you're too exposed."

"What about yourself?" she asked, reaching to touch one of the gowns.

"I'm fine. Uncomfortable as a monk in a hair habit, but I'll survive until I get home. I can sit on the carriage floor if need be."

"Then I shall, too," she said. "After all, it was my fault."

He looked at her. It was a mistake. As she sighed, her breasts rose, bringing her nipples to the forefront again.

"You will change," he said firmly, "and I shall wait outside."

He crossed the room to the open door and nearly made it out when the wicked reprobate in him added, "That is, unless you need assistance."

The strangest expression crossed Miss Bright's face, and she chewed upon her lower lip, driving a shard of lust straight to his loins.

Send me away, he commanded silently.

"You could be of assistance," she said in a soft voice.

He slammed the door shut and found himself still on the same side as this beautiful woman.

"What can I do?" His voice croaked like a frog, and he cleared it.

"Perhaps you could simply untie my dress. It's a little hard to reach the ribbon."

He moved closer again. "Is it?" It seemed to him she could easily reach around back and pull the long decorative ribbon that didn't actually seem to be doing anything substantial in the way of holding her gown in place.

Regardless, he did as she asked, tugging the end until the bow collapsed.

"Now what?" he asked.

"Why are you whispering?" she asked in return.

He cleared his throat again. "Was I?"

She turned to face him. Of course, they were much too close and by her small smile, this innocent minx knew exactly what she was doing, torturing him to madness.

Clasping his fingers around her upper arms, he drew her against him and claimed her lips as he'd been wanting to do all day.

Tongues fencing, hearts pounding, they let the warmth of their bodies seep through their sodden clothing. Then he slid his hands down her back to that delectable bottom he recalled and hauled her against his rock-hard arousal. She gasped, further inflaming him.

"You're very wet," he murmured against her lips.

"I am," she said. "When you kiss me, I feel it between my legs."

Shocked by her admission, he said, "I meant with river water."

"Oh." She started to pull away.

What a dunce he was for embarrassing her!

"You are sweet for telling me. As you can feel, you affect me equally."

He pressed his hardened shaft against her. "*That* is because of you."

"Oh," she said again and relaxed. Her fingers interlaced behind his neck and held him tightly, and he could think of nothing else except the taste and feel and scent of her.

Pungent river water!

"Let's get you out of this soggy garment," he said.

"I can do it," she confessed, whipping her gown over her head.

It didn't even have any buttons that needed undoing. She stood before him in a limp shift and half-stays, which she was already untying in the front.

Quickly, Philip shrugged out of his jacket and yanked on his cravat. Boots, trousers, stockings, all came off until he wore only a loose linen shirt.

At the same time, he'd had the extreme pleasure of watching her divest herself of the last shreds of cloth. He expected to awaken from this blissful dream of Miranda naked before him, her hair down, a damp lock curling over her left breast.

And then they were together again, skin to skin, her breasts against his chest as he devoured her mouth under his. He couldn't help letting one of his hands drift down between them, dipping a finger between the curls at her cleft to sample the wetness she'd mentioned.

"Mm," she moaned at his touch.

He stroked her, feeling her honey sweetness, as her fingers traced a pattern on his shoulders. When he touched her nubbin, those same fingers dug into his skin as her eyelids closed.

"Ohh," she gasped.

He caressed her again, over and over, feeling her nipples grow taut against him as she curled her hips into his hand and started to tremble. With his other hand supporting her lower back, he was rewarded by her body already beginning to tense as she moaned loudly.

Finding her release more quickly than he could have imagined, she relaxed and opened her eyes, now glazed with languid pleasure.

To his delight, she brought her hand to his nipple and flicked it playfully.

"What happens next?" she asked, her tone thick, sounding drugged as if with opium.

Philip could barely think with his shaft aching and pressed low against her stomach. He looked beyond her. *The bed! What a fool?* Why on earth had he made this lovely creature stand during her climax?

As if waltzing, he kept Miranda in his arms while moving her backward until they tumbled against the bed. In a heartbeat, he was settling between her legs, supporting himself on his forearms and looking down into her expectant face.

"You ensnare me with your warmth and beauty," he told her, nudging the head of his cock against her wet passage.

"You impress me with your kindness," she countered. "Every little act of it that I've seen."

He liked that she had a good opinion of him. Most people he knew didn't. Even his friends wouldn't look past his reputation to consider him a kind man.

Moreover, he wanted to be the man she seemed to think him to be.

Except at that moment, he simply wanted her.

The innocent, adorable, Miss Miranda Bright. *The magistrate's daughter!*

The devil take him! He was a blasted cur, and with the madness of craving her, he'd forgotten his promise to her father.

Looking down at her sweet face, with her hair spread across the counterpane as she willingly offered herself to him, he groaned.

"What is it?" she asked. "Are you in pain?"

He deserved to be whipped and to suffer the torture of being dragged behind his own horse. His punishment would have to be his throbbing arousal which must be denied.

"I've behaved badly." He began to climb off her, but her arms tightened around him.

"Then *we* have behaved badly," she said. "Yet I enjoyed every minute of it thus far. Shall we continue?"

What manner of temptress was she? "We cannot, not without repercussions of which you seem woefully unaware."

Miranda glanced away, pondering something, and he took the opportunity to lower his mouth to her pert nipple and draw it in. Happily, he let his tongue play across it.

"That feels very good, too."

With a measure of desperation, Philip rested his forehead on her bare skin and laughed ruefully.

She wasn't going to let him go easily. "Cannot you ensure there are no, as you say, *repercussions*?" she asked, stroking his hair as if he were a favorite pet. "I know you are referring to getting me with child, but I have read there are ways to prevent that from happening."

He let out an exclamation of exasperation. "It's not merely that. It is everything! You're trying to find a husband. He will expect to be the first in the position which I currently find myself."

"Yet I will not be *his* first," she said softly.

"That's neither here nor there, and you know it. We are not about to have a conversation on the different expectations for males versus females, are we?"

She sighed, and he took the opportunity to worship her other nipple, feeling her sink her fingers into his hair. When he flicked it with his tongue, she lifted her hips, and he pressed inside her just a little.

It was agony to stay still when he wanted to drive balls-deep inside her tight passage. Again, Philip withdrew, tore loose from her grasping fingers, and thumped himself down upon the bed beside her. A second later, the entire mattress sank to the floor, slipping between the four posts, and rolling Miranda and him together.

"I believe the ropes have broken," she said, her voice muted since her face was buried against his side.

They were as two sausages wrapped in pastry.

"So it would seem," he agreed.

They both tried to climb out of the nest that had been created. After struggling together, he got out first before reaching back to pull her after him.

They looked at one another then back at the mess they'd made. Her eyes widened, but then she smiled. Her smile became a chuckle. That made him laugh in return until they were both bent over, helpless with hilarity.

The door popped open, and they silenced and straightened as a maid entered.

"Dear lord!" she exclaimed, looking at them, naked as needles before she backed out, slamming the door shut.

They only laughed harder. Miranda's breasts were even more glorious when bouncing due to happiness. Philip didn't recall when he'd felt so full of mirth.

"Oh dear," she said, going to the wardrobe without an ounce of uneasiness.

Opening a drawer, she drew out a cotton shift and yanked it over her head. It dimmed his own joy at once. Then, barely looking at her choices, she snatched out a pale rose gown and pulled it on.

"There," she said. "At least I am presentable now, which is more than I can say for you."

A pounding on the door was followed by a man's voice. "Who are you and what's going on in there?"

Miranda shrugged as if to say she'd warned him this would happen, and Philip sprang into action putting on his wet clothes. Meanwhile, she went to the door and cracked it open.

"Are you the Duke of Northumberland's butler? We met you earlier. Our rowboat overturned as everyone was leaving. Excuse our intrusion, but we didn't see anyone downstairs, and I was soaked through and beginning to shiver. I have borrowed one of your lady's dresses or some lady's, at any rate."

She glanced behind her at Philip, as he tried to restore order to his cravat.

"However, my companion has decided to wear his own clothing home as we've given it a chance to air out. Lord and Lady Coxley mentioned we might borrow a carriage to take us back to Kew Bridge. That's where we started, before the picnic and the rowing, you understand."

Philip was amazed the butler was silent through all this, but Miss Bright could talk a storm when needed. Gathering up her wet things, he surveyed the room to make sure they'd left nothing.

Nothing but a broken bed!

Coxley would find it funny, but his lady perhaps not as much. After all, she'd been the hostess responsible for Miss Bright's safety and reputation. Moreover, they would have to explain it to Northumberland at some point.

"Ready," he said, and Miranda opened the door fully, letting the butler see the disaster. His eyes bugged, but like any good head of household, his expression remained neutral.

"If you follow me," he said, "I shall arrange for tea while the horses are harnessed."

They followed him downstairs and into the parlor, but before he could disappear, Philip decided he might as well make an utter nuisance of himself.

"I'll have some of Northumberland's good brandy instead."

He was sure he heard the butler sigh, but the man only said, "As you wish, my lord."

MIRANDA WAS GLAD THEY hadn't had a discussion about their transgression. That would have been mortifying. Strangely when Lord Mercer—or Philip, as she gave herself leave to think of him—had his arms around her, even when she was undressed, she'd felt no shyness. Yet fully clothed and back in the real world, she couldn't quite look him in the eye.

She was frankly shocked at her own behavior and at how easily she'd been carried away by the pleasurable sensations

Philip had evoked. It was almost as if she was under his spell whenever he kissed her.

In his damp clothing and in thick silence, he escorted her back to where they had begun their day. The others arrived not five minutes later in their various rowboats.

Miranda thought their small party none the wiser. Yet when her father came to pick her up, Lady Coxley herself walked her to his carriage, giving her a stern look and making her fear her hosts already suspected. In any case, they would soon know the extent of the misbehavior if the duke's maid and butler told tales. *And whose servants didn't gossip?*

Since the Coxleys were Philip's friends, Miranda could only hope they would remain silent. After all, they wouldn't want their own reputation as hosts to suffer. Notwithstanding, the capsizing adventure would make good fodder for her novel with the participants carefully disguised, exactly as Lady Harriet had advised.

When she turned to bid Philip good-bye, he nodded but his expression was grim.

Now, a day later, she was still in a state of disbelief at having had a naked man on top of her. It had been temporary madness, but it had also been a state of bliss. Writing about it had helped, although she was still unsure how to behave when next they met.

Since she didn't expect him until early the following day when they would travel all the way to Ascot in East Berkshire together, his unexpected appearance in her foyer filled Miranda with mixed emotions—embarrassment as well as happiness. To say she'd grown fond of him was an understatement, and Helen had recently written back advising her to guard her heart.

But Helen didn't know how this man had awakened passion in her, nor how easily he coaxed it to blossom.

"Good day, Lord Mercer. Have I forgotten an event to which you are taking me today?"

"No, Miss Bright," he said somberly. "I am certain you have forgotten nothing."

They locked gazes, and her cheeks warmed.

He took off his hat, put it back on, and then removed it again before tucking it under his arm.

"I am here to see your father."

CHAPTER THIRTEEN

Miranda nearly gasped, managing to stifle herself. Instead, she bit her lip to halt the excitement bubbling up inside her. *Lord Philip Mercer was going to offer for her!*

After all, he'd nearly taken her innocence. Any decent man—well, any decent one wouldn't have stripped himself bare in the first place, but having done so, he would extend an offer for her hand and give her his name in return. Yet she had never expected such gallantry from the baron.

"I tried his court first," Lord Mercer continued, "and they said he was here."

Her heart swelled with joy. She could see herself as his wife, enjoying their conversations, laughing together, and, of course, kissing and engaging in true love-making. Their life would be one of sheer happiness.

"Yes," she blurted, answering his unspoken question far too loudly and exuberantly. Trying to recover her composure, she turned quickly from him. "My father is at home. Come this way."

She led him down the passage and knocked on the study door, which was uncharacteristically closed as he was deliberating a difficult judgment. Nonetheless, for the chance to marry off his daughter, her father would wish to be interrupted.

"Papa, Lord Mercer is here to see you."

"Come in," he replied.

Miranda pushed the door open, then backed away, letting Philip go by. Without another word, he closed the door in her face.

She grimaced. *Why did men have to speak with the father before speaking to the woman they wanted to marry?* It was downright medieval!

Pressing an ear to the door, she could hear nothing but murmurs. Frustrated, she returned to the parlor. If her father said yes, which he would, then Philip would join her shortly and ask for her hand.

However, a few minutes later, Lord Mercer went down the hall, straight past the door she'd left ajar, and departed.

"Papa," she yelled, already on her feet and hurrying to his study. Without waiting she opened the door. By his severe expression, something was wrong.

"Did you tell him no?" she asked.

"I most certainly did!" Her father leaned back in his chair, folded his arms across his chest and glowered.

Exasperated, Miranda threw her hands in the air. "But why? I like him. I would be pleased to marry him despite his reputation."

"Marry him?" Her father shook his head. "Darling daughter, have you taken leave of all your wits? You know he's a rake. He is not interested in marrying. Not you, nor anyone."

Feeling the sharp lance of disappointment, she sat in the leather chair, seeing Philip's imprint just before she did. It was still warm.

"Then what did he come here to ask you?"

"The scoundrel wanted to be let out of our arrangement."

"Oh!" That was unexpected, not to mention hurtful. "Did he say why?"

"Only that he felt four weeks was enough, and he had done his duty. It would seem Mercer cannot bear being on good behavior any longer." Then he narrowed his eyes at her.

"He *has* been respectful, has he not?"

Miranda kept her gaze on him. If she looked away, her father would know the truth. All she could do was nod and swallow the lies she didn't want to speak.

"He had better be," her father added. "He thinks he is safe where Miss Waltham's uncle is concerned, too." Her father gave a mirthless laugh. "Yet I could destroy his brandy deal fast enough to make his head spin."

"Papa!" she admonished, but her heart hurt. Philip no longer wanted to escort her. Knowing that, she couldn't possibly continue as they had.

"Don't worry, my dear. I told him in no uncertain terms that he will complete our agreement through the final fortnight. After all, you've had a few callers. I'm sure you can secure an engagement from one of them before the Season's end. But not if you suddenly disappear from society, and certainly not if you continue to harbor a ninny-pated notion that Mercer will ever offer for you."

Sighing, he leaned forward and picked up his pipe. "Run along. I have work to finish." He had dismissed her.

Slowly, Miranda rose. "I no longer wish to go the races with him tomorrow. Nor anywhere for that matter."

Her father looked up, astonished. "Whyever not?"

"Because Lord Mercer doesn't want to take me," she pointed out.

Her father barked out a laugh. "He *never* wanted to take you if you recall. This was always a business contract. Nothing has changed. Now don't be foolish. Fetch me a pot of tea like a good girl."

Miranda did as he asked while considering her options. She supposed hiding in her room and refusing to go downstairs when Philip arrived would be out of the question. Besides, as her father would say, cutting off her nose to spite her face was a fool's act. She wanted to finish her novel with the last events of the Season.

Nevertheless, she would firmly withdraw her admiration for the baron and stop being as friendly as a lapdog. And she would never let him kiss her again.

"IT'S JUST ANOTHER HORSERACE," Philip reminded himself. *So why was he on edge?* As his driver halted the carriage before Sir William's home at first light, he pulled his flask from his pocket and took a long draw of brandy. It was not something he usually did at that early hour.

And then he didn't move a muscle. For the first time, he acted like the proper nobleman he was and let his footman go to the door, knock, and collect Miranda and her aunt, not to mention their luggage.

From the beginning, he'd been far too familiar with her. Specifically, he should never have kissed her within minutes of meeting, and he most assuredly should not have stripped off his wet clothes and broken a bed with her.

For this entire outing, including spending the night at Ascot, he would be on his best behavior. For that matter, at the next ball the following week and the last one after that, he had already promised himself they would have no more than a single dance. And then this seemingly endless arrangement would be at an end.

But he had to get through the next two days first.

The carriage door opened, and he looked down into Miranda's lovely face, making him catch his breath. Assisted by the footman, she climbed in and took the seat opposite, quickly followed by Mrs. Cumbersome who sat beside her.

"Good morning, ladies," he said. "I hope you are both well."

When Miranda offered him the smallest of polite smiles, he knew. She was aware of his attempt to end their intolerable and torturous entanglement. If not, her smile would be the usual radiant one that always sent a ray of happiness straight to his heart.

This one was like those from the ladies of the *ton*, false and frosty.

However, after a long moment, she added, "Good evening, my lord. I hope you are well."

Except for feeling lower than sheep dung, he was fine.

"I am, thank you. And both of you?" With embarrassment, he realized he had already asked and been answered. Regardless, Philip turned to include her aunt, hoping conversation with her would flow more easily.

Apparently, by Mrs. Cumbersome's sour expression, she had been told something, too. The older lady raised an eyebrow and turned to look out the window. This made Miranda sigh, one of his favorite actions as her breasts always rose plump and perfect above her décolletage.

Dammit! Not two minutes in her company and he was already thinking of her breasts. *And those sweet, rosy nipples!*

"We are well, thank you," she replied. "I am well. My aunt is well. My father is well. My sister up in Yorkshire is well, I don't doubt. If we have thoroughly exhausted that line of conversation, perhaps we could continue the ride in peaceful silence until we reach our destination."

Philip would have applauded her set down if he hadn't been astounded. Her aunt mirrored his emotion with a stunned expression. Yet Miranda didn't seem to care if she'd offended, simply sitting straight-backed and calm, looking out the window as they got underway.

They went by Fulham, over Putney Bridge and through Richmond Park. Naturally, neither he nor Miranda could look at one another so close to the scene of their lunatic actions on the other side of the Thames. And when they stopped by nine o'clock at the Star and Garter Inn at Richmond Hill, Philip wasn't trying to remind her of their sensual encounter by eating at a restaurant with river views.

He knew of nowhere else close by that could provide such an elegant and tasty breakfast.

In the large dining room, they took their meal in almost complete silence except for what they could hear of other diners, many of whom were also on their way to Ascot Heath that morning.

When finished, they eschewed a walk on the terrace despite knowing it would assist in their food's digestion, and instead climbed into the carriage to resume their cheerless journey. Philip could think of no way to clear the tension that lay thick between them and wished it were otherwise.

Finally, they spoke only to debate whether to stop at Hampton Court Palace which they would pass. He had it on authority the State Apartments were open for viewing along with its sixty acres of gardens. Eventually, they decided against the diversion since they didn't want to miss the first race.

"Perhaps on the way back to London," he offered, "when we are not pressed for time."

Miranda shrugged as if it was of no consequence, nor could she be bothered to speak another word to him. Instead, she turned to her aunt.

"I would like to go to the palace and be able to write to Helen and Peter about it."

Her aunt cocked her head. "You don't recall, but you went once, you and your sister, when your mother was alive. Mad little girls running and screaming down the Great Hall, not even noticing the king's expensive tapestries as you were too busy chasing each other like dogs."

Philip chuckled, earning Miranda's quick disapproving glance. A few days ago, she would have joined in with laughter. Now, she pursed her lips and fell silent again. They spoke not another word for the eleven miles to Staines where they stopped to let the horses rest and to take refreshments at the Bush Inn.

"We are making very good time," Philip began, but Miranda merely turned away to stretch her legs with a walk around the outside of the inn. She did not invite him to accompany her, which was just as well. In order to bring back the joyful, curious, and pleasant Miss Bright, he might have found it necessary to take her to a secluded spot and coax her return with a kiss.

Of course, Mrs. Cumbersome would have prevented such a thing.

Their next stop was Ascot Heath and the racecourse that had been hosting the fastest horses since Queen Anne declared it the perfect place for horse-racing in the year 1711. Around them, people were arriving on foot and by wagon and by hired post-chaise, the latter costing at least sixpence a mile.

The massive racetrack with its long stands of seating finally caused Miranda to sound like her previous wonder-filled self.

"I have never seen such a crowd of people in my life." She was practically skipping with excitement. "Even at Brighton, where my sister and I went once with Papa to the races, there were not nearly so many watching."

"Over there are the Royal Stands." Philip gestured to the section with an awning flying the King's standard to show members of the royal family were in attendance. "We have time to walk a little before we must take our seats."

Mrs. Cumbersome groaned. "I never thought I would be displeased at having to rest somewhere, but after that ride, I would almost rather stand for the races."

This made Miranda laugh until she caught him watching and sobered. He hated that he dampened her amusement. *What a shame they could not be easy friends!* Yet the most important thing was to maintain his distance and, if he could, direct a suitable gentleman her way.

Instantly, he dismissed the latter thought. Helping her find a husband was not his responsibility nor part of the bargain. Moreover, over the past month, he didn't think he had noticed any buck who was good enough for her. In truth, he'd only foisted Wesley on her because he knew the man was too much of a clodhopper to make a good impression.

Soon, they had taken their seats for the first exciting race of Ladies' Day. It would culminate in the Gold Cup, on which all three of them had placed small wagers with the local blacklegs at the track's betting stand. Philip had also placed a more sizable wager at Tattersall's in Town, hoping to win back some of his shipping deposit in case it was lost to him.

After the races, from which only Mrs. Cumbersome came away with a profit of ten shillings, Miranda tried the shooting gallery with some success, and both females marveled at the jugglers and the performing dogs. By six o'clock, the stands and the entire area was clearing out.

"We have rooms booked at The Thatched Tavern," Philip mentioned as they got back into his carriage.

"A tavern?" Mrs. Cumbersome echoed.

"Not merely a tap-house. I assure you we have two safe rooms upstairs. The alternative, The Carpenter's Inn, was fully booked. Besides, the food is better at the tavern."

In a short while, they drew up in front of the white-painted brick building with its cheerful red shutters and thatched roof. After their bags were taken up to their rooms in the two-hundred-year-old establishment, they were seated in a private dining area with dark oiled beams overhead.

At a table by the welcoming hearth, Philip was pleased to note Miranda's chilly disposition had thawed during the diversion of the races and the merriment that had come after.

Now, with a glass of wine in hand and a plate of roasted shoulder of lamb and vegetable pie before her, she was chatting with him and her aunt as if she'd entirely forgotten to be annoyed.

He thought it a good thing until he found himself leaning back in his chair, admiring the way the lamplight reflected in her eyes and on her caramel-colored hair. He dragged his attention back to his own dinner. It was far safer when she barely spoke to him and kept her glance averted. Somehow, her easygoing manner made her more desirable than the most beautiful lady who simpered and batted her eyes.

Fortunately, Mrs. Cumbersome would be sleeping right beside her niece the entire night.

⌒⌒

MIRANDA COULD HARDLY CLOSE her eyes. The day had been filled with new and interesting amusements. The Ascot track, while not her first, had been the most splendid she'd ever seen. She'd held her breath more than once as the horses thundered by. Luckily, there had been no accidents, which Philip said was not always the case.

When he'd helped her to shoot straight at the shooting range, she had wanted to make him proud of her.

Moreover, she'd had a hard time maintaining her resentment toward him. Her pride had been stung, but her father was right. The baron had simply made a business deal, one he'd grown to regret as it inhibited his normal activities. He had no interest in her beyond the physical attraction they shared, and he could have the exact same with any number of women. Indeed, if the newspapers were to be believed, he did have.

Yet he had behaved impeccably the entire day, remained attentive, and explained everything she'd asked. Accordingly, she'd decided to get over her snit and enjoy herself, which she had. *Tremendously!* Right down to the evening meal and the card games they'd played in the common room afterward.

Then why was she staring at the low ceiling of the bed chamber? The room had turned out to be small, but clean and perfectly acceptable. Her aunt lay beside her wearing a nightcap and snoring wheezily in a deep sleep, and Miranda wished she could fall into such a slumber.

Listening to crickets and the occasional owl, she fidgeted and rolled over, then rolled again, getting her long braid wound round her neck as she did. Disturbed, Aunt Lucinda snuffled into quietness and turned over to face the curtained window, but a minute later, she was louder than ever.

Miranda sighed. She knew what her father did when he couldn't sleep. He drank a glass of brandy. He said it helped his digestion, and it was what Philip had enjoyed after dinner while she and her aunt had drunk port, which Miranda didn't care for. Therefore, she'd left most of it in her glass.

Perhaps her father and Philip had the right of it. Without giving it too much thought, she swung her legs over the side and got out of bed. Donning her dressing gown and slippers, she left the safety of her room.

Of course she would never go into the tap-room, even though her dressing gown was perfectly respectable, but there might still be villagers or male guests drinking. In any case, she didn't need to. The tavern workers said they had only to ask any of them for whatever they needed, be it an extra blanket or something to drink.

Miranda simply had to find someone. Creeping along the hall, she passed the few other closed doors, including Philip's, and promptly tripped over a dog sleeping near the top of the stairs. The mutt started to bark.

"Blast," she swore under her breath, then dropped to her knees to pet the pup. *"Shh,"* she soothed. "You'll awaken everyone."

Almost immediately, the dog put its head down and closed its eyes, and Miranda stepped over it and went down the stairs, considering herself lucky she hadn't gone head over heels.

Outside the common room, she was lucky enough to encounter a maid.

"I wonder if I can have a glass of brandy, and you can put it on the account of Lord Mercer."

"Yes, miss. Having trouble sleeping, are you?"

"Yes, exactly so."

"Wait here, miss. I'll be back quick as a whip."

But Miranda felt odd standing in the doorway and she entered the now-deserted room where they'd played *Vingt-et-Un* after dinner. Through the wall, she could hear men still in the tap-room, and knew her aunt wouldn't approve were she to wake up and discover her niece downstairs.

Shifting her weight from foot to foot, she hoped the maid was as good as her word.

When she heard footsteps, however, and turned, a bearded stranger was in the doorway. Stocky, blond, and staggering drunk.

CHAPTER FOURTEEN

"A lassie in a perfect state of undress," the unruly man said, taking a step forward and boldly reaching out toward the belt of her gown.

Miranda smacked his hand and backed up.

"You are rude and inebriated," she chided.

In response, he laughed. "True, but I'm a damn good swiver, even when I'm far in my cups. How much?"

Her mouth dropped open. *How much?* She looked past him, hoping to see the maid.

"If you're looking for someone better, lass, there's none." He took another step forward.

She glanced around for something she could wield against the brute. Although fear was beginning to take hold, she also knew she was close enough to others she could let out a loud yell and help would come. *Wouldn't it?* But that would also bring curious eyes and maybe other guests. Her being alone downstairs at that hour would appear reckless and even wanton.

Wrapping her fingers around a candlestick whose candle had long since melted down during the evening, she waved it in front of her.

"Leave me in peace."

The stranger laughed. "Come along, lass. Name your price." He rubbed a hand over his greasy hair. "Don't tell me I'm not good enough for you."

Maybe she could reason with him. "It's not that. I am engaged to be married."

He stared silently, leaning to the side as if he might fall over. Finally, he said, "That's no matter. I'll share you. It seems there are two of you anyway."

Such a swill-tub, he had bunged his eyes with strong drink. More disgusted than frightened, she pointed the candlestick at him again as the maid returned.

"Murphy! Stop pestering our guests. You know you're not supposed to take a step past the tap-room."

"I thought I was going home, but I ended up in here."

"You went out the wrong door, you dunce," the maid scolded.

The stocky man grabbed the brandy she held and downed it in one swallow. Then he belched loudly.

"Now I'm going home." He turned and staggered back into the tap-room.

"Terribly sorry, miss. He's here most every night. Harmless really. I'll go get you another glass of brandy."

"No, that's not necessary. I've changed my mind." Miranda decided she had best get back to her room before trouble ensued. Climbing the stairs again, she tried to tread quietly and to step over the dog without waking him. She was unsuccessful, and he erupted in another burst of barking.

Thinking of the other guests trying to sleep, particularly her aunt, Miranda patted his head. "Please, *shh*."

When a hand touched her back, she whirled around, her braid flying, and struck out with the candlestick, which she'd forgotten to set down.

"Oof," Philip said, grabbing her wrist. "That hurt." His free hand touched his ribs through his silk banyan.

"It's you." Miranda relaxed under his warm touch. "I thought it was Murphy."

She couldn't see him too well, as the only light was what drifted up the stairs from below, but he raised his eyebrows.

"Who the devil is Murphy?"

"A drunkard from the tap-room."

He stared at her. "You went down to the tap-room?"

"Of course not! I'm not a fool." Miranda yanked her arm back. "I simply went downstairs for a glass of brandy since I couldn't sleep. And a man . . . ," she trailed off with a shrug.

"A man what? Why are you holding a candlestick? Are you in your dressing gown?"

She stared at him, and he returned her gaze, waiting.

"A man offered to pay me money."

"What?" Philip roared.

He was as bad as the dog. "Hush. You'll wake up the guests."

"I don't give a damn about the guests. I'm going down there to demand satisfaction."

"No, you're not. He's gone home. It was a misunderstanding. I forgot to put back the candlestick."

"That you picked up to defend yourself? How dare he! I'll find his home and throttle him."

"You will not. No harm was done."

He snatched the candlestick from her and set it on the floor next to the dog.

"A paying guest should not have to resort to household objects for her defense. On the other hand, you shouldn't have gone downstairs in the first place." Then he cocked his head. "Where's the brandy?"

"The drunk man got to it first."

Philip looked like he was about to roar again, so she added, "It's of no consequence. I shall return to my half of the bed, pray my aunt has stopped driving noisy hogs on her side, and hope the dustman sweeps me up quickly."

"Brandy would help to be sure. I always have some with me."

"Here? Now?"

"Not in the hallway," he quipped. "In my room. Come along. A few sips and you'll rapidly reach the land of nod when you return to your bed."

"Very well." Miranda agreed before he came to his senses and changed his mind. For surely he knew the absolute lunacy of her accompanying him to his room. She would stay for only a few sips of brandy and would be back in her own bed within five minutes.

He gestured her inside and left the door wide open. Whether that was smart or incredibly stupid, she couldn't say. When he lit the lamp, the disarray of his counterpane and sheets were revealed. She averted her eyes from the warm bed where doubtless he had recently lay utterly unclothed—his broad shoulders taking up most of the room, his muscular legs spread out to take up the rest, his private parts tenting the covers.

Did they do that? She wondered if she could ask him about how the male member behaved when he was alone. Most certainly it wasn't always like a blind man's staff when uncovered.

"Every time I thought to go to sleep, that mutt began barking," Philip explained.

She smiled sheepishly. "That was my fault. Stepping over him. Twice! I believe he's there to guard us."

"Guard us? *Ha!* Then why did he let a drunken man accost you?"

She waved his question away. "I was downstairs when it happened. More to the point, why did he let you sneak up on me?"

Philip frowned. "I didn't sneak up on you. You didn't hear me because of the dog." He was digging in the pocket of his coat draped over the only chair in the room. Drawing out a silver flask, he opened it and handed it to her.

"Is this your own stock?" She sniffed it.

"Naturally. It is my hope that gentlemen all over the British Isles will shortly be imbibing my superior brandy. Go ahead and taste it."

"I confess I don't have much to compare it to, being more apt to drink a glass of wine." But she raised the flask to her lips and sipped.

Smoother than she'd feared, while warm going down the back of her throat, it didn't make her want to choke. Still, she couldn't help a small cough and covered her mouth politely.

"Very pleasant," she told him before taking another sip and then another. By the fourth one, the brandy was relaxing her already. As she returned the flask to him. their fingers touched and she shuddered.

"Have you spent many nights in inns with married and single women, or do you usually reserve your amorous escapades for doxies in the finer brothels of London?"

He shook his head. "You cannot ask me such a thing."

"Why not?"

"Because I say you cannot." He took a sip of the brandy, closed the flask, and put it away. She watched all his actions, the way his hands moved and the way his muscles were outlined against his silk dressing gown. He was the most magnificent male she could imagine, and all too quickly, they would no longer be in each other's company.

"How will I learn the ways of men?" she wondered aloud.

"You don't need to learn the ways of men. You need to get a husband and learn only his ways."

Sighing, she sat heavily upon his bed and yawned. "That seems a most backward way to go about things. Marrying someone first and then discovering what he is like. What if I marry an absolute arse?" She chuckled at the word, then realized it wouldn't actually be funny.

"I might end up belonging to a man who abuses me or won't let me see my family or who visits me only to beget children but spends all his time drinking and whoring."

Looking decidedly uncomfortable, the baron crossed his strong arms and leaned against the wall.

"Your imagination is running away with you. Your father will determine the character of any of your suitors who ask for your hand, and assuredly, he'll investigate into the man's past as well."

"I suppose." She traced her hand across the rumpled counterpane. "And when *you* marry, will you give up all other women for your wife?"

Feeling as if she could fall asleep right there on his bed, she stretched out on her side, resting her head upon her hand. Suddenly, she was tired enough to curl upon the floor and fall asleep, just like the dog. She giggled.

"Miranda, you must not stay here any longer." His words were serious, even gruff.

"But the door is open. Hence, we are obviously being perfectly proper. Perfectly, properly proper. Try to say that three times as quickly as you can."

He remained silent, looking like a man battling with demons, what with his gaze darting over her and a small muscle twitching in his clenched jaw.

"You didn't answer my question," she pointed out.

"Luckily, I've forgotten it."

"I have not. Will you be a brute to your wife?"

"Of course not!"

"Will you break her heart by continuing your raffish ways?"

He sighed. "Not that it is any of your business, but I hope when I find the lady with whom I shall pledge my troth I shall be so much in love I will not ever think of straying."

Miranda smiled. "That's good. I wouldn't like you to be that awful kind of man I've read about. You're a better person than those other blackguards who are always named as going around to parties with their mistresses."

"Like our Prince Regent?" he quipped.

"Yes, precisely. Maybe he should be the only one allowed to behave thusly." She closed her eyes. At once, she felt his hands on hers, pulling her to her feet, and she opened her lids once again.

"Why am I exhausted?"

"You've had a long day," he said, drawing her toward the open door. "We got up extremely early, if you can still recall. Now return to your room before—"

She stood on tiptoe and kissed him. She'd wanted to do it since she'd entered his room, but even more after the brandy had warmed her body and relaxed her.

"Mm," she murmured against his firmly closed mouth. She licked his lower lip. *Still closed.*

Nor was he putting his arms around her and pulling her close. He wasn't touching her at all!

Finally, she drew back, keeping her fingers locked behind his neck. She looked up at him. His eyes were closed, and he appeared to be in pain.

She laughed again. "Is it particularly difficult for you to behave as a gentleman? Why, I believe you're perspiring with the challenging task."

"Out," he ordered.

"Is it possible regardless of what I do, you will resist me?" She watched his Adam's apple bob as he swallowed.

"Because you are a gentleman who has given your word to my father. In fact, you must be on your best behavior, even if I stroke your chin."

She did exactly that. It was like having her own life-sized man-doll. Almost as good as asking him questions was being able to touch him in any manner she wanted.

"And if I want to feel the breadth of your shoulders," she said while stroking her hands across the top of each, "and then touch your muscled arms," and she caressed him from shoulder to elbow, "then you still won't sweep me against you and ravish my mouth with your tongue?"

He made a strange groaning sound but opened his eyes, piercing her with their dark depths.

"If I slip my hands inside your banyan," she began, and wantonly, she did, feeling the skin of his chest, smooth until she encountered the short curling hair. She froze.

"I have to see," she told him before yanking wider the opening of his blue and gold silk gown.

"You saw my chest before," he protested, "after the rowboat capsized."

"I confess I was distracted by what you were doing to me to really notice." She ran her fingers across the landscape of his body. "You are beautiful yet so different at the same time."

Then she looked down to see his arousal jutting forward, and with a butterfly-soft touch, she stroked the length of it. It twitched, jerking against her hand as if it were a barely contained wild beast.

Nervously, she looked again into Philip's eyes. They were blazing, even in the mere light of a single lamp.

"You must leave," he whispered, sounding strangled.

She nodded. She knew she ought to. Instead, she went to the door and closed it.

CHAPTER FIFTEEN

"Miss Bright!" he exclaimed. "You were on your way to bed."

"And I shall get there," Miranda said agreeably, "but in just another few minutes."

Philip felt helpless to gainsay her because more than anything, he wanted to know what she would do next. He hoped she would slip off her dressing gown and show him her treasures.

Instead, she undid the belt at his waist and parted his banyan once more to look her fill.

"You are remarkable." Her tone was low and breathless.

He tried to speak, but whatever he wanted to say and hoped to tell her came out as a croak.

Philip cleared his throat, but then her soft, pale hand grasped his cock, rendering him speechless. If he growled and roared like he wanted to do, he would scare her and probably bring her slumbering aunt as well as the tavern dog to her rescue. If he carried her to his bed and worshiped her body as he desperately wished—with his tongue first and then his hands—he would not be able to stop.

Truly, he would ruin her, take her innocence, and send his seed deep into her womb for he couldn't imagine how he would pull out of such an enticing creature.

They would both be lost.

When her father discovered Philip's treachery, the magistrate would take his vengeance quickly. Sir William had been quite clear on that point. He would make it unlawful for Philip to import a wedge of cheese from France, never mind barrel after barrel of brandy.

Yet Miranda Bright stood before him, holding him where he most ached for her.

"Please," he said, softly enough he wondered if she'd heard him.

Her glance flew to his, her hazel eyes looking like a fairy's twin flames.

Nodding, she stroked him. *Again. Again.* He cupped his hand over hers to guide her. It took him less time to reach the pinnacle of his pleasure than it had since he was a randy youth.

"Yes," he hissed. Head back, eyes shut, gasping, he hoped he didn't crush her hand as together they rubbed him through his long, powerful climax. At least he remembered to turn his body to avoid spending on the front of her dressing gown.

Drawing in a shaky breath, he opened his eyes. Her own were large and wondering. She was probably frightened, but better that had happened *outside* her body than inside.

"I didn't know you could do that," she said, sounding anything but afraid. She was back to being inquisitive.

Hastily, he freed himself from her grasp and did up his robe while she stared at her own hand, then back at him.

"You were soft and hot under my fingers but also firm as a . . . as a," she trailed off while considering. "I am not sure I have the correct word.

"Please don't tell me you've got a piece of paper and a pencil in your pocket," Philip said, unable to keep from smiling. He was now so relaxed he had no need of brandy. He would sleep as soon as his head hit the pillow.

"I should return to my room," she said.

It was the first sensible thing she'd said, and he concurred wholeheartedly.

"Yes, immediately. If your aunt awakens—"

"I will tell her I had no wish to use the chamber pot and went in search of the inn's water closet."

"Good thinking." Although he could hardly believe their conversation had descended to speaking about such things. He would vow he had not ever had such a discussion with a female before.

Yet why was she still standing there, gazing at him with those lovely eyes? She ought to be scurrying back across the hall.

"You must make haste."

"Are you not going to kiss me?" she asked, looking adorable and alluring at the same time.

If he kissed her, he might as well open the door and yell from the rooftops that he intended to bed her next, for that's where it would lead.

"Absolutely not," he said, spinning her away from him, opening the door, and propelling her out into the hallway with a hand at her back.

WE STOPPED AT HAMPTON Court Palace on the way home. It was as magnificent as you have ever heard it described, but I shall try to do it justice.

Miranda told Helen and Peter everything she'd seen from the hammerbeam roof in the medieval-style Great Hall to Anne Boleyn's gate with the amazingly accurate astronomical clock in its tower that showed not only the time but the moon's phases, the month, the year's quarter, and the sun and star signs.

It even tells you when the river is at its highest at far-away London Bridge. Such a marvel. I cannot imagine the engineering behind such a clock.

Philip had explained the importance of the last piece of information to those visiting the palace from London in previous centuries when they traveled there predominantly by barge. Knowing the high water helped with speed of arrival and also made sure the return trip didn't put a barge near London Bridge during times of its greatest tidal ebb. Doing so would risk the barge being swept into the starlings when the Thames height might differ by six feet on either side of the bridge.

"You've heard the saying," Philip had reminded her. "London Bridge is for wise men to pass over, and for fools to pass under."

Miranda continued with her description for her cousins.

As for architecture, I preferred the sections by Sir Christopher Wren with the perfect symmetry of his Fountain Court and all its columns and the elegance of the south front, with its colorful red brick and white trim and windows. I wish you both could have been with me.

Instead, she'd toured with her well-rested aunt and the rather subdued Lord Mercer. On her part, Miranda had fallen directly asleep to awaken bemused by what had taken place the night before. The brandy had certainly relaxed her, but also had put her into a mischievous, careless state. She couldn't imagine why else she would have behaved as boldly and recklessly as she had.

She'd held Philip's arousal in her hand!

All day long that thought had passed through her mind, making her glance often at him, distracting her from Hampton Court's tapestries and gardens. Recalling how he'd put his head back and spent onto the floor beside them, she was shocked at what she'd done but glad to have pleased him the way he had for her on the day of the boating incident.

When he had dropped her and Aunt Lucinda off at home by dinnertime, she'd wished they could have had a single moment alone, although what she wanted to tell him or to hear in return, she had no idea.

"Thank you, Lord Mercer. I had a perfect time," was all she'd said while Aunt Lucinda looked on.

His cheeks had seemed to darken. He nodded and bid her good evening.

Sighing, she'd watched him leave, keenly aware once again that he had wanted to end their arrangement before they had gone to the races. Perhaps at the next ball, she might make him tell her why or whether he had changed his mind.

WHEN THEY ARRIVED AT the ball, the difference in Philip's behavior became apparent. He found two chairs by the edge of the great room, one for her and one for her aunt. And then, he had promptly abandoned them. Or at least, Miranda felt it thusly, for he didn't even ask for the first dance as an escort should.

In the carriage, he had not engaged beyond niceties. Miranda considered it fortunate the ride between her home and the exclusive Hanover Square wasn't terribly long.

"Lord Mercer is in a tweague over something," Aunt Lucinda said, as they watched him stride across the ballroom and out of sight.

Miranda shrugged. She couldn't tell her aunt anything about what might be bothering him and, therefore, said nothing.

"There you are," Lady Harriet said, approaching with Lady Emily and her brother, Lord Beaumont, who was often her chaperone. "I love your dress! It is divine. Isn't her dress divine?" she asked her friend.

"Absolutely," Lady Emily concurred. Lord Beaumont looked bored as usual.

"Where is your escort?" Lady Harriet asked after all proper greetings had been given and received.

"I'm afraid I do not know," Miranda confessed.

"But the first dance will start soon," Lady Emily said. "Has another man asked you yet?"

"No, but I needn't dance every dance," she pointed out.

"Not *every*," Lady Harriet agreed, "but the first. Especially if you are to secure a husband in the short time left. Brother!"

"What?" Lord Beaumont asked.

Miranda thought their tone nearly always sounded as though they were cross when speaking to one another.

"Do you have wool between your ears?" Lady Harriet demanded.

"Most probably," Lord Beaumont said. "Better than having it stuffed down the front of one's bodice."

Lady Emily gasped, and Miranda looked at her aunt, hardly believing a brother would say such a thing about his own sister. Yet Lady Harriet merely rolled her eyes at her brother's rudeness.

"Brother, dear, is that the best you can do? Are you going to behave like a gentleman and dance with Miss Bright or stand here like a churl?"

Miranda had no desire to dance with the sullen, insolent man and hoped to divert him.

"What of Lady Emily?"

"I *have* a partner," she said. "Lord Wesley. Excuse me or I shall miss him. Come, Harriet. I can't wander alone." And she grabbed her friend's hand.

They left the feckless Lord Beaumont behind. *What a nuisance!* However, if she begged off dancing using the only excuse she was allowed, not feeling up to it, then she would be prohibited from partnering with anyone else all night. She'd learned that rule from Philip on the way to her very first private ball.

With the threat of such a terrible price, she accepted the inevitable and waited for him to ask her politely.

He stared at her then said, "I thought you were Mercer's lady-friend."

Her glance darted to Aunt Lucinda, who looked confounded.

"Young man," her aunt said, not caring she was addressing an earl's son, "my niece is not anyone's *lady-friend*. If you have an interest in courting her, then you should ask her to dance, and tomorrow, you may come calling at her father's home during civilized hours. I warn you her line of suitors grows longer with each ball."

Miranda wanted to cheer her aunt's diatribe. And while she was correct, more suitors were showing up each time they held visiting hours, compared to what she'd seen at Lady Harriet's, her own collection of calling cards was quite modest.

Lord Beaumont appeared only slightly impressed. He glanced at Miranda as if seeing her for the first time.

"Will you do me the honor?" Yet somehow he made "honor" sound like a chore.

"The honor?" she echoed, wanting to hear him ask properly. And he had best be quick since the bell had already rung for *La Belle Assemblée*, and dancers were gathering for the first contra-dance. She half-hoped Philip would return and sweep her away.

Lord Beaumont sighed as if she were a simpleton. "Will you do me the honor of the first dance?"

How Miranda longed to say no.

She sighed even more loudly than he had done. When he realized she was mocking him, he narrowed his eyes, straightened, and stood a little taller. More respectfully, he awaited her response.

Finally, she gave in. "Yes, I will."

While dancing, as they wove in and out and up and down the line, she looked for Lord Mercer. He must have left the ballroom for the card room. *A pity!* There was nothing quite like dancing with him.

Except rolling around on a bed with him.

When the long, first dance ended, Lord Beaumont was only too happy to deposit her with her aunt. Miranda couldn't help but wonder why the brother was boorish when his sister had welcomed her into a fast friendship.

"Another gentleman asked to dance with you," Aunt Lucinda said almost as Miranda's bottom touched the velvet seat. "Here he comes."

Miranda rose again with little interest. When she was returned to her aunt the second time, she wished it was already the fifth and final dance.

"Remember," her aunt said, "any man you meet may become your husband. Isn't that exciting?"

She stifled a yawn and went off with her next partner, Lord Holland to whom Philip had introduced her weeks earlier.

PHILIP HAD STAYED AWAY as long as he could, but the notion of shirking his duty had grown until he couldn't concentrate on the cards and had lost two hands in a row. He simply needed to see Miranda was well and hopefully having a good time.

Mrs. Cumbersome was alone.

"Before you start fussing," she said, "my niece is on the dance floor, and I can see her."

He smiled. *When had he become the more cautious of the two of them?*

Taking a seat, he waited for Miranda to be escorted back. The smile she gave him as she approached unexpectedly tugged at his heart. He rose, having never expected to grow so damnable fond of the chit. More than that. He preferred her company to that of anyone else.

"Thank you for the dance," she told the swell who held her arm.

"No, the pleasure was all mine. May I call upon you tomorrow?"

"Yes, you may."

Philip was glad the man released her and left as soon as he did. The prickly annoyance he felt seeing her with him was unwelcome and utterly unreasonable. After all, she was supposed to dance with these bucks and even choose from among them.

"Did you win at cards?" she asked, taking the chair he'd vacated.

"How did you know I was in the card room?" His mood lifted merely from seeing her.

"I didn't see you dancing and assumed you were playing at cards."

Feeling happiness over her searching the dance floor for him was also irrational. He must get ahold of these wayward emotions.

"Lady Fortuna was not with me in the card room," he confessed.

Miranda tilted her head and observed him. "Are you going to ask me to dance?"

"Yes, of course. Shall we?" He offered his hand, eager now to have her in his arms.

She laughed. "There is a break at present. They've given us a few minutes for lemonade or champagne."

Glancing around, he hadn't noticed the lull, his focus thoroughly fixed upon her. At that moment, servers were going around holding trays laden with glassware.

"At many balls, they don't let the beverages come this close to the dance floor," he informed her.

"I can understand why." She gestured with a dip of her head.

Turning to look, he noticed Lord Wesley talking, laughing, and spilling all over the polished parquet.

"He might be a tad clumsy," Philip said, "but at least he didn't overturn his rowboat."

Thinking of what came after, with them naked in Northumberland's house, he wished he hadn't mentioned it, especially when she blushed so ferociously her aunt asked her if she was well.

"Fine, thank you."

After that, they sipped their champagne in silence, and Philip was glad when the bell rang to indicate it was time to dance. His fingers itched to take hold of her. He couldn't recall wanting to dance with anyone as much.

Thankfully, it was a spirited waltz. He would not have to release the bewitching creature that was Miranda Bright, not for several minutes. The musicians played the Sussex Waltz with distinct strains of Mozart, and the violin, piano, and flute presently had them twirling in a lively fashion about the floor.

When it was over, he reluctantly turned her over to Lord Lowry waiting eagerly for the next dance. Philip hoped it was a traditional country-dance but feared it would be another waltz.

Seeing her give him a backward glance as she returned to the parquet, he sent her a smile and then dragged his gaze away, wondering how he would pass the rest of the ball. He had no interest in the other young ladies. He wasn't supposed to have an interest in Miranda, for that matter. And he wished to God he didn't. She was a sweet magistrate's daughter, and he was . . . *not* so sweet.

Philip went outside onto the terrace and considered what he was and who he was. A titled man, an officer, and now a man of business. Many had labeled him a rake, and he knew he had behaved as such. He also knew men who acted differently, courting a woman, falling in love, and then marrying her. And some of those men even stayed true to their wives afterward. His father, for one.

When he'd first entered the Mayfair ballrooms six years earlier, he'd been ready to follow in his father's footsteps. However, none of the ladies captured his heart. Some wanted more than the title of baroness and left him alone. Some wanted more money and good riddance. Some accepted him, but he found them lacking in one or more aspects.

Meanwhile, his friends were having far more fun. While searching for his true love, Philip had decided to have some fun for himself. And then he'd gone to war. Coming home for short periods of time left him no choice but to continue his disreputable behavior in brothels or with lonely widows, and sometimes, although against his better judgment, with willing young ladies of the *ton*.

It was either that or be a monk, and he loved the female form too much to deny himself until marriage. After all, if someone thrust succulent peaches into his face, it would be rude not to take a bite.

Walking into the small darkened garden, he heard the familiar sounds of men and women enjoying themselves where they could. Smiling, he shook his head. Normally, that would be him, simply because he could and because it was harmless when both parties understood the rules.

Tonight, he was starting to believe it was time to grow up.

Miss Waltham had offered him such an opportunity, but he'd balked. Now he knew why. She was not Miranda Bright. *If he chose her, would the magistrate forgive him his sordid reputation?*

For certainly, Philip had taken the notion of 'having fun' to levels most of his friends had not. Moreover, by not hiding it, he'd allowed the newspapers to thrust every action in front of the public eye.

When he turned back to the house, he spied a couple in one of the rooms upstairs in a tight embrace and sighed. *Was that all men and women thought about at these assemblies?*

Chuckling to himself, he returned to the ballroom with a purpose in mind.

Again, there was no Miranda, only Mrs. Cumbersome tapping her toe to the music. This time, he wasn't alarmed. He'd helped her to become a sought-after dance partner, and he'd even heard her name on other men's lips, discussing the rare flower who'd come in their midst this Season.

Now, Philip had a mind to pluck that flower and keep her for himself. *Would she want a tarnished soul such as he?*

CHAPTER SIXTEEN

"With whom is your niece dancing?" Philip asked her aunt.

The older lady frowned. "Did not the two of you go off together?"

"That was ages ago," he pointed out.

"Yet you did not bring her back to me as was your responsibility," she said. "Thus, I assumed she was still with you."

"Don't concern yourself, madam. Your niece was taken from me by the very respectable Lord Lowry. Still, I cannot believe he didn't bring her back to you when their dance ended. Were you here the entire time?"

She rose to her feet and drew herself up to her full height, which put her forehead directly under his nose.

"I assure you I have not left my post, but my brother shall hear how you let his daughter wander away from you."

"There is no need to get peevish," Philip said. "In all likelihood, Miss Bright is on the dance floor with someone else whom Lord Lowry thought suitable."

However, scanning the dancers and watching everyone go around twice, he could not see her.

"Or she's in the ladies' retiring room," he suggested, "where I shall find her fixing her hair."

Mrs. Cumbersome's eyes widened.

"Not that *I* will go in there," he amended, "but I will ask if she's inside."

"I should go," she said.

"No, madam, you should remain here for when Miss Bright comes strolling back. Then give her a good talking to. I shall search high and low."

"You do that, my lord."

He hurried away, and he did in fact begin with the retiring room, but she was not there. He hunted low by going over every room on the ground level of the large Piccadilly home, whose ballroom was on the same floor. Then, despite no public rooms, nor any part of the assembly being held upstairs, he breached the second floor.

"Nuisance woman," he muttered to himself. Miranda had probably taken off with Lady Harriet again and her dull-witted friend, Lady Emily. As he climbed the stairs, he considered how he had become a perpetual protector and didn't like it one bit.

After boldly wandering through his host's private apartment, knowing he shouldn't be there, Philip lost his patience. Surely the minx had returned to her aunt. Halfway back to the ballroom, he recalled seeing a couple silhouetted in the second-story window when he was outside.

Heart thumping, he dashed upstairs again and raced to the back of the house, throwing open a door to a room that would overlook the garden.

There she was!

His stomach clenched. By her expression, something had happened. When she saw it was he, she dashed tears from her cheeks and raced toward him. If he hadn't caught her in his arms, she would have knocked him over.

"I want to go home," she whispered, her voice choked from crying.

Dread raced through him while he stroked her back. *How bad was the damage?*

"Tell me," he said.

"I was kissed against my will."

Philip let out his breath. Not the worst thing, thank God, but dangerous nonetheless.

"By whom?"

"Lord Lowry."

Lowry? He'd always seemed the most arrow-straight and laced-up man Philip knew.

"After we danced, he suggested we tour the house," she told him. "He said it was quite the done thing, the way you and I and my aunt toured Hampton Court."

"Hardly the same. This is a private home. If our host and hostess wanted us upstairs, they would have opened one of these rooms for drinks or cards."

She fluttered her hands, dismissing his words while keeping her cheek pressed against his chest.

"Your heart sounds very thumpy," she said softly, then hiccupped.

"Never mind that. Finish your tale. You strolled up here, touring in the darkness, and then Lowry kissed you in this room." He looked around. It appeared to be a salon. "Is that the end of it?"

"He said I looked perfect," she began.

A surge of anger flooded his veins.

"I'll tell you what would look perfect," Philip said. "My fist planted in the middle of his face."

"It's what comes of looking kissable," she said, before sighing softly.

"It's what comes of wandering away from your chaperone when I told you not to."

"I did not. I danced with Lord Lowry on *your* recommendation!"

She was right, it was his fault, except she knew better than to stray.

"You should not have left the ballroom."

"I thought there would be other people exploring the house. When we got in here," she gestured around her, "he halted and asked if he could call upon me in the morning. Naturally, I said yes."

Naturally, yet it brought another surge of some strong emotion racing through Philip. He didn't like to name it, but it was obvious.

"And then, before I realized what he was about, he wrapped his arms around me and kissed me. Rather the way you did that first day at my home."

Philip didn't like being compared either.

"I doubt it was anything similar," he said childishly.

"I suppose you're right. It lasted much longer since my father didn't interrupt us."

The devil take Lowry!

"And then he left you here?"

"He said it would be better if we didn't return to the ball at the same time. Besides, I had to arrange my clothes."

A wave of heat made his head grow hot.

"Why?" he demanded. "How disheveled could you be from a kiss?"

"As I said, it lasted a while, and his hands wandered." She stepped away from him, looking woebegone. "He asked if I had ever been alone with you."

Dumbstruck, Philip shook his head. "You didn't tell him anything, did you?"

"No," Miranda said. "Although I hesitated, thinking what to say. And then he . . . then he . . . ," she trailed off.

"Well?" Philip could hardly stand the thoughts flitting through his brain.

"He stroked my cheek."

Stroked her cheek! He breathed another sigh of relief. *Why was she crying then?*

"And then he asked if I would ever consent to being alone with him."

Philip swore under his breath. Her association with him was dragging her down as he'd feared it might, as he'd warned her father it could.

"I reminded him we were alone, but he said he meant somewhere truly private. Then he pressed me against the wall and . . . and now I wish to go home." She started crying again.

Philip felt ill. Thinking her safe, he'd foolishly let his guard down and she had been mauled as a result.

"Lord Lowry had no right to take any such liberty," Miranda insisted, "and I hope you will go downstairs and call him out."

"No," he said firmly, hoping to get through to her. "Although he had no right, you allowed him the opportunity. You shouldn't have come upstairs with him. If anyone finds out, you will be considered sullied."

She took a step away from him.

"That's how men get away with it." She stared at him, her lower lip quivering. "That's how *you* get away with it!"

"Do not lump me into your mess. I have never cornered a lady or compelled her to do anything. You brought this upon yourself by your naiveté, and even that is no excuse."

"I want to go home," she said again. "I feel out of sorts."

"Regardless, you must stay, eat dinner, and pretend nothing happened. And you must make damnable certain no one knows you were alone upstairs with a man."

She opened her mouth, perhaps to contradict him but then appeared to change her mind.

"Very well."

"Go quickly," he ordered. "Directly to the ballroom. Your aunt is awaiting your reappearance. I'll come in a few minutes. Tell her you were with Lady Harriet or Lady Emily."

Miranda turned on her heel before glancing back at him. "How do I look?"

Beautiful, he wanted to say, but that wasn't what she was asking.

"Hair and dress will pass inspection," he told her. Then he handed her his pocket handkerchief. "But blot your face on the way downstairs and smile before you enter the ballroom."

Nodding, she left him.

Philip paced, deciding whether he ought to seek out Lowry and set him down a peg. Unsure if it was in Miranda's best interest for the other man to know Philip was her confidante, he drew his flagon from his pocket. After a sip, he decided.

Only one thing would make him feel better. He clenched his hands into fists.

THE NEXT DAY, SHE read in *The Times* about "the indecent foreign dance." While she recalled how magical she'd felt whirling quickly and effortlessly in Philip's arms, with her heart pounding and the two of them entirely independent of the other dancers, the paper's editorial had a different opinion of the ever-more popular waltz:

". . . it is quite sufficient to cast one's eyes on the voluptuous intertwining of the limbs and close compressure on the bodies in their dance, to see that it is indeed far removed from the modest reserve which has hitherto been considered distinctive of English females.

So long as this obscene display was confined to prostitutes and adulteresses, we did not think it deserving of notice; but now that it is attempted to be forced on the respectable classes of society by the civil examples of their superiors, we feel it a duty to warn every parent against exposing his or her daughter to so fatal a contagion."

Miranda felt soiled before she even turned to the gossip column, and then the floor fell away.

"One cavorting miss, who is considered 'bright' as the sun due to her connection with the dazzling Lord M, found herself on the wrong floor with Lord L. When seen before the midnight supper, one couldn't help wondering if her tears were due to disappointed expectation or from being discovered by the wrong man? Or perhaps they were caused by loathsome regret? Lord M was in a tweague. Dare one say he is unused to having his game-birds poached?"

She could scarcely breathe. Carefully folding the paper, Miranda tucked it underneath her skirts just before her father came into the dining room for breakfast. She could at least spare him reading about his daughter being compared to a prostitute for waltzing and keep him from asking her whether it were true she'd been crying at the ball.

And if anyone asked her why she'd been crying, the answer would have been impossible to confess—she was in love with a rake. When Lord Lowry took her lips under his, she felt the disappointing contrast. He was handsome and a good dance partner, but his kiss left her unmoved.

Worse, it left her bereft, facing a future with a husband whose kisses were like his, and nothing like Philip's.

And she wanted Philip! When Lord Lowry's hands began to explore, she'd turned to stone. No part of her body reacted. She needed to see Lord Major Mercer's sparkling eyes, smell his familiar cologne, taste his mouth, and especially feel him under her fingertips. No one else could come close.

When he'd suddenly appeared, like an apparition, she had hoped he would express his jealous rage over another man touching her, but he'd scolded her instead. She'd lain awake most of the night wondering how she'd stupidly given her heart away to the man from whom she ought only to have gathered interesting stories.

An unsuitable man.

Soon after her father left for his courtroom, Lady Harriet arrived with her maid. With an expression of wonder, Eliza held the embossed calling card and forgot her duties.

"Come in," Miranda had to invite her friend into the parlor herself, while Lady Harriet's maid went down the passageway with Eliza to see about preparing tea precisely as her mistress enjoyed it.

Miranda understood how her maid might feel overcome, sharing the sentiment at seeing an earl's daughter in her home, and even more astonished when Lady Harriet unexpectedly took hold of both her hands.

Miranda expected either condemnation or pity.

"I read *The Times*. How wonderful for you!"

Stunned, Miranda repeated, "Wonderful? Whatever can you mean?"

Lady Harriet tilted her head. "Do you not realize? You have made it into the ranks of those discussed in the gossip columns. You *are* a somebody!" Her laugh was light. "The editors of *The Times* do not waste space on nobodies."

Miranda paused, considering. "But to be discussed in such a fashion with an implication of impropriety could cause me and my father grievous harm."

Lady Harriet shrugged. "Most likely not. I'm sure Lowry and Mercer are not wringing their hands this morning. Anyway, it's another juicy story for you to write about in our marvelous project."

"You mean my book?" Miranda asked. "I would never record what happened."

"Oh, but you must," Lady Harriet said. "You should see it as an indication of having displaced the *bon ton* from their throne in the newspapers. You really should. By your association with Mercer, you have become someone of interest. Write about it. It may be the most amusing thing you ever do. Let everyone know from *your* point of view, as Miss Blaze of course! Tell everything Lowry did, as well as anything Mercer did, too. It shall be most popular."

Miranda nodded. "I will think on it."

"I can see you're doubtful. Putting it in your book is the best way to reclaim your power, even take a little revenge, since you can describe these men any way you wish. Let me ask you this, is your father likely ever to read your story?"

Miranda laughed. "Certainly not."

"Then you have nothing to worry about. Honestly, I imagine the only one who might complain is Mercer. It shows him in a bad light, as if Lowry stole you from him. As you know, Mercer hates to be viewed as anything but the most dash-fire man about town. Rumor has it last night he was prowling in the garden in order to meet with another young lady. Unless that was you, too?"

"Absolutely not." Miranda wished it had been. She would far rather have been in the garden with Philip than upstairs being pawed by Lord Lowry.

As Lady Harriet predicted, after she left Miranda's next visitor was Lord Mercer, and he was in a foul mood.

"I half expected to receive a noon visit from Lord Lowry, even though I pushed him away to halt his kiss."

Philip scowled. "He shall not bother you again."

The baron had been surly since Eliza had shown him in, and Miranda hoped to get to the bottom of his thunderous countenance.

"How do you know Lord Lowry will leave me alone?"

"Because I told him not to darken your doorstep, nor ever to lay hand nor lip upon you in the future, not even for a dance." Philip was pacing in what she'd come to think of as his brooding move.

"And he agreed, just like that?"

Philip walked to the window and looked out, then returned to where she stood in front of her father's comfortable chair.

"He did agree *after* I held his head under the water of the nearest marble fountain for a thrashing good minute. When he came up spluttering and gasping, Lowry was most amenable to my request. If he hadn't been, I would have held him under a great deal longer the second time."

Miranda closed her mouth that had fallen open imagining the scene. *Gracious!* Philip had protected her honor in his own fashion.

"Thank you," she said. "I also believe I should offer my gratitude for your sitting with me at dinner when I believe you would have preferred to be seated with another woman."

He blinked at her. "You are as good company as any other."

Not exactly massive praise, nor did he deny there was someone else he might have wished to keep company, but she could hardly ask if he'd had a garden tryst before he'd come upstairs to find her.

Nor could she explain to him how her tears the night before were not because Lord Lowry had taken liberties. She might as well have had her lips upon a scaled cod from the Billingsgate Fish Market near the Tower as upon a living, breathing man.

Realizing she had fallen in love with Philip had been a shock to her system the night before. Today, he'd called her "good company," a tepid match to her own deep-felt emotion.

"Would you like to sit down?"

But he was scowling again. "I'm not here to speak about anything except *The Times*. Knowing how you like to read the gossip columns, I'm sure you saw it. Your behavior last night has landed you squarely in the suds."

He was correct. And it proved he cared more than he'd let on. About to thank him again, this time for his concern, he cut her off.

"If your father sees it, then my life shall be upended, and I may find my brandy business shattered unless I let myself be leg-shackled to Miss Waltham."

That explained his foul mood. He wasn't really concerned about her reputation, merely how it might affect his own future.

"I cannot order *The Times* to retract their words," she pointed out. "None of us can unread what was printed." Miranda sat on the sofa, feeling frustrated. "What would you have me do?"

Philip clenched his fists in frustration and made no move to sit.

"I would have you be more careful. It is plain you have not learned anything about my world in the weeks I have been escorting you. Even now, where is your maid? Why are we alone?"

She longed to tell him they were alone because when she'd heard him at the door, she'd told Eliza her presence was unnecessary. For any other man, Eliza would be seated in the room with them as she should. But he was special to her.

"Indeed, I have learned," she defended herself.

"Then last night would not have happened," Philip said harshly. "I cannot imagine your father will have any choice but to set me free of this impossible arrangement."

CHAPTER SEVENTEEN

Miranda knew she had to leave London. Otherwise, her father would force them to finish out the Season. She could no longer bear the humiliation of an escort who thought it such an arduous task to be with her. If he wanted his freedom, she would see to it herself.

"Only think how it will be the next time we are out together," Philip continued, not noticing her misery. "Gloved hands and fans will go up, and everyone will be whispering behind them. You are not used to being the object of rumor and innuendo, and I doubt you will enjoy being looked at askance or even cut in public."

He was merely making excuses. Lady Harriet had told her there was no harm in a little notoriety. In fact, the earl's daughter had specifically stated the nobility enjoyed being at the center of attention, their names upon everyone's lips.

Rising to her feet, she walked past him to the door.

"If things are, as you believe, too spicy for me, then I shall speak with my father and tell him I no longer wish to attend any more events. Thank you."

He looked surprised at her easy acquiescence, but then he nodded.

"Just so," he agreed. "It would be for the best."

The way he latched onto her suggestion with exceeding haste made her heart ache. Luckily before her distress overcame her expression, another one of her dance partners from the night before entered the foyer. Eliza took his card.

"If you'll excuse me, Lord Mercer, I have another visitor."

⌒

PHILIP STRODE OUT FEELING as though he had lost something even though he'd accomplished his aim—to protect Miss Bright by no longer accompanying her. Of course, that would make his own life easier, too, and return his liberty to pursue other women. That was, if he wanted to.

He had stared down the suitor, too, a fellow member of White's, a viscount's son. Miss Bright was drawing in the quality gentleman despite *The Times* nastiness. Eventually, they nodded at one another, although Philip thought the man a bit over-dressed for a morning call.

Hesitating only while making sure the maid went into the parlor and stayed there, he departed the Brights' house. Yet now the realization he was no longer going to be Miranda's escort, even for the short time remaining in the Season, pricked his initial feeling of relief, deflating it entirely by the time he reached his club.

"There's the man himself," his friend Lord Jeffrey Guilden said by way of greeting.

Guilden was a good man, a fellow soldier who'd come back earlier than Philip due to getting his hand blown off. And in marital status, he enjoyed wedded bliss.

Philip whacked him on his good shoulder and sat.

"Why am I *the man* today? Don't say it is because of *The Times* and you're interested in a pot of gossip-water!"

Guilden laughed. "My wife greatly enjoys your amorous antics in the papers despite how I try to shield her tender gaze, but I was referring to how you nearly drowned that rat Lowry."

Confounded, Philip asked, "How did you know about that? Surely Lowry didn't tell anyone of his humiliation, nor that he had to leave by the back gate since he was wet from the top of his head almost to his waist."

"No, but you were seen from the house by Holland, and he told me."

"*Huh.*" Philip settled back in his chair. "And yet it didn't make it into the Grub Street news, unless I missed it."

"Only a few of us know, those with wives who were bothered by Lowry. None of us will let it get to the papers. We wouldn't want you charged with assault, would we?" He raised his glass to Philip.

"I had no idea the man was a predator, and I thought I had his full measure."

"He usually likes other men's wives," Guilden explained. "The women are fearful of scandal, and thus, no one complains. You've had no wife, nor long-term lady-friend until now. Speaking of which, you have chosen well with the delightful Miss Bright."

Philip gestured the waiter over and ignored Guilden's words while he ordered his meal. Not only hadn't he chosen her, he had just rid himself of her. If he told his chum that, it was plain he would see a look of disappointment. Still, he could explain in some fashion.

"It was a temporary association. She and I will not be keeping company any longer."

There it was, as expected, a look of chagrin flittering across Guilden's expression, but then he brightened.

"If the lady is hoping for marriage, you might want to consider that one. My wife had a conversation with Lady Hartwell over tea and lavender ice cream at Gunter's. She said your Miss Bright was a woman of good humor *and* good sense."

"That she is." *His* Miss Bright, except when she went off with Lowry or onto the Dark Walk with Lady Harriet. "But I have some other irons in the fire at the moment."

"I see." Guilden tapped the table. "Well, there is no accounting for the heart. If you don't carry a tenderness for her, there isn't much one can do or say to force such sentiment."

A tenderness? He certainly had that. And before the Lowry incident, he'd been thinking of telling her he was becoming devoted to her in his fashion. But to see her in *The Times*, linked with him. He could only imagine the magistrate reading it and exacting vengeance for his daughter's besmirched name.

Philip had expected Miranda to be angry over the editorial.

Instead, she'd coolly and amicably released him from their arrangement. Maybe she had grown attached to someone else, that suitor he'd passed in her front hall. The man had a good head of hair, and no doubt about it.

Philip ran a hand through his own to make sure it was still thick and hadn't fallen out with the stress that had begun with the Waltham's solicitor banging on his door months earlier.

"But aren't you weary of being less than you could be?" Guilden's words brought him back to the present.

"Meaning," Philip said before sipping the coffee that had been brought in advance of his meal. It was bitter and not hot enough. *Was White's going down the slippery slope to mediocrity, or was it merely his own discontent coloring everything?*

"Every man-jack who served with you, including me, knows you're as right as rain and have a heart as big as Prinny's waistline," Guilden said. "It's fine to be rakish in our youth, but you are head of a great family. Currently, however, you're only the titular head of those who came before with nothing and no one after you. In my opinion, you should start creating the next generation of Mercers before you have to go through the ox house on your way to bed."

Philip rolled his eyes at the jest. "I am not so ancient as to need the ox house and you know it, but I take your meaning."

Guilden shrugged. "As your comrade-in-arms, I would like to see you become as happy as I am."

"You are one of the few, and if you're riotously happy, why are you here?" Philip asked sourly.

That made his friend laugh. "Part of the secret to a happy marriage is giving each other time alone. All the sweeter when I take Lady Guilden to bed later."

Philip nodded, and his thoughts turned to Miranda. She was the only woman he had ever met whom he could imagine looking forward to seeing every day of his life.

But even if he wanted to, he couldn't ask for her hand while Lord Perrin expected him to offer for *his* daughter. If he betrayed Perrin and Miss Waltham, his brandy casks would be sunk to the bottom of the Channel. He had to wait just a week and a half longer, and then Miss Waltham would be out of time, according to the magistrate's letter.

Besides Sir William's permission would be hard won, considering the man's low opinion of him, which was why a summons from him two days later did not bode well.

Arriving at the magistrate's court, hat in hand, Philip tried his best to appear as innocent as a choir boy instead of a thundering buck.

"What did you do to my daughter?" came Sir William's harsh greeting.

Philip had barely the time to look around the chamber behind the courtroom, but now he did while stalling. After all, he had no idea what answer he could give as he considered all the things he had, in fact, done to *and with* Miranda.

"You have many fine books," he finally said. "Thick ones," he added lamely. "Not only here, but also at your home, as I recall."

Sir William's nostrils flared. "I don't give a damn about the books. I saw *The Times.*"

"I see" Philip said, then hoped to add a jocular note by adding, "You seem more like a *Morning Herald* reader."

The magistrate narrowed his eyes. "Someone sent it to me."

That raised Philip's suspicion. "Sent it to you?"

"Just the one page," Sir William added, picking up the tattered single sheet that had been torn out and folded.

A dozen thoughts flitted through Philip's mind. *Who had sent it? Was it Miss Waltham or perhaps her father? And why?*

"You cannot believe anything you read in those columns," he began.

The magistrate held up his hand. "Who is 'Lord L'?"

"Lowry," Philip told him. "He did her no harm, I promise you. And I have made sure he'll never speak to her again."

This earned him a raised eyebrow.

"Have you spoken to your daughter about the incident?" Philip asked, wondering how much Miranda would have disclosed.

"I cannot. She has left London."

The words hit Philip like an unexpected belly-go-firster from one of his boxing partners at Gentleman Jackson's club.

"Where? When?" he demanded, wanting to jump in his traveling coach that very minute and go after her.

"For someone who has a stake in this matter and who shook my hand over a solemn vow, you are woefully uninformed," Sir William said, crossing his arms and causing *The Times* column to crumple in his grasp.

Philip took a breath. He hadn't thought she would leave because of the gossip.

"I spoke with Miss Bright when I first saw *The Times.* She made no mention of leaving. Will you tell me where she is?"

"My daughter went to Northampton."

"The home of the cousins she has mentioned before."

"My deceased wife's family, yes." The magistrate pursed his lips. "If you hadn't mucked up at the Piccadilly ball and let her get entangled with that Lowry fellow, then she would still be here, finding herself a husband. Two suitors called on her yesterday and she wasn't at home. What am I supposed to do with all those flowers?"

"I am sorry for the inconvenience, but I fail to see—"

"You will fetch her back," Sir William ordered, his voice raised. "And she will accept one of these swells. I am not getting any younger, dammit!"

The magistrate, seeming in full good health despite his declaration of aging, was roaring at the top of his lungs before slamming his hand upon the table.

Philip was not used to being spoken to in such a fashion. Not only because he was a baron, but as an officer, even Wellington had not addressed him thusly. In any case, he was unimpressed.

"I am not your errand boy, sir. I take it she left without asking your permission."

"On the contrary, she *told* me she was leaving," Sir William said. "She said you no longer wished to escort her."

"I explained to you weeks ago," Philip protested. "Miss Bright and I are ill-suited because of my reputation."

"Couldn't you put aside your rabid lust for a Season?" the older man demanded. "It wasn't even an entire one."

"That's hardly the point. The papers are discussing *her* indiscretion, not mine."

"Her indiscretion!" Sir William repeated, looking apoplectic. "You were supposed to keep her safe."

"As was your sister," Philip reminded him. "Where is Mrs. Cumbersome in all this muddle?"

"You shall not slander my sister. It was not as though she could accompany my daughter onto the dance floor with this cur, Lowry. Could she? Poor woman took to her bed with a fit of the vapors. I didn't understand why until someone kindly sent me the snippet." He tossed the newsprint back onto his desk.

Kindly, his arse, Philip thought. Someone was stirring up trouble.

"Delicate female feelings are at stake," the magistrate continued.

"Your sister's?" Philip asked.

"Don't be ridiculous. I meant Miranda's. My sister is as tough as Wellington's boots. The vapors were merely a ruse to avoid me while feeling ashamed. Lucinda rallied and accompanied my daughter to the country. It's *you* who should be mortified at failing to handle one easily managed young woman."

"If you don't mind my saying, sir, Miss Bright is not the docile crumpet you make her out to be."

"What!" The magistrate was back to yelling. "I do mind. Go to Northampton and bring her back. Or you can forget about your brandy and bid your freedom a fond farewell, too."

There was no point in arguing further. Philip had given Sir William too much information, and now the man was using it against him.

"I want my daughter safely back here, brought willingly *after* you have apologized. Tell her she has gentlemen callers waiting." The magistrate came around his desk and marched up to Philip. "She had watery eyes when she left. When I next look upon her, I don't want to see a single tear, nor a hair out of place. Is that clear?"

The magistrate was as formidable as any general on the battlefield.

"I shall do my best, sir."

"Your best?" the man repeated. "Then you shall succeed, my lord. I know it!"

MIRANDA LAUGHED WHEN HELEN scooped up one of the family's cats and deposited it onto her brother's lap. Peter pretended the cat was a nuisance, but quickly, he was stroking its head, letting it lean against his hand and close its eyes. She found her affable cousins to be a welcome change from the company she'd been lately keeping in London.

"I wish you could see it all for yourself," she mused.

"We may someday," Peter said, sounding unbothered about their country existence. "At any rate, I've told Helen she should spend time with you and Uncle William in Town. It would do her the world of good. She might even find herself a husband."

"I won't leave you," his sister said. "I would miss you, dear brother, far too much. I get everything I need of the London experience from Miranda's letters, and her book will be the talk of Britain. I can't wait to read it."

It was true her book would be printed shortly. Before coming away, she'd sent her stack of pages to Lady Harriet. After all, since her association with Lord Mercer was at an end, there would be no more amusing vignettes of Mayfair. She assumed if the story wasn't good enough, then Lady Harriet would toss it away.

"Besides Helen is sweet on the farmer's eldest son," Miranda reminded Peter, making her cousin's pretty cheeks turn pink.

Peter nodded. "He is a good man and will inherit a large, fertile piece of land. I hope he asks for her hand soon so she'll stop mothering me. We already have a mother, and I don't need two."

Although his tone was light, a measure of seriousness lay underneath it, and Helen shrugged.

"I don't mean to mother you, but I am loath to marry and leave you alone."

Peter rolled his eyes. "Miranda will visit as she always has, and I have our parents. I am not alone."

A second cat jumped onto his lap. "And I have these beasts always hanging on me. They're making me too hot in truth." He stroked each one before giving them a firm push off his lap which was covered with a light blanket despite it being a late-summer day.

"And I don't need this." He picked it off and tossed it aside onto the grass, the only sign he felt irritable. Normally, he would have folded it and handed it gently to one of them.

"Let's go for a stroll." He used the word despite remaining seated.

Miranda and Helen rose from their wrought iron chairs.

"Yes, let's," Miranda said, catching her cousin's eye when Helen went behind the pushchair. "Do you want assistance," she asked Peter, "or are you going to exercise those muscles of yours?"

Peter's arms were well-developed but his legs were worse than last she recalled, indicating he was not spending enough time trying to walk with his cane.

"I'll ride," he said. "Let's go down toward the river."

Helen gripped the handles of the Bath-chair and began to push.

They'd had a brief but intense summer shower the night before with thunder and lightning. The cats had all remained inside in the parlor while the three cousins and Miranda's aunt and uncle played cards.

"I'm glad I put on my boots," Miranda remarked as they went across the field toward the River Nene.

Suddenly, her uncle's large dog came bounding across the lawn to join them, already mud covered from haunch to toes.

"No, Georgie," Miranda said, then squealed with laughter as it nearly bowled her over and covered one side of her day dress in mud.

"We shall all look like Georgie when we've finished our outing," Helen said, and they continued on with the dog in the lead.

Peter began to talk about an imminent tea shortage due to some storm in the Pacific, and Miranda let her attention drift. While she'd kept them entertained with stories of London since her arrival, in quiet times, she could think of nothing but Philip. Even then, despite her interest in world events, Miranda's thoughts conjured the tall, handsome baron who'd bathed her body in flames of desire.

The mere thought of his hands and lips caused a pleasant, if somewhat frustrating, sensation to grow deep within her.

She sighed.

"Why the dissatisfaction, cousin?" asked Helen. "Is my brother boring you to death by his talk of the tea trade with the Orient?"

Miranda glanced at Peter, but he wasn't the least annoyed.

"I could talk about the terrible amount of rain were having, causing crop failures and famine," he offered, "but that seems even gloomier than a discussion of those lunatic Luddites destroying the looms at Heathcoat's factory."

"It's not you," Miranda said as they crested a gentle hill before the land sloped down to the river. "Nor the rain, nor even those poor, misguided weavers. It is a phantom in my own brain that I beg you to ignore. Shall we continue?"

They started along a path they'd taken easily two days before, with Georgie loping away and out of sight ahead of them. However, now the wheels of Peter's chair stuck fast, mired in the mud.

"It's probably worse down closer to the river," Helen pointed out.

"We must turn back, I'm afraid," Miranda said.

"I've got my cane," Peter said. "Let me give it a try."

Helen shot Miranda a worried glance.

"Wouldn't it be wiser to wait and walk *after* the ground has dried out?" she suggested. "Perhaps tomorrow?"

"Give up, dear cousin," Helen said. "If my brother has decided to try it, he shall not rest until he does. Besides, it rains nearly every other day lately."

With muscled arms from exercising, Peter hoisted himself up and off the seat, standing gingerly upright. He reached for the cane tucked in the side of the pushchair.

"I think I shall need the assistance of one of you on my other arm."

Miranda was closest, and they set off at a snail's pace with Helen pushing the empty chair before her.

"Can you manage?" Peter asked Miranda.

"Yes," but she couldn't speak more than a single word as his weight was resting on her and she didn't want to fail him.

He was walking as well as he could, one leg more smoothly than the other, which he had to drag forward while gingerly putting his weight on it. Their progress was slow, but it *was* progress until Georgie came bounding back.

In the blink of an eye, the sheepdog crashed into Miranda's side, knocking her off balance, and she, in turn, pulled Peter down with her. Both of them lay face down on the muddy ground with Helen shrieking behind them.

Stunned, she turned her head and looked at Peter. He levered himself up and looked back.

"Your face," he said.

"Yours," she said.

And they started to laugh. When Helen was assured they were well, she joined in.

"A merry group to be sure," came a familiar voice that caused Miranda to rise to her knees and look around.

CHAPTER EIGHTEEN

Philip! Here?

Helen had gone silent, her lovely gray eyes staring. And Peter was attempting to gain his footing again.

"Don't be alarmed," Miranda told them. "This is Lord Mercer."

Silence met her declaration, then Helen said, "*The* Lord Mercer? Lord *Major* Mercer?"

"No one calls me that," Philip said, "except your cousin. I was told you three might be out here, but I didn't realize mud baths were on your schedule."

"I would shake your hand," Peter said, "but I am as filthy as the farmer's pig."

Miranda turned to him and wondered if she could get him on his feet, slippery as the ground was.

"May I assist you?" Philip asked, speaking to Peter, although he first moved to Miranda and offered her his hand. She took it, feeling a sensation of relief merely from touching him again before allowing him to draw her to feet.

"I will not take offense," Peter said good-naturedly.

With graciousness, Philip helped the young man to stand, and keeping a hand under his elbow, he assisted him to return to the pushchair.

"Thank you, my lord," Peter said, settling back in his seat as Philip recovered the cane. "I am afraid you have ended up wearing some of our mud."

It was true. Not only Philip's shoes but his gloves were covered, and Georgie was welcoming him with bounding leaps, sending more mud flying everywhere until Helen called him off and told him to go home.

Miranda had never seen the baron looking less than perfect, except for when she'd capsized the rowboat.

"No matter," he said and sounded as if he meant it. "I've been covered head to toe before."

"On the battlefield?" Miranda asked.

He looked at her sharply, and not for the first time she realized he didn't like to speak about going to war.

"Actually, yes, but I was thinking of my estate in Guildford. I enjoy horses and being outdoors in all weather. The two mixed together can be a muddy mess."

She nodded. "I am surprised to see you here," she said. *Surprised and utterly delighted.*

As a group, they turned toward the house with Philip pushing the Bath-chair and the two siblings remaining silent, obviously interested in the stranger from London.

"Your father told me where to find you."

"I see." Her father had probably also told him to bring her back to London. He'd been none too pleased when she'd left. "But why are you here? I thought you were done with the Season, or at least with escorting me."

Philip didn't immediately respond. With Helen gawking at him, waiting for his answer, and Peter staring decidedly ahead as if pretending he couldn't hear them, the tension grew.

"Perhaps we should discuss this in private," Philip said at last.

"Please God! Yes," Peter muttered.

Yet thinking of the public nature of *The Times* gossip column that had upset Philip's apple cart, Miranda said, "I assure you my cousins know everything."

The baron turned his head and fixed her with his dark gaze. "Everything?"

Each intimate kiss and private moment they'd shared flickered through her memories. She caught her breath.

"Very well," Miranda agreed quickly. "I shall change and then come find you."

Ten minutes later, washed and changed, she dashed into the hallway only to bump into Helen.

"You look remarkably fresh considering you were lying in a mudpuddle less than half an hour ago."

"Thank you. How is he? Where is he?"

"You are as jittery as a woman in love," Helen jibed but in a kind voice.

"Nonsense!"

"Your entire dirty face lit up when you saw him," her cousin pointed out.

"Bah!" Miranda said.

"Stop pretending I am imagining things. There is no shame in love. You know I have given my heart to our neighbor, Mr. Wendall. And I can easily see why you would be smitten with Lord Mercer. He is a rum duke and then some."

"A rum baron," Miranda corrected, then added, "In point of fact, a brandy baron."

They both engaged in a fit of giggles.

Finally, grasping Helen's hands, Miranda said, "He is a fine figure of a man, and he's kind. You saw how he helped Peter without making him feel less worthy. However, Lord Mercer is a rake, and unlike your upstanding farmer, he will not make me a good and decent husband. I told you he was unhappy that I might have put his future at risk."

"Then why is he here?" Helen asked.

"That's what I shall find out."

"And if he's here to ask for your hand?" her cousin pressed.

Miranda rolled her eyes. "Helen, dear one, I have been guilty of filling your head with too many stories. Where is the brandy baron?"

"He had to change, too, and then Father and Mother made him sit in the parlor with them and drink tea, but I'm sure they'll let you have a few minutes of privacy." She paused. "On second thought, I am not sure of that at all. They never let me visit alone with Mr. Wendall when he comes calling."

WHEN MIRANDA SHOWED HERSELF in the parlor, Philip was on his feet before the swish of her pale green dress fell silent. She was back to her perfectly lovely self, although he hadn't minded her clad in slippery mud either.

"Miss Bright, I must speak with you in private if your aunt and uncle will afford us that courtesy."

He bowed to each in turn. Philip hadn't really asked permission and decided the best thing to do was not to await a response.

"Shall we walk in the garden?" He didn't know if there was one besides the wet field upon which he'd found Miranda sprawled, but somewhere outside he would find a place to have a word with her.

As if marshalling an unruly soldier under his command, he threaded her arm through his and marched her toward the terrace door.

"Over yonder is a wildflower garden," she directed, and he picked up the pace once again. "But we must stay in sight of the house."

"Naturally. I didn't come here to compromise you," he told her.

"Which begs the question, why did you come?" she asked. "Without me by your side, you are free to enjoy your *usual* course of action."

Philip sighed. She still thought he would prefer to be meeting women in dark gardens or up to his normal enjoyments at Covent Garden brothels. He had only himself to blame for her opinion of him.

"Without you, your father is less than amenable to helping me. Without you, I am more likely to be pressed to marry Miss Waltham, something I have no intention of doing." *Without you,* he added silently, *I am miserable.*

He could not declare anything like that until he was out from under Miss Waltham's threat and until he knew whether Miranda's father would give his permission. After their tumultuous conversation in the magistrate's court chamber, Philip thought that would be the hardest challenge of all.

In any case, the pretty minx looked unmoved. "I am happily visiting my cousins. Your problems, even as they relate to my father, are entirely your own responsibility."

He knew that to be true, but he had no intention of returning to London without her. He must give her a hint of his feelings.

"You mentioned my usual course of action, but I prefer an *unusual* one with you."

She hesitated. "You were upset over *The Times*," she reminded him. "Unlike other nobility, you don't seem to care for having your name in the newspapers, poorly disguised or not."

What was the chit on about? "No one I know cares for it, but that's not the point. Your father read the gossip rag and now believes you left London under hint of scandal and is blaming me. That's unfair, is it not?"

Miranda was frowning, biting her luscious lower lip, and more than one disturbing thought seemed to be in her lovely head. But she expressed only puzzlement.

"I am surprised my father read that section."

"Someone sent it to him so he would."

Her shocked expression confirmed it hadn't been her doing. For Philip had wondered if she hadn't sent it to spite him. Plainly, such was not the case.

"Regardless, you told me you no longer wish to escort me," she recalled. "And your name was mentioned as well as Lord Lowry's, intimating I might be allowing you to take liberties. Which I have," she pointed out. "You are, as you imagined, a terrible influence upon me. Therefore, the blame is not entirely unjustified even if another man was also at fault."

With that, she turned and walked farther into the tall tangle of flower stalks and shrubs. Philip felt rightly chastised.

"I promise I thought only to launch you into society so you could find a husband. That reminds me, your father said you have had suitors leaving posies."

She still didn't face him but merely shrugged.

"Miss Bright, I apologize for snapping at you because of *The Times*. It was wrong of me, and you are correct that I was partially to blame. I should have discovered Lowry's dubious character earlier. My only defense is that I have never had to watch over a young woman before. I've always been on the other side of things, trying to breach a female's defenses, not help shore them up, if you take my meaning."

"I do." She sounded sad.

Philip wished he knew how to make her happy again.

"If you come back with me, you can ask me anything you like, and I shall tell you. That is, if you're still interested."

She sighed and turned to face him. "I am here with my cousins. Thus, I have no need to write letters of interest."

"Wasn't there something else you were writing, something like Miss Austen's novels, except with fewer lessons in manners?"

"I finished that," she said quickly. "All done and dusted."

"I see. And are your cousins reading that, too?"

Her cheeks pinkened, and Philip wondered if he had made it into her little tale.

"Not yet, but they will. Why did you say your fellow nobility do not like to be mentioned in the society pages? I thought it gave them fame and notoriety, both desirable for those who like to be seen."

"On the contrary, I have never met a single person who cared for it. It is nearly always false or embellished or, when true, printed only to embarrass, humiliate, and do damage. Unquestionably, it is written solely to sell papers, without regard to the suffering it may cause."

"What kind of damage and suffering?" Miranda asked, looking at him with wide eyes.

"As you know one's reputation is a precious commodity, and many treasure and protect it, not only for themselves but for their families and their children. For example, Lady Sarah, whom you saw with Pastille. She is commonly known to be in a loveless marriage and also known to have loved Lord Pastille since they were young. Her parents forbade her to marry him. That wouldn't be terrible except the man she did marry is also well known to be an arse, and a vicious, miserly one at that."

Philip plucked a flower from the nearest plant. "He would cut her off without a penny if he had cause, and he would keep her from her children. Hostesses like Lady Hartwell allow her to meet safely with Pastille at their homes. It's the least one can do, as she cannot possibly obtain a divorce and keep her children."

Miranda had paled during all this. She was not of his set, and probably this seemed like a lot of machinations and intrigue.

"Does Lady Harriet know all this, about Lady Sarah, I mean?"

Philip thought her question a strange one. "Yes. As you've seen by attending balls and dinner parties, those of us in my class rather stay to ourselves. The same people, same faces. We don't need the gossip columns as we already know most everything about one another. And some of it, we hide to protect one another, too."

"I see. If you'll excuse me, my lord. I have a letter to write."

Philip took a step back. "You cannot possibly be dismissing me over a letter once again. This is too important. Besides, your cousins are here."

"I assure you this is equally important. Necessity compels me to correspond with a friend at once."

And with that, the irritating female dashed away from him and disappeared back inside the house.

MIRANDA RACED UPSTAIRS TO her room where she had a small writing desk. Quickly, she penned a letter.

Dearest Lady Harriet,

It has come to my attention that I might be causing not only distress but even danger to those whom I had no intention of harming. Please do not continue with the publication of my book. While I appreciate all you have done to bring it to light, I fear you and thus I were both misinformed as to its happy reception.

Sincerely,
Miranda Bright

Folding the paper, she sealed it with wax and addressed the plain outside. Racing back downstairs, feeling choked with worry over Lady Sarah, whose barely disguised dalliance had made it into the book, Miranda paid a stableboy to take it as far as the next inn. From there, it would be picked up by the mail coach and continue its journey to London. Luckily, it was merely a few hours away.

Then she breathed a sigh of relief although she would have to tell her uncle she'd sent off one of his servants without asking. That was the least of her worries.

Back indoors, she found Philip in conversation with Peter, and left them alone to take her place by Helen.

"Is everything well?"

"I pray so."

"And has Lord Mercer come to ask for your hand?"

"What?" Miranda's gaze shot to the baron who turned to look at her as if he felt her watching him. "Why would you ask that?"

"Because a notorious rake followed you from London and cannot take his eyes off you."

"For entirely selfish reasons, I assure you. My father wants him to take me back to London and find a husband. Lord Mercer wants me to go back to protect him from Lord Perrin *and* Miss Waltham."

"What do *you* want?" Helen asked.

"To stay here with you, of course."

"That is not precisely what I meant."

Miranda nodded. "I do not believe my wishes are important."

Helen sighed. "Well, that may be true, but at least you can enjoy the man's company while he is here. I assume he will stay the night, and then you will send him on his way."

"Yes," she agreed lightly.

At dinner, Philip was the perfect guest, conversing on many topics and earning his meal and his bed for the night with his entertaining discussion.

When he found out Peter knew something about the world of business and had successfully invested his small savings, turning a profit as his father proudly pointed out, Philip asked him questions. He was completely respectful despite her cousin's invalid status and his lack of worldly travel.

Impressed as always by the baron's manners, Miranda thought she hadn't seen Peter that animated and happy in a long time.

"Enough talk of business," her aunt declared. "You are all ignoring Cook's delicious apple cake. And I would like to hear my daughter and Miranda give a recital after we've finished."

Immediately, Philip's glance locked on Miranda, and she was carried back to their first assembly and the two sisters' varying talents. Sadly, that would be the same case with her and Helen.

"Auntie, I would prefer not to—"

"Nonsense," her aunt said. "We must have some musical entertainment before cards. You needn't sing if you're not up to it, but you must at least play one song."

Philip's smile and a small nod encouraged her, but Miranda knew how critical he could be, feeling mortified in advance that he would hear her mediocre playing.

When they adjourned to the drawing room, Philip approached her.

"I didn't know you had talent for the pianoforte."

"I am not sure as I do, at least not to your standards, my lord. But I suppose it is the price of a good meal," she said softly.

He laughed. "It will be different because it is you, Miss Bright, and we are friends. I promise, I shall not judge you. It is brave of you to perform."

"Thank you." With that encouragement, she decided the best thing to do was combine their talents, hoping no one would listen to her playing while Helen was singing, for her cousin had a decent voice.

"That's cheating," her aunt said when their first song, "The Lass of Richmond Hill," was complete. "If you are not going to sing and play separately, then you must give us another."

Her aunt had drunk too much wine, Miranda feared, and was making up rules, but she and Helen could do naught except go along with her and began "The Joys of the Country."

Finally, they were set free with Helen having done her part beyond expectation. As for herself, Miranda had missed a few notes but passingly muddled through. Philip gestured her over to where he stood by the garden windows.

"That was better than you led me to believe," he said for her ears only, making her laugh. "The two of you could certainly hold your own in any drawing room in London. Maybe your cousin would return with us and enjoy the remainder of the Season."

Her mirth fizzled. "I shall not keep you in a state of misapprehension, but rather I must tell you now that I will not go back with you tomorrow, nor any day after that."

"What of your suitors with their bouquets?" he asked, his tone like warm honey.

"I have no interest in them." That was the truth. Her only interest was in this impossible man who stood before her.

"What about my brandy business?" he asked, raising a hand as if to stroke her cheek and then dropping it abruptly. It seemed he'd forgotten fleetingly they were not at the type of country party in which he'd kissed Miss Waltham. "As my friend, will you not help me?"

She must resist his attempts to seduce her with nothing but his voice and beautiful eyes. *Were they truly friends?* She didn't think so.

"I am not returning to London," she insisted.

"Very well." He crossed his arms, making his muscles flex. "Then I shan't either, not for a day or two anyway. The longer I stay away, the less opportunity I give all those who seek to ruin my life."

"You're being a bit dramatic, are you not?"

She would swear she saw the moment he made a decision.

"I believe I must confess to you something I have told no one else."

CHAPTER NINETEEN

I f her ears could perk up like a dog's, then Miranda would describe her own as doing precisely that. She glanced over at her family, but her two cousins and their parents were already playing a round of whist.

"If you wish, you may confide in me." She was surprised he would, given as how he knew she enjoyed a little gossip. But if he trusted her with a secret, she would keep it close to her heart.

"You must not tell anyone," he insisted.

"Why do you wish to tell me?"

"I think you'll understand after I tell you," he said, looking at her family. "May we sit in the far corner?"

"Of course."

When they were as far as possible from the others, Philip said, "I hope it won't make you think less of me."

A prickle of alarm raced through her. *Was he married? Did he have children he'd abandoned? Or was it something worse? A fatal disease he'd picked up in France perhaps?*

"I am *not* as wealthy as people believe," he said quietly.

She waited. *Was that all?*

When nothing more was forthcoming, and he held her fixed by his keen gaze, she nodded thoughtfully, which was far better than laughing with relief as she had nearly done.

Finally, she asked, "You're not?" It was a tepid reply, but she could think of no other.

"I can tell you do not understand the import," he told her.

Lifting a shoulder in a slight shrug, she said, "Fewer gold coins here or there hardly seems of great significance."

"Brandy, Lord Mercer?" came her uncle's voice from across the room.

Philip startled, his eyes widening for a second. Then he turned to his host.

"Yes, please. I would like that very much."

In a minute, Philip held a glass of brandy, which first he sniffed before placing it before the lamp and inspecting the color as if were a fine jewel. Miranda accepted a glass of her aunt's delicious ratafia, and they were left alone again.

"I am not speaking of a few gold coins," he continued, and finally took a sip of the amber liquid. "It's very good, thank you, sir," he called over to his host.

"But not as good as mine," he muttered to Miranda. "Regardless, if no one ever gets to taste it, then what is the point?" he asked, seemingly to himself.

Miranda could see he was battling with words. Then he looked at her again. "If I cannot bring my brandy over to Britain, I will lose my family's estate. Is that of great enough significance?"

She gasped softly.

"I have already put everything I can into the brandy, its production, the casks, and a deposit with Waltham's shipping company. I need to bring it over and sell it before I find myself on the rocks with pockets to let."

Nearly bankrupt? Miranda could scarcely believe it.

"How did this happen?" she asked. After all, the Mercer barony was known to be a wealthy one.

"I left the wrong person in charge of my finances while I was away."

"That's terrible!" Suddenly a few things made sense, like Philip balking over the cost of her clothing and accessories for the Season.

"What's terrible?" asked Helen coming upon them unexpectedly. "Was it my singing or your piano playing?"

"Neither," Philip said, rising as a perfect gentleman. "Is it my turn to partner for cards? I believe Peter and I can beat anyone."

Miranda watched him go. The notion that Miss Waltham could bring him down by stopping her family from honoring their shipping arrangement was disturbing, and knowing she also had a hand in it by aggravating her father did not sit well.

PHILIP FELT BETTER FOR having told someone his troubles. Having done it once, he almost wanted to unburden himself to Miranda's cousin Peter, too, for the young man had good sense as well as clever ideas. From what Philip gathered, Peter had taken small money and grew it to where he could afford to move into his own home if he chose, all the while incapacitated in the country.

But keeping his own counsel, Philip went to bed like a well-behaved guest without attempting to find Miranda's room at midnight. However, in the morning, he was happy to find her alone in the dining room with a book on the table where there was nothing yet laid out except a pot of tea and some toast in a rack.

"I was thinking . . . ," he began.

"I wanted to tell you . . . ," she said at the same time.

Philip smiled.

"Go ahead, Miss Bright, while I eat this delicious breakfast of cold toast."

She laughed, a sound he'd missed and of which he was extremely fond.

"I assure you in another fifteen minutes, there will be eggs and bacon, sausage and mushrooms, and some freshly baked items. As you tasted last night, they have a superior cook."

"They do," but he couldn't take his eyes off of her. "Is it too forward to tell you I have missed you?"

He watched her cheeks grow a sweet shade of pink.

"That's kind of you. I thought I was a nuisance at best, although a useful one."

He grinned. "That's how it was at the beginning, but as I said yesterday, I think of you as a friend now."

"Good, because as a friend, I have decided to help you in whatever way I can. To that end, I shall return with you to London to soothe my father. Hopefully, at the Season's end, Miss Waltham will have decided to cease her nonsensical claims and your brandy will be released from bondage."

The weight on Philip's shoulders lifted. As he had chosen the chair beside her, she was in easy reach. He could not refrain from taking her hand, drawing her around to face him, and then pulling all of her into an awkward embrace with the table digging into his side.

As soon as the familiar, floral scent of her hit his nostrils, he leaned down and kissed her full on the lips. It was the most natural thing in the world.

She responded with pressure, kissing him in return, making his heart beat faster, even more insistently than his lower regions pulsed, which was unusual. Nibbling her lower lip, he wished they were alone. But quickly coming to his senses, he broke off the kiss.

He felt elated and strangely complete, even though all they had done was a rather chaste kiss. They grinned at each other, and he reached for the toasted bread without buttering it, taking a bite and letting crumbs go everywhere, over the plate, the tablecloth, even on his clothing.

She giggled adorably, and he might have kissed her again if her aunt hadn't entered, followed by the maid carrying the first of three trays to follow, all containing the promised hot breakfast. Philip rose to his feet and remained there as Helen entered and, lastly, Peter who was pushed by his father.

Before he could think better of it, Philip said, "I have seen men with terrible wounds heal enough to get around with a crutch. Have you considered relinquishing your Bath-chair to strengthen your limbs?"

The other three family members glanced at one another, but Peter seemed unaffected and certainly not insulted.

"Not that I mean to overstep or to pry," Philip added quickly. Perhaps there was more wrong with the young man than he knew.

"No," Peter answered, "you have not. I appreciate that you speak from experience and with concern. I have a cane, but I spend more time falling with it than walking."

"As I said, perhaps a crutch," Philip suggested.

Peter shuddered. "It is the symbol of a beggar," he pointed out.

"Even in the short time I have been here, I know you to be anything but. If you are willing and if there is a capable carpenter or better yet, a joiner, I would be happy to sketch out the best type of crutch that our soldiers use. Do you have problems with both legs?"

"I do, but to a lesser degree on my left."

"Still," Philip considered, "you could start with two. You have a strong upper body and have kept your arm muscles healthy. Using crutches, you would be able to do stairs, as well."

Silence met his last words, but after filling his plate, Peter said, "Thank you, Lord Mercer. I would appreciate seeing your drawing."

"We have very good joiner in the village," Miranda's uncle chimed in.

Philip also thought the young man should regain his freedom to travel by riding a horse once again, but he would suggest that in private in case it was too traumatic a notion. It was not terribly difficult to fasten a strap to the saddle that would hold a crutch, too.

Satisfied he had done some good, Philip tucked in to his breakfast, pleasantly surprised when Miranda readily announced to her family she had agreed to accompany him back to London.

"Of course, we must wait until Aunt Lucinda returns," she said.

Aunt Lucinda?

"Mrs. Cumbersome!" he blurted as it dawned on him. "I recall now your father said she had accompanied you. Where is that good woman?" Frankly, he'd forgotten about her existence entirely.

"Gone to visit friends, a mere day's ride away," Miranda said. "We expect her back in two days. Three at the most. If you wish to go on ahead to London, that will not offend me. If you wish me to go with you, then we must wait for my father's sister."

"I can wait," Philip said, feeling decidedly cheerful. He liked this family and their food, and now he had a task to keep him busy with the unfortunate Peter. And then there was the company of Miranda.

It seemed finally all was going well.

ALONE IN HER UNCLE'S study perusing his book collection, Miranda saw movement out of the corner of her eye. Philip poked his head around the door, only to dart away. She called out to him.

"Come back." Silence met her plea. Then finally, he appeared again.

"You're not disturbing me," she said, "if that's what you're worried about."

"Were I to be found alone with you in here, we would risk a tongue-lashing, and rightly so. We cannot flout acceptable behavior, especially in your aunt and uncle's home."

Acceptable behavior. Those words from his lips made her shiver. She was well aware how extremely *un*acceptable he could be, and she longed for another taste.

Sighing, she turned her back to him and returned the book to the shelf.

"And you call yourself a rake," she muttered, running a finger lightly across the spines.

"What's that you said?" he asked.

She heard him draw closer, but still, she didn't face him.

"Why do you do it?" she asked.

"Do what?" he returned.

He was very close now. She could practically feel the heat from him through the back of her cotton dress.

"Pretend to be a riotous man of the Town in public. You actually bask in the infamy of it."

He laughed, his breath tickling the back of her neck.

"I pretend nothing, you wench. Every man who doesn't immediately marry the first lady with whom he dances twice and calls upon the following morning is looked at with suspicion. Then when he dances with another lady— especially, God forbid, a waltz—he's labeled a rake!"

His hand stroked her spine, forging a hot, sensual path between her shoulder blades down to her bottom. She stepped forward before he reached it.

"I think there were a few other naughty actions that sullied your reputation and earned you your brand," she pointed out. "It was not merely waltzing and disappointing a lady. A few females were discovered left in your wake in a state of deshabille in a garden or while departing a carriage."

She turned and looked up at him then.

His mouth spread into a wicked grin, making her quiver.

"If you know all that—no doubt gleaned from those blasted hack sheets—then why do you call me a pretender to my hard-earned label?" He lifted a hand and stroked the side of her cheek.

Closing her eyes, Miranda took a deep breath. She wanted to lean into him, slide her fingers into his soft hair, and draw him close.

Maybe *she* was the rake!

"I remember you once said you read about people in the gossip columns who were not a part of your world," he said softly. "They were merely characters in a story. Now we have all become real to you. You must see a rake is merely a man who enjoys the company of women."

His hand had dropped from her cheek to her waist, his fingers gently kneading her through her layers of clothing.

She could hardly speak with him close, looking down into her eyes, touching her.

Footsteps drove them apart, at least a few inches before her uncle came into view.

"My brother-in-law allows you to stay without your chaperone because he knows we will keep you safe," he said. And then he stared at them both until Philip nodded and moved farther away.

"Thank you for sharing your thoughts, Miss Bright," Philip said. "I am going to walk into the village. Would you care to accompany me?"

"If she goes," her uncle said, "my wife must go as well, or my son and daughter."

Miranda considered the expedition. While she would enjoy it, she didn't want to uproot the household simply so she could spend time with Philip.

"I will see you later, Lord Mercer. Enjoy your walk."

THAT AFTERNOON, PHILIP RETURNED from the village under dark gray clouds and heavy showers. Despite such, he was feeling jubilant, having already met with the joiner. Peter would have successful crutches in a short while, a matter of a mere day and a half.

Indoors, there was an air of excitement, and he followed the sound of voices to the parlor where Miranda and Helen were poring over a book.

At his entrance, their speaking ceased and both heads whipped up. The women's gazes locked on him. Helen appeared concerned, to be sure, but Miranda looked positively stricken. Philip hoped it was merely due to overheated emotions from whatever they were reading. Perhaps they had got hold of a copy of *The Midnight Bell* or *The Mysteries of Udolpho*.

"What are you ladies reading with such enthusiasm?"

Instead of answering, Helen rose to her feet, squeezed her cousin's shoulder, and left the room with nothing but a nod to Philip.

Curious and curiouser.

"Is aught amiss?" he asked. "Normally, I don't drive women away in such a hurry, at least not before I perform some terribly raffish action as you accused me of earlier."

Miranda did not smile, and his stomach tensed. Something was terribly wrong.

"Is it your father?"

She shook her head before glancing down at the slim volume she held.

"I have done something that I believe was a mistake."

"We all make mistakes," he said. *How bad could it be?*

"This one may hurt people, such as Lady Sarah." Her soft voice caused Philip to lean forward to catch the last of her words as she added, "Or you."

"Tell me," he demanded.

"I tried to stop the publication, but it was too late. This arrived today, and apparently, it's all over London as we speak."

She held out the book to him.

"This book? I don't understand." He opened it and read its title page.

A Few Months to Remember: A Tale of London's Pleasures

He turned the page and the title was repeated, this time with the author's byline under it.

Marian Blaze

He glanced down at her. She had a palm to each of her cheeks, shaking her head. Frowning, it took but an instant to come clear. Miranda Bright was Marian Blaze!

The next page dove right into their own association with a ball at Lord Breadalbane's in which the Prince Regent put in an appearance. He supposed it was an acceptable tale since nothing untoward happened that night. But next he read a titillating account of the young lady slipping away from her chaperone to walk in the garden and receive her first kiss from her escort.

He frowned. That hadn't happened. Their first kiss had been at her father's house. *And why was she mentioning it at all?* Anyone who puzzled out who the writer was would recall *he* had been her escort all Season. Everything she described in her book would be attributed to the two of them.

Surely she wouldn't open herself up to condemnation by writing about their intimate encounters.

"Perhaps you should not read it," Miranda said, lifting her hand toward the book, but Philip held it out of her reach and began to skim through. The words "Vauxhall Pleasure Gardens" leaped from the page.

'Zounds! She'd incriminated herself along with him and everyone else she mentioned. Stunned, he looked at her, but she refused to meet his eyes, staring down at her hands on her lap, looking abashed, innocent even, and like the most unthreatening creature in the world.

CHAPTER TWENTY

P hilip began to skim through the chapters. *Please God, don't let her have included the incident after the rowboat!* There it was, their entire intimate scene at Syon House.

His throat clogged with rage and betrayal, and a healthy dose of fear, thinking of lives destroyed, not to mention his own chance to turn around his family's fortune. With his heart hammering, it was as if he'd awakened from a sound sleep surrounded by the enemy.

"I didn't think you were serious about writing a novel. Besides, this is most assuredly *not* fiction. This is real life. Our real lives!" He paused, realizing Miranda's cousin had been reading it. No wonder she could hardly look him in the eyes when he'd entered the room. Every decent person he knew would be looking at him in the same way—askance and entirely shocked.

All over London! "You said you wrote only for your cousins, not the whole bloody world!"

He was striding up and down, waving the slim volume in the air. "I didn't realize you were going to be the next Mrs. Crackenthorpe!"

"Who?" Miranda asked, rising to her feet.

197

"Crackenthorpe. Reported to be 'a lady who knows everything.' More precisely, she was the anonymous author of the *Female Tatler.*"

In the deep recesses of his club, they had a framed page from the eighteenth-century publication upon the wall. Serving as a dire warning, the single sheet mentioned three highly placed individuals, basically tarnishing their reputations for all time.

"I have never heard of her," Miranda said.

He stopped pacing. "Well, she's long dead, thus I'm not surprised."

"Then why mention her?" she asked, sounding agitated. "In any case, my silly little book is more likely to be compared to *Town and Country Magazine.* Have you ever read it or seen one?" She didn't wait for a reply.

"It's not published anymore, but my cousins found a stack of them, about a decade's worth in my uncle's library when we were children. Let's see, once a month for a decade. That's . . . ," she trailed off.

He waited for her to do the relatively simple math, but she frowned and seemed to want him to supply the answer.

"Numbers are not my friends," she said finally, wringing her hands, "and now I'm feeling so anxious, I cannot think straight."

"Obviously," he said unkindly, still in disbelief over what she'd done.

Not only his own scandalous portrayal in her heinous writings, she had willfully destroyed herself, too. Her father would have to stand in line to kill him, after Lord Perrin, Mr. Waltham, Lady Sarah, Lord Pastille, Lady Penelope, and a half dozen other wronged people mentioned and exposed.

"Ten years multiplied by twelve months is one hundred and twenty," he said, latching onto something sane and normal.

She waved the answer aside. "The magazine contained the *Tête-à-Tête* column. 'Head-to-head,' you understand?"

"Yes," he bit out. "Words *are* my friends, as you put it, even French ones."

She stared at him, a hard stare which left him feeling like a petty man, but he was too overwrought to care.

"May I continue without being insulted?" she asked, lifting her adorable chin.

At that moment, however, he was finding it easy *not* to adore her. He could finally resist the irresistible Miranda Bright, who'd brought doom upon both their heads. He wasn't sure she realized exactly what she'd done.

Philip merely gestured with his hand, indicating she should carry on.

"Each month's column would dedicate itself entirely to a single couple from *your* world of the titled and privileged. Their names would be left out of course, but the magazine would include little sketches. A perfect likeness of those they discussed. Can you imagine? How precious!"

"Precious," he repeated softly, imagining the horror of an illustration of himself on the page when damning words were bad enough. And worse, what if he found his likeness linked to a lady he didn't really care for, such as Miss Waltham. He shuddered.

"*Town and Country* gave a detailed summary of each couple's amorous activities," she continued, "and all their questionable behavior. But it is widely understood those discussed within the *Tête-à-Tête* were flattered."

He was sure his expression had turned sickly, and he was probably a distinct shade of green.

What a nightmare that publication must have been! Every last one should be found and burned.

"And you're sure it is no longer published?" he asked with a note of dread that she didn't catch.

"Sadly, it is not, but my cousins and I spent many hours trying to work out exactly to whom the articles were referring. Since they were twenty-year old magazines, for us it was like a riddle. But I understand the old coffeehouses of London would bustle with people reading about the month's featured couple."

A rake's nightmare, he thought, *and a busybody's dream!* He could imagine how the lickspittles would rattle on, ever more gleeful when they could actually see a sketch of the hapless pair. He supposed the answer was to live a life of angelic morality. *Impossible!*

"At any rate, my novel is nothing like your *Female Tatler,* nor even those intriguing magazines—" she began.

"Only because you all but named our names."

"The entire compilation was an accident," she protested. "At first, I merely wrote letters to my dear cousins, and then Lady Harriet pressed me to turn it all into a real book."

Philip shook his head, unable to believe he'd heard her correctly. He stared at the book in his hand, thinking of the damage it had done and would continue to do.

"Lady Harriet knew about this?"

"Yes," Miranda said. "She suggested it. She invited me to her home the first week after you started escorting me. We were speaking about family. Naturally, I mentioned my cousins and that led to a brief discussion of how I write letters to keep them amused." She broke off at his thunderous expression.

"Hold your tongue," he ordered and thumbed through the book, every damnable, cursed page. Finally, he looked at her again.

"Yet Harriet Beaumont is not in this . . . this compilation of horse dung."

Miranda's mouth dropped open. "That is not very nice. I know it has not the caliber of Miss Austen, but it's hardly dung!"

"Fine!" Philip spat out. "The story of a young woman's Season is passingly good. It has the style of a very abbreviated version of Fielding's *Tom Jones.* Yet why doesn't Lady Harriet grace its literary pages?"

"Because she said her family doesn't need the fame nor find it agreeable the way others do." Quieting, she considered her own words while her verdant hazel eyes grew larger.

"Now that I say it to you, it sounds implausible. But she has been so kind and given me advice on who and what to write about. She is my patron." Miranda lifted her chin. "She paid for the printing and distribution. After all that, you see I couldn't put her in unless she wished it."

Philip was beginning to see clearly as through a crystal ball. Tossing the volume onto the sofa, he walked to the window overlooking her uncle's modest acreage.

"She knew I was escorting you. She knew you would tell your cousins about me. And she probably even added a few juicy morsels, I'll warrant."

He turned at her silence. By the color of her cheeks, he would say he'd hit the nail firmly with the hammer.

"I am truly sorry," she said. "I would not hurt you for the world. In fact, if I may tell you the truth of what I am feeling—"

"The truth!" Fury rose like bile in his throat. "I think you should keep your feelings to yourself. You have already laid bare quite enough, and I for one don't think I can stomach any more."

MIRANDA LOOKED DOWN AT the book.

She'd been naïve. Lady Harriet's friendship had occurred quickly, practically overnight. She recalled wondering at the kindness of the flurry of invitations, and only now realized she'd been spoon-fed stories and suggestions like a baby with its first slip-slops.

Having thought she was figuring out the *ton* and their ways, in truth, she'd been made a fool of. Worst of all, she'd betrayed Philip.

"I'm terribly sorry."

Philip shook his head. "It's too late for that. I think it's too late to salvage anything now. I need to send a courier to London to determine the damage."

With that, he stormed from the room.

He was not going to forgive her. After he left Northampton, he would probably never speak to her again. *How could she bear it when she loved him?* And this on the heels of having decided to go back with Philip to London, even knowing how it would have bruised her heart to be near him when he didn't return her love.

Should she try again to tell him of those feelings?

Chewing her bottom lip, Miranda decided it would make little difference. Trying to express the fullness of her heart's emotions had only infuriated him further.

When Aunt Lucinda came back, Miranda would return home and face whatever consequences there might be.

Retiring to her room, she saw no one until dinner. Her aunt and uncle knew something was going on, but only Helen had read any of the pages upon the book's arrival. Her cousin's wide-eyed stare of shock had made Miranda's stomach churn. With her anonymity stripped away, everything that had seemed amusing was now simply vulgar.

If this was how she felt with family, how terrible would it be to encounter those who did not care for her. Miranda could hardly bear the humiliation.

Wearing a bleak expression at dinner, Philip made little effort to be congenial, leaving her uncle and Peter to carry the conversation. After the debacle of the book, the good news of the crutches barely raised Miranda's spirits, and Helen, too, remained subdued.

When her aunt switched to the topic of *Glenarvon*, a recently published novel by Lady Caroline Lamb, Miranda thought she would jump out of her skin. A satirical political tale, it was Lamb's cruel and bitter depiction of Lord Byron, her ex-lover, that had caused the greatest stir.

"*Glenarvon* has raised many an eyebrow and set tongues to wagging all over London!" her aunt said, echoing Miranda's words.

"Not just London," her uncle added, giving a hint he cared for gossip a little more than he let on. "It's a sensation in Dublin and Edinburgh, too."

"The stir is just reaching us," her aunt said. "I have told my husband we must get the Town papers again. We miss far too much."

The parallel was not lost upon Miranda, nor on Philip. Experiencing his dagger-filled glance, she wished the floor would open and let her fall through. As it was, she shrank farther into her seat.

Hunching over her plate so she didn't have to make eye contact with anyone else, Miranda hurried through her meal and excused herself before the dessert. No one objected since she'd been such poor company.

Choked by sorrow at how thoroughly she'd strayed from good sense, she buried her head under her pillow and didn't get out of bed for the remainder of the evening.

When it was barely light outside and the house was still silent, she crept downstairs to retrieve her copy of the book Lady Harriet had sent, having not received Miranda's letter in time to stop the publication.

After thinking about it, and watching Philip's reaction, she had a feeling Lady Harriet would not have called off the printing anyway. Miranda had been bamboozled!

However, the book had vanished, and she sat on the sofa with only her aunt's cats for company, feeling numb and more than a little afraid of what her father would say. If he'd sent Philip to fetch her upon seeing the mild few lines in *The Times*, what would he say upon seeing her book?

Drawing her knees up under her, she could only pray he never got his hands on one of the limited copies. After all, Lady Harriet was in charge of dispensing them to members of the *ton*. Why would a magistrate end up with one?

Feeling a little better, she decided to go along to the kitchen and make herself a cup of tea as if she were at home when she heard horse's hooves. For an instant, she thought Aunt Lucinda might have returned early, but the sound was of a single rider, not a carriage. Pulling the curtain back, she looked out. To her astonishment, Philip, who was up and already fully dressed at this early hour, strode out to meet whomever had arrived.

After the man dismounted, their meeting was brief and then the rider went to the stables with his horse. When Philip turned toward the house, Miranda would swear he'd seen her at the window, and she hastily let the curtain fall back into place.

Sure enough, in less than two minutes, he found her in the parlor.

"The news from London is worse than I thought. It's all anyone can talk about from the men's clubs to the ladies' salons. As my friend said, and I quote, 'It's beyond any previous scandal.'"

Philip paced the room. "And the book is not even available yet, except a few copies sent to choice recipients and then a handful of select quotations given to all the papers. Lady Harriet has had her revenge upon me and taken you and a number of others down as well."

"I sent her a letter to stop the book, but I was too late," Miranda disclosed, but then the import of his words struck her. "Why would she seek revenge against you?"

He looked away, looked back, blinked, then sighed.

"I had a brief dalliance with her once."

"No!" Miranda said, not sure why it bothered her immensely. Yet thinking of the earl's daughter's beauty and assuredness, it definitely did. "Why didn't you tell me?"

"For the same reason I don't discuss Miss Waltham or any other young lady. It's not done."

"If you had disclosed something about this, I might not have walked blindly into trouble. The entire island of Britain might not be privy to my Season's gadabouts had I known the truth about the one person who was counseling me as to what a grand idea this was."

Clenching her fists with frustration, Miranda added, "While being a gentleman regarding Lady Harriet, I assure you she was not behaving as a lady in the same honorable terms."

"I understand that now," he agreed. "But you should have known better."

"In retrospect, yes, I should have. I should somehow have realized she was only creating a bond with me, a nobody, in order to penetrate *your* shield. If I'd suspected such, I would have shown more caution. As you know, I am not entirely unaware of how the world works." She was pacing the way she'd seen him do in the past. Stopping herself, she came to stand before him.

"Now the damage has been done, why don't you break that irrational code of honor that allows you to behave like a rake while keeping as discreet as a priest and tell me why Lady Harriet sought her revenge through me?"

"Very well. She was displeased with the way our association concluded."

Miranda's imagination took flight immediately.

"Is that all you will tell me?"

He put his hand upon his hips and leaned down toward her. "She did not want it to end. Ask me why."

Miranda swallowed. He was close enough she could count his eyelashes. "Why?"

"Because I am an excellent lover," he whispered.

She trembled, knowing he spoke the truth. Then he straightened.

"All that balderdash about being one of the first and finest families! She pretends she's waiting for an earl or a duke—*ha!* She was ready and willing to fling her skirts over her head for a baron," he fumed.

Miranda took a step back.

"My apologies," he said. "I am furious at how many people she has dragged into this, including you. And for what? Merely for pure spite because she could."

"Because I let her," Miranda said.

She lowered her head, noticing for the first time how ugly the parlor carpet was in her opinion. Surely that was why she felt tears well up and why her insides ached wretchedly.

She couldn't imagine what would happen now. Philip would be forced to marry Miss Waltham or lose his brandy and his hope to rebuild his fortune. Her father would be apoplectic and probably banish her forever, maybe to live here with her cousins or with her sister, if she would have her.

With her thoughts running wildly and noisily in her head, Miranda barely heard his next words until they had hung in the air between them for a few moments.

"There is nothing else for it," he declared, "but to get married!"

CHAPTER TWENTY-ONE

Miranda lifted her gaze to meet his rich brown, serious stare.

"Married!" *What was he saying?*

"Yes, and immediately! Even as curious eyes are reading this frightful tome and my brandy casks are being rolled into the Channel."

"Immediately!" she echoed.

"Stop repeating words. It's getting on my nerves."

"Who will you marry?" Miranda could only imagine it must be Miss Waltham. It would go a long way to soothing Lord Perrin and the lady's uncle, not to mention lifting Philip from the dregs of hedonistic rakishness to the pinnacle of respectable society. He would do the right thing by a woman whom everyone thought he'd led down the garden path.

"Sometimes, Miss Bright, you seem so incredibly buffle-headed, I wonder how you get out of bed in the morning."

Now that was cruel! And unnecessary. Miranda swallowed the lump of tears and fanned her face with her hands.

He continued to stare at her.

"I am warm," she explained. At least she'd kept her tears at bay. "Despite my density of mind, I wish you a happy marriage. If you want to leave early, I shall say your goodbyes later to my family. Meanwhile, the servants are up and will help you prepare to depart."

"We must *both* prepare to depart. I can't very well get married by myself."

Miranda blinked at him. The implications were starting to become clear, but she would hate to jump to any conclusion and thereby be labeled even more of a fool.

"Will you speak plainly, my lord?"

"I thought I was. You and I must marry as soon as possible. We'll leave at once for Scotland."

"Scotland!" She'd heard of such an adventure but never, ever considered she would be involved in the long carriage ride across the border to a hasty, pagan ceremony.

"There you go repeating things again. Do you know of any easier way to get married without waiting three weeks?"

"No, I don't believe there is one," she said. "Unless you have a close friendship with an archbishop."

He smiled at her for the first time since he'd looked at her book. "Holy men and I don't generally travel in the same circles."

His gaze, still grave, held hers. "What do you say, Miss Bright? Shall we stop tongues wagging now and forever by marrying?"

That wasn't the best reason she'd ever heard, but it seemed suitable enough for a rake tired of disgrace and who hoped to salvage a legitimate brandy business.

She nodded, then reconsidered. "What about my father?"

"I am sure he'll be delighted. Far more than having a defiled daughter return to Town with her tail between her legs, the gaping-stock and laughing-stock of London. Besides, wasn't this entire arrangement designed to get you married off? Additionally, we'll save him the cost of a wedding."

"How practical," she said softly. "Yet he might feel disrespected if you don't ask him personally for my hand. I recall my sister's suitor coming to our home and being secured in my father's study with him for at least half an hour as they worked out all the details of the marriage contract. And there was her dowry to negotiate."

"I can practically guarantee your father will not give us permission. If he didn't think I was unsuitable before, he does now. What's more, I'm not interested in your dowry," he said and turned toward the door with her following closely behind.

Then he paused, and Miranda walked into him.

"Although, I shouldn't be hasty," Philip added. "Given my current financial situation, your dowry might come in handy if you have one. Do you?"

She nodded, wondering whether she'd fallen asleep on her aunt's sofa and this was all a dream.

"Good, then we won't be begging for farthings out of Newgate, at least for the first fortnight."

Had she really made him penniless?

"Come now," he said, putting a hand to her chin and tilting her head to look at him. "Don't appear as if I'm dragging you to your execution. You could do far worse than me, I warrant. I shall rally my fortunes, even if I cannot keep my London home."

"I could do worse," Miranda agreed.

He barked out a laugh. "What a glowing recommendation from my bride-to-be!"

While she was still wrangling with the tremor of excitement over that unexpected word, *bride*, he slipped his hands into her hair, anchoring her face before him.

Then he lowered his head, but instead of claiming her mouth, he trailed kisses along her chin and down her neck, and she quickly forgot everything except how her body sizzled from his touch.

Philip raised his head. "In some ways, we are a perfect pair."

Feeling light-headed, she had needed no reminding and, thus, said nothing. He shrugged.

"How quickly can you pack a few items to carry you over a night or two? We shall leave as soon as you're ready, but no longer than ten minutes. We must be away before the household gets up. Your aunt and uncle will try to stop you elsewise."

"What about Aunt Lucinda? She's not yet back. I can hardly go without a chaperone."

Philip rolled his eyes.

"I'm afraid you cannot bring anyone with you. That's *not* how Gretna Green is done."

"I know that! I'm twitterpated by all this, that's all. May I at least say goodbye to Helen?"

She was still stunned at the turn of events, and by her own meekness in going along with his outlandish plan. *Would he let her say no?* She couldn't decide if Philip was doing this strictly for his own sake or also for hers. But while this wasn't how she had ever pictured an engagement to be, she was honest enough with herself to admit she wanted to marry him nonetheless.

Apart from the rather consequential flaw of being a thundering buck, he was everything she'd ever dreamed of in a husband.

"Even your cousin may try to stop us, especially after reading that tell-all tale," he said. "I think you should do as I say and tell no one."

"Helen likes you very much, as does Peter. You've been extremely kind to them." She considered everything he'd done. "You are truly a gentle man."

She thought she detected the hint of a ruddy blush creeping up his face. Before she could be certain, however, he had hold of her arm and was tugging her toward the staircase.

"Hurry. We need to reach the blacksmith's shop by sunset tomorrow."

"Why?" she asked, rushing up the steps beside him.

"Because he's the one who shall marry us, and he closes when the sun goes down."

Miranda faltered, then regained her footing and caught up with him.

"Of course," she muttered. Why she had supposed it would be a quaint Scottish vicar who would preside over her wedding, she couldn't say.

The blacksmith! Her father was a reasonable and lenient man, but this might push him a step too far.

⌒⌒

FROM THE CONFINES OF Philip's well-sprung traveling coach, Miranda stared out the window at the passing landscape. There was little to break up the monotony outside the carriage, and within, there was only tense silence as they went up and down the occasional small hill. She let her thoughts drift to what awaited her at the end of their journey.

Since they'd started so early, Philip was confident they would reach their destination in time to perform the desired feat late the following day. And as it turned out, they didn't have to marry at the blacksmith's. There was also a perfectly satisfactory King's Head Inn nearby, where a man did nothing but weddings all day long. They'd discovered this interesting tidbit when stopping at a reputable coaching inn about two hours into their journey and a kind barmaid asked if they were headed to Gretna Green.

"We are over twenty hours away," Miranda pointed out. "How on earth did she know?"

"It must be the desperate expression you are wearing and my own dashing good looks. She imagines you to be a wealthy heiress and I, a fortune-seeking cur, manipulating you into marriage."

Miranda rolled her eyes. It was the only barely good-humored thing he'd said since leaving her aunt and uncle's home. For her part, she'd left a note on her bed addressed to Helen to explain how Lord Mercer thought this the best course of action to recover her reputation. She ought to be grateful, but she did, in fact, feel manipulated.

On the way, they would have to stay at an inn, and Miranda considered how that alone sealed her fate. Even if she wanted to change her mind, she would not be able to afterward, despite having separate rooms.

At least, she assumed they would each have a room. It would be egregious not to wait to share a bed until they were lawfully wedded after managing to avoid fornicating for what felt like an eternity.

As expected, after a long day of travelling with many stops, sometimes to let the horses rest but thrice to change them out altogether at great expense, they arrived at a large well-lit coaching inn where other north-and-south bound travelers were taking their ease. The public room was crowded, but Philip secured them a single room under the name of Mr. and Mrs. Thomas.

Miranda followed the owner's daughter up the stairs to her utter ruin.

And then they were alone.

"We were lucky to get this room, my lambkin. I couldn't face going back out on the road at this hour, could you?" Philip asked.

"Lambkin?" she repeated, standing stiffly in the center of the modest chamber.

"I was trying out a fond nickname for my soon-to-be wife. You don't like it?"

"Not particularly." Just hearing her given name from his lips would demonstrate a level of fondness she hoped would presently be surpassed by his love. In case she had neglected to in the past, she now gave him permission.

"You may call me Miranda, if you wish."

He grinned in that sensual way which made her toes curl and her body start to throb instantly.

"Miranda," he tried it out. "Now it feels like we are as close as family."

She didn't point out that they had previously been closer, unclothed and pressed together. When they were wedded, they *would* be family, although he would have all the freedom in their marriage to do as he pleased. She knew this and tamped down the fear that he would make a fool of her.

"We are fortunate no one knows who you are," she said.

"A good reason not to emblazon a family coat of arms on one's carriage," he remarked.

She couldn't tell whether he was joking, and decided he wasn't. A rake probably needed to maintain anonymity if he was dallying with another man's wife. And if he was stealing away with a woman not yet twenty-one without her father's permission, all the better.

"When your book spreads across our fair kingdom as it most certainly will, then I imagine we shall both be infamous from Land's End to John O'Groats, just like Lady Caroline Lamb," Philip said. "My friend sent word back that your book is extraordinarily sought after, although as yet unavailable, neither for love nor money. Thus, we can expect by the time we head back to London, we will find ourselves known even on the outskirts of Town."

Miranda hoped he was wrong and her mortification wouldn't spread past the boundaries of London and its outskirts, perhaps as far as Twickenham to the west, Greenwich to the east, Croydon to the south, and Wood Green to the north.

"Undeniably, I shall forever be known as the hell-born blood who ruined Lord Perrin's daughter and lost his family's fortune, who then followed up by running off with a magistrate's youngest lass. All the more fool me, as they say. The wolf betrayed by the lamb."

He was never going to forgive her, she knew.

"Don't look so morose," Philip added. "I am in a tweague to be sure, but can you blame me? I'll let it go for now. My stomach is grumbling, and my coachman is probably already having a good meal. We should do the same."

"Down there?" She considered the lively crowd, thinking everyone would know her to be an unwedded female running for the border, just as the barmaid had done earlier in the day.

"There will be a private dining area for those who can afford to pay. We still can. It won't be empty, but it won't be as full as the tap-room either. Or I can have a meal sent up here."

"Let's go down," she said quickly. "We've been cooped up like the queen's songbirds all day. Perhaps we could take a stroll around the inn after we eat."

"You don't mind being seen with me?" he jested.

Miranda shrugged. "You are my pretend husband tonight, Mr. Thomas, and by this time tomorrow, my actual one. As long as you can procure a lantern."

"Afraid of the dark?" he asked, escorting her downstairs.

"Afraid of spiders in the dark," she said.

"Ah, yes, our downfall at Brentford." The baron sounded irritated again with the reminder of why she'd toppled their boat. "I read the entire book last night in my room. You have quite a talent for writing both the dramatic and the sensual."

Wincing, she vowed to try her best not to remind him of her foolishness again.

PHILIP COULDN'T SHAKE OFF the mantle of anger that had settled over him when first he'd learned of the book that would take everything from him—both his freedom and his attempt to regain his fortune. After reading it the previous night, he'd realized Miranda would be unable to return home if she wasn't a wedded wife.

The protection of his name didn't put her beyond reproach, but their marrying diffused the notion she was a loose woman, willing to allow her own ruin. Instead, it would confirm the notion she was one of the *incomparables*, a tamer of a notorious rake.

And with any luck, marrying her would keep her father from creating a reason to toss him into Newgate jail.

Regardless, he couldn't help the occasional harsh remark or jab at his hapless fiancée. She had betrayed him to the core. Philip vowed to make an effort to recall how much he had enjoyed her company and how perfectly they'd pleasured one another. There was no reason to believe they wouldn't have happiness in the bedroom, and that, he hoped, would lead to a happy home.

It simply had to!

He had waited too bloody long to take a wife only to think he might be saddled with a colossal mistake.

Anger and hope had kept him company during the journey. Those emotions were undoubtedly responsible for locking them each in their own solitude for the past many hours, with neither knowing what the other was thinking. Philip was unable to reach out and ask her what was on her mind. Not yet, not while his own thoughts and feelings were still in turmoil.

Luckily, they found seats in the small dining room set aside for quality folks and for women traveling alone.

When wine and potato stew and roast chicken were brought, Miranda perked up a bit from the deflated creature she'd become.

"I hope you enjoy it and the room," he said. "Our trip is already costly. Even without this room and board, I believe I'm spending about three shillings per mile, when you add up all the breaks and horse changes."

Silently, she stared with her small elation at the meal dashed, and Philip remembered his manners.

"My apologies. I should not be speaking of expenses, not when we're on such a somber trip." Yet she alone understood his increasingly dire financial circumstances.

"Weddings are not supposed to be somber," she said softly.

He ignored her, not about to pretend they were gaily riding toward a marriage they'd both willingly chosen.

"We're fortunate I came away from Town with a goodly amount of coin," he added, since London bank notes were nearly useless outside the city. Sipping his wine, he vowed to stop obsessing over the cost of everything. It was difficult, however, knowing when he returned home, he would have to announce the sale of the Mercer country estate and then the London house shortly after.

"You may continue speaking frankly," she offered. "I am not uninterested in the expenses, especially since I have caused this one. I believe having saved most of my modest allowance since my fourteenth year, I can pay half."

Philip lowered his glass. He had never expected her to say anything of the sort, nor could he imagine any woman of his acquaintance offering assistance. It was as if she intended to be his true partner in life.

"The marriage price can be rather dear. These border Scots know they have us by the short-hairs."

'The short-hairs, my lord?" She'd paused with a forkful of chicken halfway to her lovely lips.

"Never mind. If it costs half a guinea or fifty pounds, it shall be worth it."

"I hope it's closer to half a guinea," she said, "unless they provide a wedding breakfast."

Philip realized she was making a joke. *Bless her heart!* If she could take this in stride, he could as well.

Besides, he was about to spend the night in the same room with her. Surely that should make him happy. *Then why was he dreading going back upstairs?*

He knew why—given all that had transpired recently, he did not want her to believe him incapable of behaving like a true gentleman. And being alone with her, given how much he had longed to tup her for weeks, the temptation would be great to behave badly.

When their dinner was at an end, he asked, "Shall we see if they have decent brandy?"

She shook her head.

"Would you like to play at cards?" he suggested, thinking of ways to put off retiring.

"No, thank you."

"What about that walk you desired?"

Miranda rose to her feet. "I confess I am exhausted. As we shall rise early, I wonder at your reluctance to go to sleep."

Reluctance to go to bed was more accurate, but he jumped to his feet and escorted her upstairs.

CHAPTER TWENTY-TWO

C losing the door behind them, Philip surveyed the size of their accommodations. The room seemed to have shrunk greatly, especially as she was removing her spencer. Then she sat upon the bed to take off her ankle-high shoes.

"Shall I step outside while you undress?" he offered.

Her glance fell sharply upon him. "I have taken off everything I intend to." Then she rose again. Walking in her stocking feet to the washstand, she used the cold water and cheap cake of soap to wash her hands and face.

The only clue she wasn't as calm as she appeared was when she began to feel around the area with her eyes closed having forgotten to take note of the drying cloth.

Quickly, he stepped forward and yanked the small piece of clean cotton from the hook, pressing it into her hands.

"Thank you," she mumbled into the cloth, then patted her face dry. "That feels a little better. I brought tooth-powder, too."

Philip watched while she retrieved a toothbrush and tooth-powders from her small leather satchel, as if this were an entirely normal occurrence to be performing one's ablutions in the company of a stranger. With clean water from the pitcher poured over the bristles, she dipped her toothbrush into the tin case of powder before using it to freshen her mouth.

He knew he oughtn't to be staring, but he'd never seen another person doing these things, at least not a soft female, only a few fellow officers in the confines of a tent. His heart squeezed to see her in such a personal moment.

"Frankly, I am rather surprised at your willingness to stay in this room with me," he blurted.

She shook her toothbrush with a few quick flicks of her wrist and put it away, leaving the powder tin on the small washstand.

"You may use the tooth-powder if you have none of your own. I wouldn't want a husband to lose his teeth because I wouldn't share."

Miranda was making light again. And the more normally she behaved, even generous with her silly tooth-powder, the more attractive she became. If she'd been in a great and terrible snit while raging over her fate, then he would have felt resentment and even despised her just a little.

Instead, he wished to strip her down before sweeping her onto the bed and under his body, so he could pleasure her until she cried out his name. He was puzzled at how much he still wanted to do that when she'd caused the very chain of events he'd been trying to avoid with Miss Waltham.

In any case, he would refrain from touching her until she invited him. And by her sleeping fully dressed except for her shoes, she was definitely not offering an invitation.

Lying down as close to the edge of the bed as seemed possible without her tumbling off, she settled her head upon the pillow, arms crossed over her middle, and stared at the ceiling, eyes open.

Philip couldn't help it. He laughed.

Without sitting up, she asked, "And what do you find funny about our situation?"

"Nothing, I assure you. But I beg you to make yourself more comfortable. I promise not to pounce like a cat upon a mouse."

"I am perfectly comfortable," she said, wriggling around slightly.

Sighing, he went about his own ministrations, undressing to his small clothes, washing his face, and brushing his teeth, all the while feeling her gaze upon him. When he lifted the counterpane and slid under, she tensed.

"Ahh," he said. "It is good to lie down, is it not?"

"Yes," she said stiffly.

"What if you grow cold? There are no spare blankets with which I can cover you. You should get under the covers. I can feel the air cooling already."

"I am fine," Miranda said. "But you forgot to put out the lamp."

"I left it on for you, thinking you would sleep more easily if you could see your surroundings."

"Ridiculous," she said. "My eyes will be firmly closed, as will yours. At least, that is how I sleep."

He got up brought the lamp to the table on his side of the bed. Once under the covers again, he doused it, shrouding the room in darkness.

"Good night, Miss Bright."

"Good night, Lord Major Mercer."

WHEN THEY'D PAID THE last toll before the Scottish border and then crossed the River Sark over a small bridge, Miranda put her head back and closed her eyes. She was sick of the coach, the jostling, the boredom, and her own terrible reproachful thoughts.

Finally, they were minutes away from being married!

Her insides quaked with the enormity of what she was doing. By mid-morning the day before, her aunt and uncle would have sent word back to London, and her father would have learned of her choice.

The previous night, she'd lain awake despite her tiredness. Knowing Philip's warm and powerful body was inches away, she'd been distracted. Where he'd touched her before, she pulsated simply from his presence and from hearing his steady breathing.

The wayward part of her had considered stripping off and quenching her longing for him, letting him douse the blaze he'd ignited when from their first kiss. It wasn't as if they wouldn't be performing the marital act the following night after they were lawfully wedded, even if it was a chancy Scottish ceremony.

However, since he hadn't offered, she'd steeled herself against appearing desperately depraved.

Unfortunately, Philip had been right—she *was* uncomfortable. Her dress bunched up under her back and her skirts rucked up and twisted. Yet she made herself lie still to keep him unaware of her discomfort. Eventually, she must have fallen asleep for when she awakened at earliest light, he had flipped his half of the counterpane over her.

More a gentleman than a rake just when she would have enjoyed the scandalous, sensual facets of his nature.

"We shall go to the inn first," he said, breaking into her thoughts. "Mayhap we can wed there and spend the last hour before sunset strolling the village as a married—"

The coach lurched to one side and stopped at an angle.

"What the devil?" Philip asked, pushing open the door on his side, which was higher, while Miranda had been thrown against her side of the carriage.

"Wait here," he said, which she'd fully intended to do since her right shoulder was awkwardly pressed against the door and her cheek flattened on the window.

He climbed out. "Blast it all!" she heard him swear.

The next minute, he peered in.

"It will take longer than we've got to fix the wheel. Bloody decrepit roads! Where are the Romans when you need them? Come along, Miss Bright. We shall have to walk the rest of the way. Are you game?"

"Yes," she answered softly. There was no point in not being game anymore.

Lifting her hand toward him, Philip reached in and hauled her out like the last herring in a brine barrel.

"Shall we bring anything?" she asked when he had her upright on her own two feet.

"No, my coachman will keep watch over our bags, and he is well-armed. Eventually, he'll find us in the village." He patted his pockets. "I've got money and my gloves."

"I've got my reticule. Is my bonnet still tidy?"

Hurriedly, he glanced her way, but when she caught his eye, he paused and really looked at her. Finally, he said, "Let me assist."

With that, the baron straightened her bonnet and retied her bow. When he'd finished, he nodded at his handiwork.

"As well done as any lady's maid, I dare say."

She smiled. "Then I am ready."

He offered her his arm, which she took, and they proceeded along the main road, which went from Carlisle on the English side all the way up to Glasgow many miles north. And of course, just a little way on, a few hundred yards, was the small village of Gretna Green. A cluster of clay houses met Miranda's gaze.

But they turned right onto a footpath with a sign toward Springfield.

"I don't understand," she said, hurrying to keep up as the sun was dropping quickly toward the horizon, and Philip increased his pace.

"I think the inn up ahead is closer than the blacksmith's at the Headlesscross."

"The what?" she asked.

"Where the five roads meet in Gretna Green."

Before she could ask anymore, a collection of buildings that didn't amount to enough even to warrant the designation of a village came into view. With only one large structure, the white-washed, two-story inn proclaimed itself "The King's Head" by its sign. Apparently, thirty paces from the road, they'd arrived in Springfield.

Miranda had expected something a little merrier, but the inn had no flowers, nor a blade of grass out front, not even a shrub or a tree. The only welcoming signal was the smoke pouring out of its two chimneys, one on either end of the roof.

"It's not as pretty as last night's inn," she pointed out.

Regardless, Philip didn't hesitate to draw her toward the single door between two sash windows with three more over the top.

"We'll try here first," Philip said. "I have no doubt I shall be able to hire a wainwright and send him back to fix our carriage."

Inside the hostelry, however, they were met with disappointing news.

"A wainwright I can send to your coach, and no problem," said the manager, a middle-aged man who was as round as he was tall. "I even have a nice room with a good view of the Solway for your night's stay, but our anvil priest, as we call him, Mr. Elliot, has already left. You missed him by a quarter of an hour."

"The devil!" Philip muttered. Then he looked at the man again. "Can't you perform the ceremony, such as it is?"

The manager's cheeks reddened. "That's not the way we do things in Scotland."

Philip sighed with exasperation. "That is exactly the way you do things in Scotland, my good man. That's why we've come."

Miranda waited for the man to be insulted, but instead he began to laugh. He laughed so hard he had to wipe his eyes on a handkerchief he pulled from his sleeve.

"You've got me there, sir, and no mistake. But I mean to say is we have an understanding here in Springfield and with the next village over, Gretna Green, as to who will do the honors and who takes the money, and then—"

"We have no time for the entire workings of this dodgy arrangement," Philip said. "Will the blacksmith still be open?"

The inn's manager made a great show of looking out the window and then even lugging his impressive girth outside to stare west toward Bowness and beyond where the River Esk spilled out into bay known as the Solway Firth.

Finally, he proclaimed, "The sun be going down fast."

"Blast it all, man! We know that," Philip said.

Miranda couldn't help the nervous laugh that escaped her.

"You'd best hurry then," the manager said. "You don't have to go back on the path, just go up that way and then take the first turning."

Philip was already tugging her along. "We can see it from here," he snapped. "It's less than half a mile. I don't even know why you call it another village!"

"Thank you," Miranda called behind her. After all, they might be spending the night in that establishment, graceless as it was, and she didn't want to be given soiled sheets for her baron's churlishness.

"I'm sorry about this," Philip said, striding even more quickly than before.

Miranda's legs were pumping to keep up, and she feared her bonnet would be askew once again. It didn't take long for them to run up the road and take a left since there was no right.

At last, they headed toward the long, low building with large open doors and a thatched roof at the crossroads. It had to be the entrance to the blacksmith's.

A spotted hound was lying outside, looking content. It lifted its head as they approached.

"Hail," Philip called out while they were yards away.

A man stepped out, a tankard of ale in one hand, wearing a stained leather apron. They came to a halt in front of him, both breathing hard. Miranda thought her heart would pound out of her chest, as she bent over gasping and noticing how filthy her shoes had become.

"Will you marry us?" Philip asked without preamble.

At first the man said nothing. Then he lifted his ale. "Finished for the day," he said.

"If it's a question of cost, I shall pay double your normal rate," Philip added.

The man's eyes flicked over him and then over Miranda.

"Suppose I can do one more. Need two witnesses though."

Philip exclaimed in frustration.

"We've got the dog for one," he said, only half-joking.

The blacksmith shook his head. "That'll never do, Lord Mercer."

Miranda gasped while Philip cocked his head. "How do you know my name?"

"Because *I* told him," said a second, all-too familiar voice.

With disbelieving eyes, Miranda watched her father come out from the dark interior of the blacksmith's shop.

"Greetings, dear daughter."

CHAPTER TWENTY-THREE

"Papa!" she exclaimed.

Philip's blood chilled as if he'd been plunged into the sea. The magistrate must have raced like the devil himself to beat them, and he couldn't have slept a wink in the past two days.

Surprisingly, as if she had no fear of recrimination, Miranda ran into her father's arms.

Sir William encircled his daughter in a bear hug. Looking over her head at Philip, he said, "A mangy dog as witness? Truly?"

Philip shrugged. "Improvising, sir, as I would on the field of battle."

The magistrate shook his head. Then he pried his daughter from him, holding her by her forearms so he could look into her eyes.

"Do you want to marry this blasted prig?"

"I say, I have never cheated anyone in my life," Philip protested the insult.

Sir William glared at him.

"Tell me, Miranda, is this sorry cur, this slippery, niffy-naffy rascal the person to whom you wish to be joined in wedlock?"

Philip was only pleased the magistrate hadn't called him something worse. It would be a difficult start if his father-in-law thought him a shoddy fellow. All three men awaited Miranda's answer, no one more eagerly than Philip.

"It seems to be the wisest course of action, Papa, given the terrible mistake I've made. You see, I wrote a—"

"A book. I know it well. It seems I cannot turn around without a courier delivering more unwelcome news about you. First *The Times*, then the book, then the missive from my sister-in-law of your elopement."

Philip watched Miranda pale, undoubtedly at the notion of her father reading the literary telltale, even if the magistrate didn't know all of the thinly disguised characters.

Miranda glanced at Philip. He nodded, hoping that gave her some reassurance. She looked at her father again.

"Given the book, his lordship and I thought a speedy marriage to be the best course of action," she finished. "Did you come to stop us?"

"I came to make sure you weren't being forced into something. Just because I want you married, that doesn't mean I wish you to marry any old swell."

"Lord Mercer is not any old swell," she said.

Philip appreciated her standing up for him. However, when she opened her mouth again, he wished she would stop at what she'd already said.

"It's true he's been in too many gossip columns with too many young ladies."

Philip winced.

"But I have also seen him perform acts of kindness, even recently toward cousin Peter. I think I shall, at least, not be beaten."

"Beaten?" Philip spluttered. "Of course you won't! I do not hold with those who strike a woman. I am an officer and a gentleman, and in my upbringing, neither of those afforded room for tormenting the weaker sex."

"What about her allowance?" Sir William asked. "I intend to provide a dowry, but I vow it should belong to her to spend on whatever she needs, particularly if you turn out to be a miser."

Philip wisely knew it was best not to mention how they might need her allowance to live on until he could recoup his losses.

"Miss Bright may spend her money how she sees fit," he promised.

Although if she wanted to eat, she might see fit to spend it on the butcher, the baker, and the green grocer, Philip thought. Again, he knew better than to say it.

Her father dropped his hands from her arms.

"Then I shall not stand in the way, and there's only one thing left to do."

Philip nodded and looked to the blacksmith who'd downed the rest of his ale while listening to the small drama play out before him.

"Yes," the magistrate said, and he swept his daughter to the side and took a step toward Philip. "I must give you a sound thrashing for ruining my daughter. We'll start with a blow to your lying mouth," he said, "and then a good plump in your breadbasket."

"Papa!" Miranda said. "Please do not resort to violence."

"This is about your honor," Sir William said. "I told him to keep your reputation pure, but he has already milked the cow if I'm not mistaken."

Miranda's cheeks went red as an apple.

"No, sir," Philip protested. "We have not done what you fear."

"You haven't shared a bed?"

"Papa," she moaned out an embarrassed protest.

The blacksmith turned heel and went inside. Even the dog disappeared, perhaps not wanting to be party to this mortifying discussion.

Philip stood his ground. "We have not."

"Last night?" Sir William asked.

"Oh." Philip had not forgotten the inn, yet he hardly thought that was what the magistrate meant. "We did share a bed since the inn was otherwise full, but your daughter stayed fully dressed and lay atop the counterpane."

The man's eyes grew larger. Then he looked around at his daughter.

"Did you truly?"

"Yes, Papa."

"And this cur didn't touch you?"

"No, Papa."

The magistrate turned to Philip again. Stepping forward, he reached out, and Philip flinched ever so slightly, feeling foolish when all the man did was slap his shoulder.

"I never thought I would say thank you to a rake for his honorable actions," Sir William said, "but I'm sure her mother, bless her soul, would be pleased."

Before Philip could digest this compliment, the closing of one half of the shop doors indicated the blacksmith was about to end his day.

"I suppose we don't have to hurry now that we know you are not trying to stop us," Philip said.

Did his bride want to delay for a nicer venue?

"Now we don't have to rush if you wish to wait for Mr. Elliot tomorrow at the inn or even try the vicar at the local parish church," Philip offered.

Miranda opened her mouth, but her father spoke first.

"She'll marry now and not a minute later. Just because you didn't sin last night does not forgive the rest. Remember, I have read the book."

With that, he turned and went inside, leaving them alone.

"If you're ready, Miss Bright." Philip wished he could say he would be honored or some such flowery nonsense, but they both knew this was a marriage of rescue and redemption. It was exactly what he had always striven to avoid, with the undesirable feeling of being forced, snared like a weak rabbit in a hunter's trap.

"Yes," she said, somewhat stoically. "I am ready."

They followed her father into the blacksmith's shop, dimly lit as there was no fire in the doused forge. Philip and

Miranda approached the anvil where the blacksmith and her father awaited.

"We still need another witness," her father said, as if that made this truly legitimate. "And I would know the name of the man performing my daughter's wedding."

"Lang. David Lang," the blacksmith stated. "I'm the nephew to old Paisley."

Philip looked at the other two, equally baffled by the pronouncement.

"Why," the man exclaimed. "Don't say you never heard of my uncle? He was doing weddings in this very spot since 1754, or some such date. Died a couple years back."

"I had a London wedding," the magistrate said firmly, "as did my eldest daughter."

The blacksmith looked at Philip, who shrugged, having never heard of Paisley either.

With a sigh, the man whistled loudly, and for a moment, Philip thought they were actually going to use the dog as their second witness, but footsteps in the rafters brought a young man scrambling down the ladder.

"My son, Simon," Mr. Lang said. "Old enough to witness, never you mind." Then he tugged a parson's hat from a hook on the wall and shoved it upon his own head. It looked strange, indeed, combined with the blackened apron.

Seeing their stares, the man reminded them, "I am an anvil *priest*." He tapped his hat. "Some even call me Bishop Lang." He grinned, his teeth looking surprisingly white in his grimy face. "Who is paying for this wedding?"

Sir William looked squarely at Philip. Swiftly, he drew out a purse from his pocket.

"How much?"

"Fifty pounds of the king's coin," Mr. Lang stated firmly.

"At the high end, then," Philip said drolly, counting out the money.

"How can you put a price on love?" the blacksmith quipped.

Philip scowled. "Is that a riddle because you just did put a price on it. At least on the ceremony if not on love itself, no matter if this be a practical Smithfield bargain or a marriage of two destined hearts."

Mr. Lang laughed as if Philip had said something amusing.

"Come stand before the anvil," he entreated, taking his place on the other side of it. "What are your names and where is your permanent abode?"

"I thought you knew both our names and where we're from," Miranda said. "My father told you." She glanced at Sir William who nodded.

"I have to ask, miss, but you go first, my lord."

Philip could hardly believe the ceremony was starting. He was truly getting married. Strangely, he didn't feel the expected churning in his gut.

"Philip Mercer of London." Then he looked at Miranda. "Hold on a minute. Miss Bright likes her bonnet straight." And he carefully set it to rights for her.

"Thank you," she said softly.

He winked at her, hoping she wasn't filled with regret. "Your turn," he reminded her.

She coughed softly into her gloved hand then spoke, "Miranda Bright of London."

"Are you both single?" Mr. Lang asked.

"You know we are," Miranda said.

The blacksmith threw his hands in the air and turned to her father.

"You've raised a right sauce-mouth, and no mistake."

"I am single," Philip said steadily, glancing at Miranda to follow suit.

"I am single," she confirmed.

"Did you come here of your own free will and accord?"

"I've just determined that fact, Mr. Lang," Miranda's father said. "You may continue."

The blacksmith rolled his eyes. "I'm asking *them*, and I need *them* to answer. I must tell you this is the longest wedding I've ever performed."

Miranda laughed softly, and Philip smiled to hear her. It was a pretty sound, one he would get to hear often, he hoped.

"I came of my own free will," he said.

"As did I," Miranda added.

"Simon, bring me a certificate and a pen, boy. Hurry up. Your mother will have our dinner on the table, I expect."

The lad snatched up the requested items from a nearby cabinet and brought them to his father, who scrawled a few illegible words. Philip presumed it was their names.

"Do you take this woman to be your lawful wedded wife, forsaking all others, keeping to her as long as you both shall live?"

Philip glanced sideways to see Miranda staring at him, her gorgeous hazel eyes as big as saucers. He hadn't expected any traditional words, only a mere handfasting as if they were country clodhoppers.

"I will," he said, surprised at his own husky tone and heightened emotions as he looked at the woman who was rapidly becoming his wife.

"Do you take this man to be your lawful wedded husband, forsaking all others, keeping to him as long as you both shall live?"

"I will," Miranda answered, her voice a little too quiet for Philip's liking.

"Take hold of each other's hands," Mr. Lang instructed. "What God and I have joined together, let no man put asunder." Then he paused, before adding, "Do either of you have a ring?"

"No," Philip said, while Miranda simply shook her head.

Her father looked disappointed as if his new son-in-law should have planned a spontaneous wedding more thoughtfully and brought along a gold bejeweled band. But a wedding had not been on Philip's horizon when he'd left London for Northampton.

"For as much as this man and this woman have consented to go together, I, David Lang, sometimes called Bishop Lang—"

This was interrupted by Miranda's nervous laughter at the ridiculous moniker. She used her free hand, waving slightly as a gesture for the man to continue.

The blacksmith cleared his throat and finished, "I declare them to be man and wife before God and these witnesses in the name of the Father, Son, and Holy Ghost, Amen."

And then he reached for the hammer resting against the base of the anvil, brought it up and slammed it down a little too close for Philip's liking. He and Miranda both whipped their hands away as the ringing sound of metal-on-metal half deafened them while it reverberated through the shop and out the open door.

"Now the village knows another couple has been joined," Mr. Lang declared solemnly. He shoved the single piece of paper into Philip's hands.

"You can both sign it, but do it elsewhere. It's past our dinnertime. Come along, Simon."

MIRANDA AND PHILIP WALKED back toward the King's Head Inn slowly, silently. Her father had mounted his horse and gone on ahead. She didn't feel any differently as a married woman, but she was relieved not to be running like a hunted fox from place to place.

More importantly, she now had a husband by her side.

"Baroness Mercer," Philip said suddenly, startling her.

"I had forgotten my name would change," she confessed.

"Much more than that will change," he said.

She took in a long breath. He might be referring to where she would live or how people would treat her. Or something else entirely.

As good as his word, the manager had sent a wainwright to fix the wheel for now Philip's handsome coach was parked in front of the inn. The hostelry didn't look so shabby in the gathering dusk due to the warm glow of lamplight shining out from each of the five windows facing the street.

Inside, the manager congratulated them both.

"Sir William is in the tap-room and asked me to send you to join him."

"Do you think he is actually going to buy us a celebratory meal?" Philip asked.

Miranda recalled her sister's special day. "Perhaps he will make it an evening wedding 'breakfast,'" she said. "But you might have to eat eggs and rashers for your dinner."

Neither was the case. Her father was sipping wine and had already ordered himself a plate of roast beef and parsnips, which they placed before him as Miranda and Philip took their seats.

"I will be falling over if I don't go up to bed shortly," Sir William said. "Unlike you two, I rode through the night. Hence, I shall leave you to enjoy your first married meal." He rapidly shoveled in another forkful, and then another.

"Will we see you in the morning, Papa?"

"I doubt it. I shall leave at first light. While I won't attempt to reach London as quickly as I did Gretna Green, I must return to my bench in three days. We are not all wealthy noblemen like my new son-in-law, able to fritter away their leisure time while gallivanting around the countryside."

At her father's words, Miranda glanced sideways at Philip. He might not be a wealthy nobleman for long. It didn't bother her except for how Philip would lose his family's estate. She knew that was a crushing blow.

Her husband, looking a little grim, merely ordered for the two of them.

"I put mine on your account, too," her father said to Philip. "After all, it's your fault I am eating away from home instead of in my own cozy dining room."

"Of course," Philip said. "I am only too happy to pay."

But Miranda didn't think he was overly happy, not by the hard line of his mouth.

Suddenly, her father barked out a short laugh.

"What is funny, Papa?" she asked, thinking they could use some good humor.

"I was just thinking how you outsmarted the prince of prurience, here, when he was doing all he could to wriggle and slither and remain unshackled."

He laughed again. Miranda's gaze lifted to Philip's face, a mask of cool politeness, with the telltale tightening of his jaw. Her father made it sound like she'd planned it.

Without any further discussion—after all, what could be said about a disgraceful daughter and a scandal-clad rake fleeing to Scotland—her father finished eating and bid them goodnight and farewell until they met again in London.

There had been no toast to the momentous occasion, after all. And in the long stretch of silence while they ate, she tried and failed to keep her thoughts from skittering wildly to what came next. Unafraid of the wedding night after having experienced the awakenings of passion with Philip already, still, she had a fluttering of anticipation. She also had her share of regrets.

Instead of a marriage to salvage something of both their reputations, she wished her dashing major had whisked her away due to a surge of romantic feelings, or dare she dream, even for love's sake.

"You must be exhausted," Philip said, not sounding particularly romantic. "I certainly am. Like your father, we can return home at a more leisurely pace." Then he laughed. "Isn't that exactly how Congreve's wit decreed it? 'Married in haste, we may repent at leisure.'"

Miranda didn't think that was funny in the least. She didn't want to consider a long lifetime of regret over their Gretna Green wedding.

"At least I am not like Shakespeare's Katherine," she countered, "fearing her Petruchio wooed in haste and meant to wed at leisure, or as she believed, not wed her at all."

Philip offered a tight smile. "Even without a ring, which I shall rectify when we are back in Town, we are definitely married. I would not have let you sink in the sea of shame in which you had carelessly cast yourself."

Her words of gratitude stuck in her throat. *Was she going to feel beholden to him for the rest of her days?* Gratitude seemed a poor substitute for love. Perhaps the marriage bed would unite them physically and, thus, emotionally, too.

"Shall we go to bed?" he asked, perchance reading her thoughts.

CHAPTER TWENTY-FOUR

Their room purportedly had a fine view of the Solway, Port Carlisle, Bowness, and even the Cumberland hills, or it would have if the sun hadn't gone down.

Miranda didn't care much about the view as the chambermaid described it while leading them up the stairs to the correct door. She wanted a hot bath and to sleep in her softest shift.

"Can a bath be arranged this late in the evening?" Miranda asked the maid.

"Oh, yes. We have lots of young ladies wanting a bath before their first night as a wife, especially if their new husbands will spare no expense."

Miranda knew that was hardly the case, but she ordered a bath anyway. Soon, she found herself in a tin tub on an oilskin in the middle of their modest-sized room, sunk down as low as she could go while her Philip returned to the public room for a glass of brandy to spare his new wife any embarrassment.

This surprised her as much as anything. After all, a bath could be a passionate, lusty exercise. Or she'd read as much in a wicked novel from the previous century.

Since he'd asked her to save the water, she'd bathed quickly and was under the bedcovers when he returned. They locked gazes.

"I suppose you'll have to stay and watch," he quipped, "since you can hardly go down to the tap-room in your shift. You *are* wearing one, are you not?" he asked.

She nodded, feeling as if he could see right through the counterpane.

"I will cover my eyes," she offered, while continuing to stare at him as he began to undress.

"I was only speaking in jest. I didn't mind you watching me *before* you became my wife, and now you can ogle me without fear of debasement."

With those words, he stripped bare as a needle in under a minute and climbed into the tub, facing away from her.

"Not as large as my bathtub back home," he remarked, splashing water about as he picked up the cake of soap and also a washcloth.

"You were very clean," he added. "I can still see my toes through the water."

This made her giggle.

"Are you ready?" he asked.

And just as quickly, her humor stuck in her throat.

"Ready?" she croaked, and a shiver of anticipation ran down her back.

"To be a baroness, to run my household wherever we end up, to face London's upper class who will not accept you at first and probably sneer at you? And to meet my family?"

She sighed. "I thought you were asking me if I was ready for my first tupping."

The soap squeezed from his hand and shot across the room to hit the wall.

After a brief silence, he said, "I suppose that would be a better question. Are you?"

"Yes." In truth, Miranda wanted him to begin so she could relax.

"Very well. I suppose consummation is the best way to seal a marriage."

Philip rose from the tub, dried himself off, including scrubbing the cotton cloth through his hair until it stood out wildly in all directions, and then he approached the bed.

"The light," she reminded him.

"I think it might be nice to see each other." Then he drew back the covers and took in the view of her in her shift.

Not wishing to lie there like a sacrificial virgin of ancient Greece, she sat up and whipped it over her head before holding it against her.

But he reached out and tugged it from her grasp, dropping it beside them on the mattress.

With his gaze fastened on her naked body, Miranda swallowed. She had some gazing of her own to do, glad she'd seen it before. His muscular planes weren't a surprise, nor the thick thatch of curls from which his member thrust out.

"Well," she murmured, about to ask what came next when he stroked the inside of her ankle. She stared at his hand, watching him while trying not to grow tense.

He caressed her from ankle to the juncture of her thighs, and when she held her breath thinking he might touch her at her curls, he stroked down her other leg. Her blood was thrumming already, and her skin tingled where he touched. But mostly, her female parts now throbbed, awaiting his attention.

Unsmiling, he replaced his fingers with his mouth, making her gasp, as he kissed and nibbled his way up her leg, but this time, he settled on his stomach between her legs and parted her soft folds with his capable fingers.

Holding her breath, unable to look away, she watched him lower his mouth to her core. When the tip of his tongue touched the little aching bud, she lay back, unable to support herself any longer. With the gentlest of licks feathered across her nubbin, he had her writhing and sinking her fingers into his damp hair in order to hold him to her.

With unexpected speed, she felt the blossoming of fulfillment. Her muscles tensed and squeezed even as she splayed herself to give him full access. From breathing hard one instant, she held her breath the next as the edge of her climax drew swiftly closer. Bliss hovered just out of reach until . . .

Philip traced a circle around the pulse of her desire with his warm, firm tongue and then flicked the tip across her now-hardened bud.

"Yes," Miranda cried out before she could stop herself, releasing his hair and stretching her arms out to the sides. Gripping the sheets between her fingers, she lifted her trembling hips for his greedy feasting kiss.

With her eyes tightly closed, her head arched back, she welcomed the satisfying sensations that crashed over her like waves, shuddering through the powerful crest until she sank back down onto the mattress and breathed steadily.

Feeling Philip rise to his knees, she opened her eyes, almost dizzy with pleasure. He said nothing, but stared at her with his darkened gaze, his pupils large with his own desire. With a feather-light touch, he stroked her breasts, tugging gently on each nipple, as if worshiping her.

Spreading her thighs farther, she held her hands out to him. Into her welcoming embrace, he lowered himself. He guided his sturdy shaft into her dampness and slowly, thickly, begin to impale her.

Time slowed from the rapid, feverish pulsing of moments before. With unhurried movements, Philip eased inside her. She knew of the pain she ought to experience, but when it came, it was less than a bee sting. At once, their glances locked and she nodded.

With her silent invitation, he rocked his hips, gliding deeper inside, leaving them perfectly intwined. While she adjusted to the feeling of being stretched and filled, he dropped a kiss to her right breast before beginning to draw out again. To her delight, he set up a rhythm she could easily match with the lifting and settling of her hips.

In this sensual dance, he continued to kiss first one nipple, then her other, each time he embedded himself deep in her channel.

When he began to thrust more quickly, she watched his face. Pushing up onto his hands, he closed his eyes and sheathed himself fully, withdrew, and repeated the action. In a very short while, she could see he was close to spending. Suddenly lowering onto to his forearm, he slid the other hand between their bodies and stroked her quivering core.

As before, the sensation crested and crashed through her, only this time, she heard him groan as he pumped to his own powerful release, flooding her with liquid warmth.

When Philip finally stilled, he collapsed atop her briefly, then rolled to the side, lying on his back, eyes closed.

She wanted to thank him, but doing so felt awkward. Instead, she offered praise.

"It was beyond anything I expected."

He didn't look at her when he spoke. "I have not deflowered many maidens. I am only glad we didn't break the innkeeper's bed."

She didn't like how he made light of her first time, nor the mention of other women. She would far rather he rolled over and kissed her tenderly. And then she realized—Philip had not kissed her on the lips, not since finding out about the book.

Should she be worried?

"More than adequate," she said, then yawned broadly, enjoying the utter relaxation of her body. But she would not beg him for a kiss.

THEY DID NOT GET up early, and Miranda didn't see her father ride away. They roused at the civilized hour of nine o'clock because, as Philip said, he had spent too many mornings awakening at dawn on an uncomfortable wool blanket in a tent full of pungent men.

She'd hoped after their swiving, they would regain their easy manner with one another. However, after a quiet breakfast in which he seemed preoccupied, they climbed into his carriage and started home under a cloud of solemnity.

Philip had bought all the newspapers he could find at the first coaching inn across the border in England and then buried his nose in them. Miranda took one gingerly after he slammed it down onto the squabs.

The news from London was all mundane. Parliamentary bills explained, word of King George's health, the opening of a national penitentiary at Millbank Prison in London, and the creation of a society promoting "permanent and universal peace." Yet the society pages were anything but peaceful.

It was an all-out battle as to who could print more outrageously scintillating quotes from her own book as well as the excited reactions of those quality folks who claimed to know who was who, and the denials of those being identified.

After the third paper with similar scribblings, she leaned back into the corner and closed her eyes.

Like a bolt of lightning, Philip suddenly sent a harsh question across the carriage's interior, "What *were* you thinking?"

Miranda knew what he was asking but didn't answer. It was futile trying to excuse herself when she had no defense.

"I confessed personal matters to you," he continued. "Things I had shared with no one else, and you managed to work them into your book as if they were nothing more than silly stories about a stranger."

She closed her eyes against his wounded tone.

"Look at me," he said harshly.

Snapping open her eyes, she gazed at him, her husband, wishing fervently she could go back and do everything differently. On the other hand, then they would not be married.

Was that what he wished most of all?

"In all other ways, you seem reasonable, even clever," he added. "And yet by writing this book, you managed to overshadow all your good qualities."

It was like a sword blade to her heart. He would never forgive her. Their marriage was doomed for he would grow more and more resentful and then restless.

"If I am such a detestable female, then why did you rush headlong toward our wedding?"

"I saw no other course of action, and I learned from Wellington how to cut my losses and take the best if only path to victory."

"A hollow victory," she said. He may have gallantly saved her honor, yet he all but despised her.

Recalling their prior relaxed way with one another, their shared laughter, the passionate kisses, this was a bitter lesson. Better to have let herself be scorned, shunned, and banished from London and away from those who did not matter to her than to marry the one who mattered most and live with his severe judgment.

"Not a hollow victory," he disagreed. "And I never said you were detestable. You were led astray by Lady Harriet who saw a weakness and exploited it."

He picked up another paper, then put it aside. "I am used to my exploits amusing my peers, but you mentioned the private predicament in which I find myself with Miss Waltham. When I go to my club, the other men who know of my brandy venture may put two and two together. Believing the Walthams have ruined me, they'll think I am already a pauper. And when I put my house on the market, I won't be able to say it is due to an unacceptable abundance of vermin or a leaky roof. Everyone will know it is because I cannot afford to keep it."

Miranda felt smaller and smaller. She opened her mouth to tell him again how she'd tried to stop the printing presses, but it was pointless. After all, by then the book had been written. Much as she enjoyed gossip, it had not been worth it.

"The thing of it is," he continued, "the story is amusing. If only you had better disguised those involved. I vow if it weren't my own life on those pages, I would have praised the writing of your little book."

"And now you are stuck with a wife you don't like."

Philip sighed. Reaching the short distance between them, he placed his large hand on her arm, grabbed hold, and dragged her onto his side of the carriage where she sat in a heap beside him.

"Just because I didn't go short by the knees and plead for your hand, doesn't mean I dislike having you for a wife," he said.

Not disliking her was hardly loving her!

And she would have settled for him going down on at least *one* knee and asking with some small enthusiasm for her hand.

Philip draped an arm around the back of the seat, lightly touching her. She tried not to stiffen but couldn't relax the rigidity that had taken hold of her shoulders.

"Once I have faced the gawkers in Town and got past the initial humiliation, I will ignore them," he said, not sounding as sure as he ought to.

Closing her eyes, she wished there was a way she could fix this, but she had betrayed the man she loved.

CHAPTER TWENTY-FIVE

Philip hadn't thought it could be worse than he'd feared, but it was. Some arse who believed himself humorous had even hung black crape over his doorway and along the wrought iron fence in front. It must have recently happened or his butler would have taken it down.

Unless perhaps his butler was the one who did it!

Snatching at it, tearing off a swag of fabric as he tossed open his door, he then recalled his manners and stepped to the side.

"After you, Lady Mercer."

Philip wished she hadn't flinched when he said those words. In any case, she entered his home, now hers, at least until he sold it. It was mid-afternoon, as they had taken their time to get back. The only good thing about the long journey had been their two nights of passionate swiving. When they were stripped to bare skin, saying nothing, they communicated perfectly.

His butler appeared from the back of the house at a quick pace, looking grim-faced for having been caught unawares.

"I am home, Mr. Cherville."

"Yes, my lord."

"And this is Lady Mercer, my wife."

"Welcome, my lady," his butler greeted her respectfully, his thoughts on the matter of a hasty marriage unknown as always.

"See to it her ladyship's bags are—"

"Bag, just one," Miranda interrupted him, then turned to his butler.

"You see, I was visiting my cousins in Northampton. Thus, I had only one small trunk with me anyway, and then we went to Scotland on a moment's notice, so I have even less at present. Tomorrow, I will go home and pack up my things. Home," she explained to Mr. Cherville who was manfully trying to follow her tale, "is on Russell Square. My father is Sir William Bright, the magistrate."

His butler nodded, his face placid.

Then she turned to Philip. "May I send a courier for my trunk in Northampton?"

"You are thinking of everything at once. All in good time. First, I'll show you your room and then—"

"*My* room?" she repeated. "Am I to have my own room? Are we not to share one? My parents never slept apart. I know the nobility try to emulate royalty, but—"

"Miranda," he cut her off, sending Mr. Cherville an apologetic look. Undoubtedly the man must be wondering what type of creature his employer had brought into their home.

"Send the lady's single bag up to *our* room, along with mine. We'll take tea in the upstairs salon. And bring all my correspondence there, too. I imagine there is quite a lot of it."

"Yes, my lord."

Philip gestured for her to precede him upstairs.

With her lips pursed, she nodded and ascended.

"Up one more flight if you wish to see our bedroom," he told her, and up they went with him enjoying the view of her backside. At least he still had that. "Do you have a lady's maid you wish to bring from home?"

"No," she said. "My father is partial to retaining the people he knows and trusts. Eliza shall remain in his employ."

"Very well. I have housemaids. Perhaps one will do as your personal maid. If not, you may hire one," he said, reaching his door ahead of her and opening it. How he would afford another servant, he couldn't imagine.

"I am more than happy to share my bedroom with you," he continued, "but you may want to have privacy at times and a place of your own. When you do, there is another chamber next door. For the time being, my house affords us more than enough space."

He shouldn't have added that. It sounded like another jab at her, especially not while she was standing in the center of his bedroom for the first time, her dainty feet on his soft Persian carpet, surveying the gold and white wallpaper, and the large four-poster bed that had been his grandfather's.

Her head whipped around to face him.

"How long have you lived here?"

He swallowed. "All my life. My parents bought it when they were newly married." A surge of anger tried to take him over again, and he tamped it down.

Besides, she looked as miserable as he felt for having failed his family. Her book was merely the final doomed battle in his epic defeat.

"I think I should like to see my room after all," she said softly.

They blinked at one another. It was probably for the better.

"Through there." He nodded to the connecting door and gestured for Miranda to go explore. She passed by him, but he didn't follow.

"It might need freshening," he said, peering past her at the blue and white room. "Mr. Cherville is an efficient man, as good as any general. He'll send up a housemaid to set things to rights at once. After you've settled in, there is a salon one floor down, toward the back of the house, overlooking the garden. I shall await you there."

She opened her mouth to say something and changed her mind.

Spinning on his heel, Philip left her, going downstairs to the salon. He knew what would be awaiting him.

As expected, a stack of missives from shocked friends which he put aside, invitations from people who were *not* his friends but who wanted him as the attraction at a party, which he crumpled up and tossed into the hearth, a letter from his mother, and lastly, an urgent message from Lord Perrin.

First, he scanned his mother's shocked and saddened words at his behavior. She did not yet know she finally had a daughter-in-law. Then he turned to Miss Waltham's father's curt note.

When Miranda entered five minutes later, having removed her bonnet, gloves, and spencer, he was unable to keep his fury at bay any longer.

"I have been *summoned* by Lord Perrin." He slapped the paper while pacing up and down the peach-colored room. Supposedly, it was a soothing color for walls and furnishings, but it annoyed him right then. He wanted to see vivid red to match his mood. "Summoned!"

"What happens if you don't comply?" she asked.

He stopped and frowned. Truthfully, he hadn't considered ignoring the viscount. But it would gain him nothing.

"That would only delay the inevitable."

"Which is?" she asked.

"He may call me out to duel over the honor of his daughter."

"That's preposterous!" she said. "You are innocent of all but a kiss."

"He may simply want to tell me he sank the blasted ships rather than transport my brandy." Philip sat, then jumped

248

up since she was still standing. "Now I cannot even sit in my own house when I wish to."

With those unkind words, he drove off his new wife who, with her back ramrod straight, left him alone with only his ire for company. Instantly, he regretted it. Having Miranda in his life was truly the only bright spot.

Bright spot! He smiled wryly and vowed to do better. It was fear of what would happen next that drove his seesawing emotions, and he knew better, as a soldier, than to let fear control him.

MIRANDA WONDERED IF THEY would survive the evening, never mind a lifetime of wedded war. She was ready to take herself home and tell her father she had made a dreadful mistake.

Many of them, actually!

However, she'd brought it all upon herself. Mayhap tomorrow she would pay a call upon Lady Harriet and punch her in the nose!

After exploring the house on her own, Miranda looked up from the shelf of books in the study at the sound of a throat being cleared.

"Dinner will be served shortly, my lady," Mr. Cherville said. "His lordship asked me to bring you to the dining room."

While still marveling over being transformed into "a lady" by a hammer being struck upon an anvil, Miranda followed him.

Unfortunately, the meal was another silent affair as it had been at the inn the night before. Recalling how pleasantly they'd spent the hours afterward, her husband probably expected her to offer herself in his chamber at bedtime.

Instead, she retired to her new room by herself. True to his word, one of the maids arrived to assist their new baroness.

"I hardly need help to undress," she protested after the young woman introduced herself as Jane.

"Perhaps I can brush out your hair, my lady."

"Honestly," Miranda was about to send her away when she realized the maid's face was growing red, and she appeared ready to cry.

"Are you well?"

"It's a plum position is all, my lady. I would much prefer it to being a maid-of-all-work. I vow I will make you a good personal maid."

Doubtless, it paid better, too. But Miranda was well aware they would have to cut the fat as Philip's accounts dwindled further, and any of the household positions would be at risk except the butler's, the cook's, and the housekeeper's.

"I am sure you will do fine," Miranda said. "I simply don't know what to have you do. It's rather new to me, I'm afraid."

Not that she hadn't had Eliza's help in the past, but never a maid devoted entirely to her person.

"Let's start with taking down your hair. I'll be able to do a fancier coiffure if you wish next time you go out with his lordship."

Hardly necessary when Philip said he would have to give up his family's box both at the rebuilt Theatre Royal and at the Lyceum. If he was correct, they would be shunned and left to become dried-up hermits in some hovel in Chipping-Norton or the outskirts of Bath.

"Thank you." Miranda sat on the ottoman by the dresser and let Jane begin. Soon, the young woman started to chat.

"And if you have any secrets, my lady, I shall keep them in my bosom. I know sometimes one needs to tell somebody. Or if you wish to gossip, I know a great deal as we talk downstairs about everything we hear."

Miranda hid a smile at the contradictory statements, reminding herself never to tell Jane anything of a private nature. It would seem a word to her maid in the evening would be warmed over by the Cook at breakfast.

"I also can deliver a *billet-doux*," the maid added. "Not that I expect you'll be writing those, given how bonny the master is."

Miranda no longer felt like smiling. She was married to the most dash-fire man, but he didn't love her and had even stopped kissing her. But she let Jane continue brushing her hair for it felt delightfully relaxing, somewhat easing her tension.

"Hoping to cause no offense, but Lord Mercer was expected to marry Miss Waltham, my lady. Since you snagged him instead, I can't imagine you would—"

"Jane," Miranda exclaimed, standing so quickly the brush got wrenched from the maid's hand and entangled in her hair.

While working to free it, Miranda said, "I do have something to send to a man. And it must be done this very evening. Will you help me?"

PHILIP WAITED ON THE other side of his closed door. Feeling incredibly foolish, he leaned his back against it.

Would Miranda come to him?

Should he go to her?

He finally had a legal right to a legitimate wife who bore his name, and yet he was uncertain whether she welcomed his advances.

Without the enforced closeness of a crowded inn, they had nothing to drive them together, except passion. And such had been sorely lacking during the daytime hours. He blamed himself, always reminding her of the blasted book and being in a tweague over his financial situation.

If he hadn't behaved like a rake in truth, then Miranda wouldn't have had much to write about. From the kiss with Miss Waltham, which he hadn't even done out of desire but from his own stupid self-indulgence, all the way to the incident at Northumberland's gracious Syon House, which he definitely had done out of desperate desire for Miranda, Philip had provided her all the ammunition she'd needed.

Lady Harriet had merely lined up the soldiers and taken him down.

But he could not say he minded being married to the magistrate's daughter. He could think of many worse females, and try as he might, he could think of none better among those of his acquaintance, none he preferred to his beautiful, fun, untitled wife.

No one else had ever come close to setting up a home in his heart the way she had.

After waiting a while, he came to the realization she would not be coming to him that night. And rather than suffer a devastating wound to his pride, he refrained from going humbly to her room in case she didn't open the door to him.

Tomorrow, he would try to mend bridges.

However, the following morning, Miranda's trunk arrived from her cousin Helen as well as a long letter. With a squeal of delight, his wife left the intimate salon where they were enjoying a quiet breakfast and secured herself in her room for the unpacking of her things and to read the precious letter.

After that, dressed in a new gown that made him jealous of whomever would see her in it that day, she hurried out the door with barely a backward wave of her hand.

He wondered how he would bear it until she returned and he could beg her forgiveness for being sore-headed. But then another missive arrived from Miss Waltham's father, even more strongly worded than the one he'd found awaiting him the day before. Perrin knew he had returned.

Only back in London one day, and it was time to pay the piper.

CHAPTER TWENTY-SIX

Miranda waited while her brand-new calling card, which was merely one of Philip's with *Lady Mercer* written neatly across the top in her own handwriting, was taken by the Beaumonts' butler. Quite quickly, he reappeared.

"Lady Harriet is in."

"Naturally," Miranda said, enjoying her moment, even more so when the butler faced the open doorway to the second-floor drawing room and announced, "The Right Honorable Lady Mercer."

"I shall never get tired of hearing that," Miranda said in an overly cheerful tone with a big false smile.

Strolling into the familiar yellow room, she was not surprised to see Lord Beaumont there as well, lounging rudely, not bothering to stand. Apparently, Lady Harriet assumed an ugly scene and wanted her brother either to support her or witness it for his amusement.

"Good day to my patron," Miranda greeted.

"Good day," Lady Harriet said, already looking doubtful. No doubt, she'd expected Miranda to be in tears.

"Congratulations are in order," Miranda said. "To me, of course! You saw my calling card. Why, if I'd known my little book would result in such a happy outcome, I would have written it sooner."

Lord Beaumont laughed. It seemed he didn't mind amusing himself at his sister's expense.

"You had a very warm *tendre* for the baron a while back, didn't you?" he asked Lady Harriet. "You might have tried doing the same, dear sister, since you know as much about everyone's business as anyone. Then *you* would be Lady Mercer."

"Shut up, Geoffrey. That's the last thing I want!" Lady Harriet insisted, lifting her chin with her cheeks growing rosy.

Ignoring their banter, Miranda took a plump seat despite none being offered and waited while Lady Harriet resumed hers.

"Will there be tea?" Miranda asked. "Never mind, I won't stay too long. Only to thank you for being my patron. What a brilliant idea you gave me! And I must thank you for sending exactly the correct number of copies out into the world to the right people, although I do believe we could make a small fortune if we wanted to do a larger printing."

"Oh, but we will," Lady Harriet said, clearly thinking Miranda a simpleton not to realize what damage had been done with the first few volumes and what more would be done when her book was spread all over London.

"Oh, but we won't," Miranda said unequivocally. "While my father appreciated my little jestful tale, my husband has advised me that others won't be as understanding. Truly, some of those mentioned are flagrant buffoons or wickedly debauched dogs, but others are innocent. They might get hurt through no fault of their own as their tales are told with their identities too thinly disguised."

"That *is* the point," Lady Harriet said. "The printer has started the presses up again and—"

While she blathered on, Miranda took out the precious copy of the old *Tête-à-Tête* column, which had arrived from Helen with her trunk. She'd thanked her lucky stars for such a clever cousin, rolled the page and slipped it into her reticule that morning.

Interrupting the earl's daughter midstream, Miranda made a great show of yawning loudly.

When she had both the siblings' attention, she smiled.

"You are aware I have a cousin who loves gossip nearly as much as I do. And bless her heart, she had an old copy from your parents' day when some intrepid fellow had done a little digging in the back garden of knowledge. Only look at these adorable sketches of your mother and father, just before you were born."

Giving the fine paper a little shake, Miranda held it in front of her, and Lord Beaumont sat up for the first time to peer more closely.

"Those are bloody good likenesses," he said.

"You should mind your manners and not use such words in the presence of ladies," Miranda scolded lightly. "You will never get a wife that way. Speaking of which, you might not get one at all should word of your family's humble, even distasteful origins get out. A few too many babes on the wrong side of the blanket. *Tsk, tsk,*" she added. "One might conclude you're not even in line for a legitimate title."

Lord Beaumont looked confused, but Lady Harriet seemed to know exactly what she was talking about.

"And to think your great-grandfather wasn't even English."

Lady Harriet paled.

Miranda pressed home her advantage. "The strange thing is, upon my first entering society, everyone told me your family members were *la crème de la crème* of English bloodlines. You can only imagine my surprise, nay, my shock to find out that is a lie. A lie!" she repeated for emphasis. "Egregious flim-flam with more fiction than my own little book."

"What are you going to do?" Lady Harriet asked, her voice barely above a whisper.

"I am going straight to every editor of every London paper with this little sheet." With that, she rolled it up again. "You did tell me once that all the nobility likes to see their names in the gossip rags."

"Why would you tell her that?" Lord Beaumont demanded of his sister.

"If you would prefer, I'll keep this to myself," Miranda said.

Lady Harriet's gaze darted to her brother then back to Miranda.

"Yes, I would prefer, as would my parents."

"Then I shall do exactly that," Miranda said, sending her another smile before standing. This time, she stared hard at Lord Beaumont.

Finally, his sister said, "You're being rude, brother. You must stand when a lady stands."

"But you said—"

"Shut your cake-hole!" Lady Harriet snapped.

Miranda laughed as if they were all three good friends. Touching her bonnet to make sure it was straight, she added, "You shall deliver any copies of my book in your possession as well as those still at the printers directly to my new home on Cavendish Square, along with the manuscript, too."

"Yes, of course." Lady Harriet looked positively ill but compliant.

"Then we have finished our brief association as writer and patron. I wish you good-day."

Miranda walked to the door, and without turning, she added, "By this afternoon, mind you. If there's any delay, I shall be visiting the various offices of all the papers for their evening edition."

And she strode out and down the stairs, feeling as if she'd finally mastered the business of being one of the quality folk.

IN HIS STUDY, LORD Perrin looked grim, and Philip girded himself for battle.

"She's gone," the viscount said.

"Your daughter?" Philip guessed, having only just been ushered in, not yet offered a chair or coffee.

"Yes!" The older man folded his arms. "Her mother is beside herself with worry, even though our girl has only gone as far as our country estate in Kent."

"I take it Miss Waltham received a copy of a certain scandal-filled book."

"No, I did," Perrin ground out. "I would have spared her, but I thought it important she read it. She ought to learn that her actions have consequences." Then he put his fisted hands on his waist. "You should have well understood that *before* playing games with her."

Philip shook his head. "As you must have read in the book, which in some instances is quite close to factual, I did nothing more than kiss your daughter, and for that I am beyond apologetic, I assure you."

"I don't care for your apology. I want you to go after her and marry her."

Perrin hadn't heard the news, and Philip was certain the man wouldn't be overjoyed to learn the truth. Yet there was no other recourse except to tell him at once.

"I cannot marry your daughter because I am already married."

The viscount narrowed his eyes. "What tale are you telling now?"

"It is true. I eloped to Scotland recently."

Silence met his response. Then the man asked, "Did you ruin another young lady?"

Philip took a deep breath. He would not discuss his new wife with another man. Besides, Perrin had only to read the book to figure out who his bride was.

"That is not your business," Philip said.

"No, it's not," the viscount agreed. "But your brandy *is* my business."

Philip was prepared for this. It was wrong of the viscount and his brother to penalize him, but he had known it would happen eventually.

A pounding on the outer door interrupted their conversation.

A second later, Lord Rowantry rushed in ahead of Perrin's butler who dutifully trailed in and announced him.

"Lord Rowantry to see you, my lord."

Not only was the young man's cravat hanging loose, but his jacket was swinging open and his waistcoat unbuttoned as if all had been hastily donned while on the move. And to cap the image, his thick hair stood up in a frightful mess, none of it befitting a marquess's son, unless he had an extremely poorly trained valet.

Philip doubted that was the case. Something had caused Rowantry to be in a state of distress, and Philip had a good idea what it was, or rather *who* it was.

"What the devil!" Perrin exclaimed. "You are interrupting, not to mention you look unhinged. Collect yourself, and I will see you anon."

"I must speak with her. Where is Miss Waltham?"

Philip watched the viscount's interest perk. Perrin circled the desk, coming close to the young man.

"Why? What do you want with her?"

"To marry her. I demand you allow it. Don't let this scoundrel have her."

Philip took a step back. *How had he become involved again?*

"I say, watch your tongue," he protested. There was no cause to throw insults, especially when they both knew who the real scoundrel was.

"If you'd asked politely," Philip continued, "I would have told you that you may have Miss Waltham with my blessing. I am already married, and happily so."

"Then I'll forgive the kiss I read about," Rowantry said, still glaring at him. But then he focused on Perrin. "Why did no one tell me of Miss Waltham's dire circumstances?"

Perrin shook his head. "I suppose my daughter thought you knew and didn't care. You do know how the reproduction of the human species works, don't you, boy? First you talk sweetly to a female, then there's the *pully hawly*, and then you make feet for children's stockings. But you're supposed to do that after you are married. *After*, I say! In any case, now you've made the blasted feet, you had better provide for the stockings!"

Rowantry looked suitably chagrinned. Philip was glad Perrin wasn't to be his father-in-law. In comparison, he'd got off easily with Bright.

"Nevertheless, I give my permission," Perrin continued. "Since you've ruined her, I assume you'll forego her dowry?"

"Yes," Rowantry assured him. "That is if she'll have me."

"She will have you if I have anything to say about it, and I assure you I do," Perrin said.

Philip hoped Miss Waltham was amenable because it was clear she would be given no choice.

"Where is she?" Rowantry asked. "I am desperate to see her and ease her worries."

"Let us not be hasty," the viscount said. "We must discuss her allowance."

Philip decided to leave the men alone to finish up their negotiations.

"I shall visit with your brother tomorrow at the Custom House, to see how quickly my brandy will be arriving, yes?"

"What?" Perrin asked, then his eyes focused, realizing Philip was no longer of interest to him. He had a marquess's son on the hook. "Yes, yes. Tomorrow. My brother will handle everything."

After Philip stepped outside, he made his hands into fists and punched the air. *By God, he was not ruined!* His brandy would start to flow across the Channel and the Mercer estate would be saved.

And all because his talented wife wrote a book.

"YOU WERE RIGHT," HE called out as soon as he walked through his own front doorway. *Where was his minx?*

"Cherville, where is my lady wife?"

"Not at home, my lord. She had *important business* to which she had to attend."

Philip handed him his hat and gloves.

"Do tell."

"That is an exact quotation from earlier, when she left with Jane as her companion. I know nothing more, my lord."

Philip wanted to see her immediately. It was most inconvenient for her to be out. He had the urge to wrap his arms around her and kiss her senseless. He was well aware he hadn't kissed her in a donkey's age, ever since the anger at her betrayal had caught him in its grasp. They'd swived like eager rabbits on more than one occasion, but the intimacy of a kiss had been beyond him.

He'd imagined it would be a Judas kiss. But no longer!

Now he knew it all to be nonsense. While she'd done nothing purposefully to harm anyone, those around her including Lady Harriet and Lord Perrin, used their positions to control and injure as they saw fit. What he'd seen as betrayal was blind ignorance of the group of vipers to which he'd introduced her.

"Brandy, Cherville." Then he thought better of it. *What would Miranda like?* "It's too early for that. Tea in the upstairs salon, and send Lady Mercer to me directly she returns."

As the hours passed, however, and the day went from tea time to actual brandy time, Philip became increasingly alarmed. The infernal woman would be made to leave her itinerary next time she went out. After all, she could be anywhere and with anyone! Few knew of their marriage yet, leaving her relatively defenseless except for the protection afforded her as a magistrate's daughter.

The growling sound he heard was his own impatience emanating involuntarily from deep within. What's more, he had started to pace. *Did she realize how greatly he cared for her? Dammit all!* Much more than that. At least to himself he could admit he loved the chit. Elsewise, he never would have married her, not even to save her from ruin. And now she'd vanished.

As his imagination began to go wild with thoughts of every dreadful accident befalling her and in ways he'd never worried over a woman before, he heard her voice.

"In the salon? Yes, Cherville. I shall go at once."

Hastily, Philip sat down and picked up the first thing to occupy his hands from the sofa cushion, hoping to appear as if he'd been entirely relaxed and not going out of his mind for the woman he loved.

Miranda came in looking dazzlingly beautiful in a lavender and cream dress.

"I have returned," she announced. "Did you miss me?"

"Were you gone?" Philip asked, rising slowly to his feet.

She laughed, the warm and lusty sound of her happiness setting his loins to aching for her.

"What is so funny?" he asked.

"You are holding *my* needlepoint."

He looked down at what he was fiddling with. *The devil!*

"I was examining the skill of your handiwork." He held it before his eyes and peered at the stretched canvas interwoven with many colors of thread. It seemed she was creating a cat or a lion. Perhaps it was a bear. Whatever it was, it was dreadful.

"Satisfactory," he proclaimed it and tossed it onto the sofa while she laughed again. "Very well. Tell me where you were these past many hours."

"I had an important visit to make, which I shall tell you all about in a minute. But afterward, I went home. With Eliza—you recall my father's housemaid—and with Jane's help, I packed up all my worldly goods and brought them here."

"This is your *home*," he reminded her. And now it would be forever, since he would not have to sell.

"Yes, of course," she said. "Wherever my husband is shall be my home."

He must tell her immediately how her book had saved them.

"Take a seat," he told her and crossed to the bell-pull. "Wine, brandy, tea, what do you desire?"

Her cheeks flooded with color, and he knew what she desired. *By God, he was a lucky man!*

"Wine," she said softly and kept her gaze on him as he pulled the cord and waited for Mr. Cherville. "Someday," she added, "I would like our cook to make whipped syllabub if you think she could."

Soon, they were relaxing together like any man and wife, and Philip was ready to tell her how he would eat his words about the book when she opened her reticule and drew out a rolled piece of paper. This, she smoothed upon her lap.

"It's a *Tête-à-Tête* from an old monthly *Town and Country*. You may remember I mentioned them when we were at my aunt and uncle's home."

Philip frowned, before recalling his distaste over the magazine that delved into the personal lives of the upper class. With annoyance, he snatched it from her.

"I would have hoped you'd had enough of dangerous gossip." Without looking at it, he went to tear it in half.

"Don't!" she yelled, reaching out to stay his hand. "It's my only copy. And my possession of it has changed the path of our ignominy."

He glanced down at the worn sheet, taking a moment to read the headline. "It's about the Beaumont family!"

"Indeed, it is!" Miranda practically sang the words. "The true and unpolished facts about Lord and Lady Beaumont. Only see who Lady Harriet's great-grandfather is."

He read the entire column before he looked up at her, grinning like a fiend.

"Does she know you have this information?"

"She does. I paid her my first visit as Lady Mercer. There will be no more copies of my book printed. In fact, I expect a delivery of any stray ones in Lady Harriet's possession to come tonight. While I cannot get back the few she sent out, no one else will receive one, nor will there be any more quotations from it sent to the papers."

Handing her back her precious page, it was his turn for good news.

"You were correct," Philip said simply.

Miranda's hazel eyes, looking mostly green that night, twinkled in delight. Philip thought he could dive in and swim in their clear, verdant depths.

"Was I?" she asked.

"Yes. You advised me when we first met to go to the marquess's son and tell him about Miss Waltham's plight and how she was trying to point her boney finger at me."

"I recall nothing about her boney finger," she said. "Only about her lips being against yours."

He sighed. "I vow there will never be another woman's lips against mine ever again." With that, he leaned the few inches between them and claimed her mouth.

Nothing ever felt better or more like coming home, not any of the instances when he'd returned from the Continent to this very room, nor enjoyed a woman after a long absence.

Never had his entire body sizzled with heat at the mere touch of soft lips under his. This was love, pure and deep and everlasting!

CHAPTER TWENTY-SEVEN

Miranda slid her hands up and around his neck, and he drew her against him. When she parted her lips, Philip delved inside, his tongue dancing with hers until he was ready to toss her skirts up and—

"We're crushing the *Tête-à-Tête,*" she said.

"I vow that gossip will not come between us again." He took the single sheet that laid bare the lies of the Beaumont family's lack of antiquity and bloodlines and set it on the low table in front of him. Then he went to the salon door and looked out. Not a servant in sight. *Good!*

Closing it, he returned to the arms of his wife and did exactly as he'd wanted to from the first time he'd met her. He ruined her wickedly and thoroughly on their sofa, both keeping their clothing on, merely loosening it and drawing it up or down as necessary.

All his mouth needed was access to her lips, her plump breasts, and her pearled nipples, and all his jutting arousal needed was the sweet, damp place between her soft thighs.

MIRANDA COULD HAVE FALLEN asleep on the sofa in the salon, so languid did she feel after their swiving. Rousing herself, she pulled up her bodice and drew down her skirts while Philip fastened his breeches and tucked in his linen shirt.

"That was different," she said. Neither better nor worse than in a bed, she'd experienced the same blissful ending as had her husband.

He laughed. "I hope you don't mind if we try different places often."

She was more than willing. "Not at all." But she couldn't help wondering where they would end up after he sold everything.

Hoping not to offend his male pride, she had an idea.

"After the sale of this house, we could move in with my father. He has room and will be retiring in a few years. Thus, he might—"

Philip shook his head, and she stopped, but then tried again.

"We could move in with your mother," she offered, wondering if she would be under the Dowager Lady Mercer's thumb. They'd had a successful meeting in which Philip's mother had graciously thanked Miranda for taming her wayward son.

Again, her husband shook his head, and then he gave her his winsome smile.

"We are not moving anywhere for I am not selling our home. Can you imagine why?"

"No," Miranda said truthfully. Her saved allowance was not enough to support the household. "Has your officer's half-pay been increased?"

"Hardly that. Your outrageous book has altered our fortunes for the better." He tucked one of her errant locks of hair behind her ear. "I have devastated your coiffure while ravishing you," he added, looking pleased.

He *had* ravished her, but it was his little gesture with her hair that made her feel cared for, causing her breath to catch in her throat as her heart clenched.

"Tell me. How did my book do that?"

"As I said before we got carried away, you were correct. *About what?* you ask, for I know my inquisitive wife. Rowantry did not know anything about Miss Waltham's plight. I should have done as you suggested in the beginning and contacted him. I heard him myself declare he wants to marry her. As expected, Perrin is in full agreement." Philip rubbed his hands together with happiness.

"Consequently, my brandy will no longer be held hostage. By late tonight, Rowantry shall have arrived at Perrin's estate in Kent. He fully intends to go short by the knees and beg Miss Waltham to marry him. All very romantic."

Miranda felt a dropping sensation in her stomach.

"Miss Waltham will get a husband who loves her after all. I dare say the first of the banns will be announced this Sunday, and in three weeks, they'll have the wedding of their dreams. Nothing like ours, I warrant."

An undeniable shard of sadness sliced through her, perhaps even a wee drop of anger trickled down her spine, too, at his comparison to their own wedding, not to mention the state of their marriage. He'd kissed her and ravished her, but did that make her any more to him than any other woman he'd tupped in his life?

Rising from the sofa, she took up her reticule and her precious magazine column she'd used to blackmail Lady Harriet.

"Then everything worked out for the best," she said, her tone involuntarily stiff. "I think I'll go tidy up before dinner."

For some reason, she wanted to have a good cry and shriek into her pillow at the same time. For while Miss Waltham had been duplicitous from the start and tried to play Philip falsely, she'd managed to gain the love of her intended. Miranda had been truthful with her baron from the beginning and ended up with her hand nearly smashed upon an anvil!

Glancing at where they'd recently been making the two-backed beast in earnest, she wondered if the act between men and women was superior for a couple in love versus those who merely lusted.

"A good idea," Philip agreed. "I cannot play your lady's maid well enough to repair the damage I've caused to your hair. And my baroness must be presentable," he teased.

"Like a well-groomed dog," she muttered.

"Miranda, is something the matter?"

"Not at all! By the way, your own appearance is the worse for wear due to joining giblets."

His expression rearranged itself into one of shock.

"Joining giblets!" he exclaimed.

"Yes, you know, the goat's jig, riding St. George, to strap and strum, to wap, and all that."

"Yes, *I* do know, but you shouldn't have one and twenty ways to say *swiving*. What sort of education did you get at that Ladies' Seminary?"

Miranda stomped her foot. Her own husband didn't know her very well.

"That was my sister," she finished on a hiss.

"I was speaking in jest. Why are you angry?"

"Isn't that all we were doing? The same as you've done with every other lady of your acquaintance?"

"Not *every* lady, no." He was mocking her, and it sent her ire into a glimflashy passion.

"Each one with whom you graced with your . . . your manly parts, I mean. Every time you had a flyer, as we just did, still dressed, or you gave some woman a green gown on the grass of a Mayfair mansion in the darkness."

Miranda was getting worked up, but the notion she'd married a hell-hound who might as easily have married any other woman who'd written a stupid story about him hit her like a bag of Brighton pebbles.

Philip crossed the room in two strides and took hold of her.

"Tell me truly, wife, why are you angry?" he asked.

"Because I never wanted to end up married to a man who did not want to marry me, fervently and ardently and with his whole heart." She shook herself free of him because just his fingers gripping her upper arms made her desire him again.

He was an obsession for her, just as much as those who couldn't get enough gin or cheese or sponge-cake.

"I never thought I would be envious of Miss Waltham, but she gets to marry a man who loves her, while I am handfast to a rake."

"Well then!" he exclaimed, stomping across the room, looking childish. "I guess we both have cause to hiss and shout."

"Truly?" she snapped, standing stiffly in the middle of the salon while a case of the blue devils and the red furies mingled together inside her. "And why are *you* angry? You have your precious brandy business back."

"Because I never wanted to be forced into marriage without the opportunity to ask for the hand of the woman I love," he raged before her like a gathering thunderstorm. "I've ended up leg-shackled to someone who doesn't love me but looks upon me as nothing but a buck of the first head who allows his cock to rule him!"

She cringed at his bitter tone, but then stamped her foot again. He spoke as if he was the only one whose dreams had been dashed. But then she replayed his words for she'd heard him mention love.

"Are you saying you wished you could have asked some woman whom you love to marry you, or are you saying you wished you had been able to ask me properly for my hand?"

"Yours, of course!" he snapped. "You are the only woman I love. And instead of getting to do it right, on my knees or at least presenting you with a ring as a token, I had to endure an exhausting trip, a silent, surly bride, and an ugly 'bishop.'"

A bubble of laughter escaped her.

"My disillusionment is amusing to you, is it? Just because I've been raffish in the past does not mean I don't have deep feelings, or that they cannot be wounded."

Miranda took a step toward him.

"I know that, Philip."

His glance shot to hers, his gorgeous coffee-brown eyes widened.

"I promise you haven't ended up leg-shackled to a woman who does not love you. For I do. With my whole heart, I do."

Dropping her reticule and the *Tête-à-Tête* upon the floor, she rushed at him. Luckily, he opened his arms as she reached him or they would have gone tumbling over the lamp table and into the hearth.

"Say it," she demanded.

"I love you," he answered. And then he dropped to his knees, clenching both of her hands in his.

"Will you be my wife for the rest of our days, keeping yourself only to me?"

"I will," she whispered, with tears pricking her eyes so she could hardly see him. "And you?"

"I will." He rose to his feet, took her upturned face between his palms, and kissed her.

"Philip," she said when he released her many minutes later, "what did Lady Harriet mean when she said there are *mushrooms* in the gossip column?"

He smiled, and then he started to chuckle. He laughed hard enough he needed to sit, dragging her onto his lap when he did.

"I promise to answer every question you ever ask me concerning the strange ways of the nobility, as long as you promise never to write another book about us."

Taking his face in her palms, she said, "I promise."

EPILOGUE

As the music came to an end, Philip and Miranda heard the bell. He took her hand, and they hurried off the dance floor near the Turkish Tent and into the darkness beyond the Grove.

The night was warm and the Vauxhall Pleasure Gardens were filled with happy guests, but the newlyweds managed to beat the throng, meeting up with Helen and Peter, who'd gone early to the copse that contained the famed Cascade.

"Everything has been wondrous," Helen said. "I don't see how this can top the other entertainment or even the lamp-lighting."

"It will," Miranda assured her, linking her arm through her cousin's. "This shall make your visit to London worthwhile."

Helen laughed. "Too late for that. My stay in Town has exceeded my every expectation."

"Then my letters didn't do it justice?" Miranda asked.

"Not by half," her cousin said.

Peter shushed her. "It's starting."

He had merely a single crutch tucked under his right arm. Sometimes, if the walk was short, he used only a cane. His legs had strengthened with the use of two crutches for months, allowing him to walk better than he had in years.

When Peter had come to London to handle Philip's brandy imports, managing the business with his keen mind, Miranda's kind husband had made certain her cousin was in the capable care of a former army doctor who'd had great success with all types of physical rehabilitation.

At first, Helen had not accompanied her brother. And Miranda realized her cousin had stayed in the country all those years not because she'd needed to tend her brother but because of her own timidity.

While still proclaiming the neighboring farmer's son had possession of her heart, Helen finally agreed to a month's visit. They were two weeks into it, and Miranda had an idea her cousin would like to stay for the upcoming Season, but they would decide later.

After the artful scene played out with the roaring cascade and the false pedestrians and carriages crossing the bridge, the crowd clapped and cheered. Philip reclaimed his wife's arm, and they turned toward the exit with Peter and Helen following. They had come by boat this time, much to Miranda's delight, and they would return by a wherry lit with lanterns through the darkness that stretched over the Thames.

"I am deliriously happy," Miranda said.

"I will be *after* I get you alone. It seems we are always in a party of four lately."

"Shh," she whispered, but she was thrilled by his unceasing desire, especially when he leaned close and brushed his mouth across her temple.

As usual, he'd been very generous to her cousins. But she couldn't deny how she looked forward to their time alone and the passion she and Philip shared nearly every night, and some mornings, too.

"I'm glad we did not wait forty years to return to the Cascade," he said.